D0410037

A GOOD DAY TO DIE

A GOOD DAY TO DIE

AMEN ALONGE

QUERCUS

First published in Great Britain in 2022 by

QUERCUS

Quercus Editions Ltd
Carmelite House
50 Victoria Embankment
London EC4Y 0DZ

An Hachette UK company

A CIP catalogue record for this book is available from the British Library

HB ISBN 978 1 52941 518 6

10 9 8 7 6 5 4 3 2 1

Typeset by CC Book Production
Printed and bound in Great Britain by Clays Ltd, Elcograf S.p.A.

Papers used by Quercus are from well-managed forests and other responsible sources.

To my wonderful wife.

ABOUT TWO YEARS BEFORE

'Forgive me'

Meiling sits alone at the large centrepiece table in an impressively opulent banquet hall. She's bored and unimpressed by the grandeur, but she's enjoying the sultry solo jazz performer on the stage and her fourth glass of champagne of the night.

From her seat, she can see across the palatial hall, and it seems everyone but her husband is staring at her. They don't smile or look away when she locks eyes with them either. She could easily pretend to be having a good time because she's good at pretending. She once had a burgeoning career as an actress, but she quit. Dreams are for little girls, she told herself.

Her husband has been working the crowd for half an hour and hasn't looked in her direction once. She turns away from the stage to search for him again in the lively room. All the men look almost identical in black tuxedos, but she easily spots him. She watches him, and he looks alien to her in a tuxedo, but it handsomely fits his tall and lean frame. She sighs; she knows the worst is over as the dinner will finish soon. But just before she turns back to the stage, her husband catches her eye with a smile.

At fifty-one, age has been good to him. He has the vigour of a younger man and still has all his jet-black hair. He walks towards her, and a plump man follows him closely. She wears a well-practised smile and stands as they approach. In her high heels, she is the same height as her husband and almost a foot taller than the other man.

'Monica, my beautiful wife,' Meiling's husband says to the other man.

'Frank Robert, Hampstead and Kilburn MP,' the man introduces himself with pride.

'Nice to meet you, Frank,' she says, and shakes his outstretched hand. He stands on his toes to kiss her on both cheeks. 'Forgive my husband, call me Meiling; only my gran calls me Monica.'

'Very well, Meiling,' Frank says. 'Your husband speaks highly of you, says you organised this all by yourself.'

'Yes, she did,' her husband interjects. 'The Camden Children Together charity is very dear to her heart. Her father, you know, they took care of him as a boy.'

He turns to Meiling for confirmation, and she nods.

'You've done a wonderful job,' Frank says. 'I thank you on behalf of Hampstead and Kilburn.'

'My pleasure,' she says and glances at her husband with a subtle but peculiar expression that only he will recognise – her simmering annoyance.

'Go on, Frank,' he says. 'Enjoy yourself. I'll see you soon, we'll finish our chat.'

'Sure,' Frank says.

Frank politely smiles at Meiling, and she smiles back. Meiling continues to smile as she watches Frank walk away, and soon as Frank rejoins the crowd, she glares at her husband. But he's oblivious to her glare because he's watching the room.

He turns to her and genuinely smiles as he admires her.

'Monica?' she asks.

He shrugs. 'Forgive me,' he says. 'But . . .'

'But what?' she asks and shakes her head in disgust. 'Meiling is not good enough for your new friends? And no one else can hear you, so just talk normally.'

'Ah, fuck,' he mutters. 'What's wrong now?' he asks in his true coarse London accent, which has a faint hint of Irish in it.

'Nothing,' she snaps. 'I don't like this place. These people look at me like trash.'

'Who did?'

She chuckles. 'What are you going to do about it?' she asks. 'Tell Frank?'

'What?'

'This isn't you. You don't belong here, and these stuck-up fucks know it. They know who you are. Everybody in London knows.'

'I'm not hiding it, am I?' he retorts. 'This lot think I'm a changed man with more money than sense. That's what matters here. Plus, they came, didn't they? And there are press and paps in here and no one's shying away from taking a photo with me . . . enjoying my booze, my food. If this comes off, I'm sweet with this lot. Even get Frank's job in a few years. You'll live the life, and you'll enjoy it. For now, all you need to do is smile, okay?'

She shakes her head, and this angers him.

'Stop that shit,' he commands. 'There are people fucking watching. And smile, for fuck's sake.'

His tone stuns her, and she glares at him, but he looks away. She snatches a customised cigarette case from the table.

'What are you doing?' he asks.

'Going outside for a fag. What does it look like?'

'You're going to leave the bag?' he says, and gestures to a large handbag on the table.

'Yes, it's fucking heavy, you know that.'

'I know, and that's why you'll take it with you. I can't be watching it, and we can't leave that amount of cash lying around these vultures.'

'Why don't you—'

'Don't argue.'

He reaches into the bag and picks out a platinum security bracelet that's attached to it. He grabs her wrist and locks the security bracelet above an exquisite diamond bracelet, which deftly disguises it.

'Fuck this,' she says, and grabs the bag.

She attempts to strut past him, but he places a hand on her belly to stop her.

'Let one of the boys know you are outside,' he softly says. 'Don't want you out there alone looking this ravishing.'

She forces a smile, and he smiles back. She walks across the busy hall to a fire exit and barges out. The night is quiet and sparsely lit. She scans the street, and it's desolate. She walks a few steps to an area of the pavement not lit up by the streetlights, and with every step her stiletto heel produces a sharp sound that echoes into the night.

She places a cigarette between her lips and takes her time to light it. She takes a long drag and savours it before she slowly exhales.

The chill of the April night seeps through her thin dress, and she shivers. She could have gotten her jacket, but she didn't leave through the main entrance, past the cloakroom, because she didn't want one of her husband's boys guarding the entrance to follow her. She's grown tired of their constant presence in her life.

From the moment she started dating her husband – while he was still in his first marriage – her life became one of constant paranoia. Not hers, but his. He has her followed and guarded every minute of the day. He's without a doubt a jealous man, which has something to do with it, but he has a justified fear that she's a prime target for the vast collection of enemies he's amassed through his infamously violent decades in the London underworld.

She takes a last drag and tosses the stub to the ground. She snaps open the cigarette case.

'Gimme the bag!' someone says from behind her.

She turns around to two men wearing full head masks. The taller weedy man wears a Tony Blair mask, and the shorter stocky man wears a Gordon Brown mask. Tony Blair holds a sawed-off shotgun to her face, but Gordon Brown is unarmed.

'Gimme the bag!' Tony Blair repeats in the most assertive voice he can muster in a whisper.

She takes a moment to study both men and grins before she blows the smoke in her mouth from her last drag towards Tony Blair.

'What?' Tony Blair asks. 'You want to die?'

She doesn't respond, and Tony Blair turns to Gordon Brown.

'Why doesn't anyone listen to me?' Tony Blair asks.

Gordon Brown grunts and doesn't take his eyes off her. Tony Blair shrugs and turns back to her.

'Maybe cos you whine like a bitch,' she says.

He's surprised by her defiance and forces a chuckle. 'Gimme the fucking bag now, or—'

'Do you know who my husband is?' she interrupts.

'I don't give a shit.'

She nods. She opens her mouth to speak but decides not to. She doesn't want to indulge any further.

'Please, talk, let's hear it,' Tony Blair says.

'Just to make me happy,' she says. 'My husband will cut you both to pieces and feed you to his dogs. He loves those dogs. I don't much care for them, but they've got to be fed.'

'Believe me,' Tony Blair says. 'If not for the masks you'd see the horror in our faces.' He chuckles. 'Give me the fucking bag.'

'No.'

Tony Blair shakes his head in frustration, and she smiles.

'You expected me to be overwhelmed with fear and just

hand you the bag,' she says. 'But I'm not, and now you're fucked. Because you know who I am, you know who my husband is, and you can't touch me. Plus, I don't suppose you were just walking past on the prowl . . . wearing these ludicrous masks. Someone sent you for the bag. Someone on the inside.'

She shakes her head in disgust, and Tony Blair attempts to speak.

'No,' she commands. 'You're done. But I'll give you five seconds' head start before I scream, and my husband's boys come running. And you can tell whoever sent you that you couldn't have gotten the bag anyway.'

She extends her left arm to show that the bag is secured to her wrist, but Tony Blair is captivated by the glistening diamond bracelet.

'No . . .' she says.

In one sudden motion, Gordon Brown pulls a cleaver from his jacket and swings with full force clean through her wrist. The bag falls to the ground with her hand still attached, and before she can react, he hurls a fist onto the side of her head, and she collapses, unconscious.

'Suka,' Gordon Brown mutters in a deep, mature voice.

Tony Blair is stunned. 'Ah, shit! Holy fucking shit!' he says. 'Why the fuck did you do that?'

Gordon Brown ignores him and picks up the bag and the attached hand.

'You fucked me,' Tony Blair says. 'You fucking fucked me, man. Fucking hell!'

'Shut up. Let's go!' Gordon Brown says with a pronounced Russian accent.

'Fuck no!' Tony Blair says, and runs away.

Gordon Brown grunts and runs off in the opposite direction.

06:45

'You got any candy for me, big man?'

The muffled funk beats of 'Super Freak' begin; it's finally 06:45. Yes, it's 2012 and 'Super Freak' is my alarm tone, and in case you're wondering, no, I wasn't born when the song was released, I've just always loved the song – although I've never cared much for Rick James. But the alarm doesn't wake me because I'm not asleep; I couldn't sleep. I pull my phone from underneath the pillow to stop the alarm and step off the bed. I carefully stretch every limb and then begin my morning workout.

Eighty squats later, I walk around the small second-rate hotel room to relax my legs. I stop at the window and part the curtains to look outside. It's bright and sunny for a spring day, just as the forecast said. Good start. I drop to the floor for a hundred push-ups, turn over for a hundred sit-ups, and then stretch for another five minutes to finish. I've kept up the same routine for almost a decade. Some days I add more exercises, but that's an arbitrary decision; my days haven't exactly been busy for a while now.

I walk to the sink in the tiny bathroom and immediately spot my anxiety in the mirror over the sink. I look away and brush my teeth without even a glance back at the mirror. I've hardly slept the past forty-eight hours, so for a moment I try to convince myself that tiredness is what I saw in the mirror, but no, it was anxiety. I try to enjoy a hot shower, but my mind can't help going over what's ahead today. I've done my best to plan and plan and plan again, but with me, things rarely work out as planned. Today, good luck, or maybe even just average luck, is crucial.

I dry myself with a towel and walk to a chair beside the bed. My jeans and t-shirt are folded on the chair, my duffel bag and trainers are underneath, and my leather jacket hangs over the back. I dress, wear my watch, and slot my phone into a jacket pocket. I sling the duffel bag across my back and put the towel and toothbrush into a plastic bag.

I walk out of the cheap hotel just minutes away from Waterloo station and head towards the McDonald's I'd seen on my way from the station last night. I toss the plastic bag into a half-full skip I'd also seen last night.

The McDonald's is busy, but I make sure to sit at the table closest to the only way in and out. I observe the restaurant as I eat, and there's nothing out of the ordinary. I check my watch; it's 07:54. It's time. I take a moment to enjoy the last piece of my double bacon and sausage bagel, which tastes much better than I remember, before I make the call. The call rings once before it's answered, but no one speaks on the other end.

'Topper?' I say.

'Yeah, who the fuck wants to know?' the voice on the other end says with a thick Caribbean accent.

'I'm sure I'm the only one left that calls you Topper, Topper.'

'Shit, you, brother,' Topper excitedly says.

'What's the closest station to yours?'

'Station? What, you mean train station?'

'Yeah.'

'Nah, brother! You don't move shit like that using the fucking tube.'

'It's okay,' I say, and glance at the duffel bag between my feet. 'I'll worry about that.'

'Get a cab, I'll pay.'

I smile. 'I'm not broke, Topper.'

'Aright, man,' he says, and laughs. 'You just get to Kilburn station. I'll send someone pick you up.'

'All right. I'll be there in about twenty minutes.'

'Aright, my youth will be there, still.'

'Okay.'

I end the call.

Tyrone is the rather overweight man sitting in the back seat of a speeding Audi A6 Saloon. He oozes the aura befitting his station – that of a successful man in a cutthroat business. The business is selling drugs, and not pharmaceuticals either, but if the price is right, Tyrone will sell you those too. A handful of people call him Topper, a name he adopted in his early teenage years as a bad grime rapper – bad as in awful. He's third-generation British Jamaican, and although he's never been to Jamaica, he sure acts like a yardie. And like most untrained actors, his performance is exaggerated, but so is his propensity for violence. His fuse is beyond short, and the resulting violence is always dramatic, but that keeps the doubters quiet.

Tyrone tosses his phone onto the seat and turns to the light-skinned black man with long dreadlocks in the passenger seat.

'Colin,' Tyrone says. 'Call Nori n tell im go Kilburn station to pick up the product we expecting.'

Tyrone takes his time to relight a spliff, and Colin watches with complete attention.

'He bring the man with the product to the castle,' Tyrone says, and takes a long drag of the spliff. 'I don't want Nori chatting to my man, yeah? Nori chats too fucking much. And you tell Nori to best be careful with my man, cos man's a pure killer.'

'Sure thing, boss,' Colin says.

'Blizzard coming for the northwest, you get me,' Tyrone says, excited.

Colin nods, and Tyrone takes another long drag. Tyrone laughs to himself and turns to the driver.

'Stop at Mickey Dees, yeah,' Tyrone says. 'Man wants a fucking bagel. Man wants two fucking bagels, you know.'

Tyrone laughs, and Colin forces a smile. Colin considers reminding Tyrone of his diet – he ought to be on a strict diet recently imposed by a nutritionist to contain his diabetes – but thinks better of it and turns away.

I haven't thought about the London Underground in years, so I had no idea I'd missed it so much. The platform is congested, but as always, no one seems aware of the next person. It's even more peculiar on the train because my carriage is crammed and it's obvious that everyone is avoiding eye contact, which is fine with me. It's amusing to watch, but anxiety and thoughts of what's ahead in the coming hours soon bury the pleasure.

The train moves overground at Finchley Road station, two stops from Kilburn, and I consider calling Topper but decide to wait till I get to Kilburn. A few minutes later, the train arrives at Kilburn station, and I step off with about fifty other people. I shuffle along amid the crowd, which moves slowly down the stairs to the barriers. I look through the crowd for what is causing the slow pace and call Topper.

He instantly answers. 'Feds at the station, brother, and they got sniffers,' he frantically says, and I see the police officers at the barriers with two keen dogs.

'Oh, I'm sorry, Auntie,' I calmly say. 'I thought you meant Kilburn station. I'll be on my way to Kilburn Park now.'

'What the—' he says.

'I know, Auntie, I'm sorry,' I interrupt and chuckle. 'Okay . . . all right, I'll hurry. See you soon.'

'Aright, aright.'

I end the call and turn around to walk back up the stairs. I wade through the crowd and smile politely at everyone I brush past. I get to the top of the stairs, and there is no train at either platform. If the police noticed me turn around, I'm fucked.

I walk to the southbound platform and mix in with the people dotted along it. I'm on edge but try to appear as calm as possible. I focus on the details of my trainers, trying to hide my face and stop my urge to look around. I can't stop myself; I turn to the stairs.

I watch people walk up the steps and disperse onto the platforms, and I relax, but then a police officer marches up the steps. I turn to the tracks and see a southbound train approaching. I take a deep breath, and another, and then glance at the stairs, but the police officer is nowhere in sight.

The train stops at the platform, and I join the queue waiting at the closest carriage door. I search for the police officer as people get off the train, and I see him a couple steps away, approaching. My heart rate erupts, and I instinctively clench my fists as I study the officer. We seem the same age, but that's where our similarities end. I'm bigger, stronger, and without doubt, I will be meaner than he could ever be. He has no firearm, just a Taser and a baton. I will hurt him, bad. But then he smiles at me, and my fight instinct disappears. I smile back, a genuine smile too, and I don't know where it came from. I look away and realise the queue ahead has entered the train and the train doors are about to close. I hop in.

The train doors close and I watch the police officer continue down the platform. The train departs, and I relax. That was close, or was it? There are no empty seats, so I wipe my sweaty palms on my jeans and grab a support pole in the middle of the carriage. I call Topper, and it rings once before he answers.

'You aright, brother?' he asks.

'I'm on my way to Kilburn Park.'

'Bless, brother. My youth will be there. Why you hide your number though? Was trying to ring you . . .'

'It's okay, Topper. I'll call when we need to talk.'

'Aright, brother. My youth name Noriega. He's wearing a black Adidas jumper and a black cap. Dark-skinned boy. Got a scar on the face . . . big ugly thing, you can't miss it. He'll be waiting for you.'

'Okay,' I say, and end the call.

Getting to Kilburn Park station doesn't take as much time as I expected and, in contrast to Kilburn station, it's not busy. Soon as I step off the escalator, I see Noriega leaning on the wall beyond the barriers and spot the scar across his face that cuts through his lips. He nonchalantly watches me step through the barriers and approach him.

'Noriega?' I ask.

'Yeah, bruv, you?' Noriega asks, with a squeaky voice reminiscent of the Chipmunks.

The voice startles me, and I have to fight back a smile. 'Where's the car?' I ask.

'Outside.'

I wait for him to lead the way, but he doesn't move; he just stares at my bag.

'Noriega,' I say, somewhat sternly. 'Let's get to the car, yeah?'

He looks up from my bag and stares at me for a couple more seconds before he cracks a peculiar smile. 'All right,' he says, and bounces off the wall.

He leads out of the station, and I wear my sunglasses as we walk across the road to a line of cars parked along the street. He pushes a button on a key fob, and a fresh Mercedes CLK parked ahead unlocks. This surprises me, and I study the car before I turn to him, and he smirks as he walks around to the driver side. I step into the passenger seat, and the car still has that new car smell. I look through the interior as he steps into the driver's seat, and it's pristine. He continues to smirk as he starts the car and drives.

Noriega drives at considerable speed through the busy high road. We narrowly beat a red traffic light, and I worry about being stopped. Ordinarily, a person of Noriega's age, race, and appearance driving such an expensive car arouses suspicion, and to add to that, he's driving like a mad man. For all I know, the car could be stolen too . . . fuck! I need to stop my mind going deeper down this hole.

'I see Topper's doing very well for himself,' I say.

'Who Topper?' he asks.

'Tyrone.'

'Who's Tyrone?'

My paranoia resurfaces, but I fight to remain calm. 'Your boss,' I say.

'Snowman? Nobody calls him Topper or Tyrone. We call him Snowman,' he says and grins. 'Bossman controls the snow in northwest, you get me.'

Snowman, really? But then I'm not surprised, it is Tyrone. Plus, Noriega's amusing voice isn't helping. We stop at a traffic light, and he turns to me.

'The fuck-up now, yeah, is what we selling is weak, bruv, and mandem in South got some power ting,' he says, and glances at the traffic light. 'Snowman try get mandem connect, yeah, but mandem acting all tight and that. We're going have to get active with mandem soon, you know.'

I nod, but I'm struggling with what he said. Not that I think it's a lie, although I'm sure there is a fair bit of embellishment. But why is this kid telling me? I didn't even ask, and even if I did, he ought to know not to tell. This isn't a good look for Topper's operation.

'How old are you?' I ask.

'Twenty-one.'

I nod. I thought Noriega was young, but he looks older than twenty-one. Maybe because of the scar across the lips. He stops at an intersection and turns to me with his peculiar smile.

'Got this Merc last week . . . part of a promotion package.'

I nod. It's obvious Noriega wants me to ask about his *promotion*, but I don't indulge. As I expect, he tells me anyway.

'Me and my brethren were the top boys round these ends for a long time,' he says. 'Now, I'm the top man.'

'That's . . . nice.'

He makes a sharp turn into a street and parks in front of a dishevelled house. He switches off the car, and I scan the near-dilapidated houses on both sides of the street for as far as the eye can see.

'Are we here?' I ask.

'Nah, bruv, just checking my *food*,' he says with that smirk, and steps out the car.

This fucking idiot has taken me on a detour just to show his spot . . . where he's the 'top boy'.

'You coming, bruv?' he asks. 'I don't think you want to wait in the car. The kids out here are wildings.'

I nod and step out of the car. The street is full of kids from about seven years old to mid-teens. More boys, but then a lot more girls than I expected. Most of the kids are dressed identically. Hoodies with jeans or track bottoms that sag at the hips and reveal underwear or another pair of track bottoms. And expensive trainers, mostly Air Jordans it appears from a quick glance. Did I dress like this at their age? I don't think so, but then I can't be sure.

Most of the kids just loiter, but a group of the older kids excitedly provoke a large Pitbull Mastiff, which is being held back with a chain leash by an equally large kid. I think this is a school day . . . well, maybe not . . . I really don't know. But regardless, I suppose this is where these kids learn the tools they think they need to thrive. And to their credit, here they are bright and early, dressed in uniform, ready to learn.

I scan the street, and litter and graffiti are everywhere. I appreciate art, but there was no attempt to make the graffiti art. I suppose neither Banksy nor a street sweeper would venture this way. You can feel the lost hope and angst in the air. I recognise the feeling anywhere because I was raised in the depths of it, somewhere not too far from here.

Noriega acknowledges a few of the kids with a nod and leads me to the door. We approach the house, and I recognise its distinctive repugnant odour. A mixture of dried sweat, faeces, piss, vomit, and other things your mind doesn't want or need to comprehend – it's the eclectic odour of a crack house. Noriega knocks the sturdy front door twice and gestures a middle finger at the peephole.

'A lot of brethren lost their lives or in pen for this here,' Noriega says, somewhat poignantly, but then he smirks. 'But better them than me, you get me?'

I don't care. I have no business here, but I nod and take off my sunglasses. Let's just get this over with. There is a thud from a heavy latch, and a kid no older than sixteen pulls the door open. The kid is exhausted and flinches at the daylight. He raises his hands to cover his eyes, and I see a converted handgun tucked in his track bottoms. Noriega shoves the kid aside and leads me into the hallway with several lifeless junkies sprawled across the floor.

The kid shuts the door, and the hallway becomes dark. I side-step the bodies as we walk through the hallway, but Noriega shows no such grace; he walks on the bodies and deliberately steps on their heads. The junkies don't seem to mind because they can't get any worse for wear. I step on a syringe, and it crushes underneath my trainers. Oh, fuck!

'Don't walk on the floor, bruv. You don't know what's there. Use the human carpet,' Noriega says and laughs. 'And don't touch the walls.'

I want to charge at him and cut his throat with a piece of the shattered syringe, but I take a moment to calm myself. I tiptoe around the bodies into what ought to be the living room. Soon as we step into the room, a petite teenage girl runs to Noriega and attempts to speak, but he shoves her, and she crashes to the floor.

'Wait here, yeah? I'll go check the food quick,' Noriega says to me. 'And best hold your cock, bruv.'

He laughs and walks towards a door across the room. I scan the room, and it's filled with junkies; most are women, only two men. Most of the junkies are lifeless, but in a corner of the room, a woman kneels at the feet of a man, and he has a hand full of her hair as she sucks his cock. I can't tell if he's enjoying it because he just looks crazed. Across the room, the other man urinates on the wall. In the centre of the room, a thick naked woman rummages through the carpet for crack rocks.

Noriega unlocks the door with a key and quietly opens it. He steps through the door into the kitchen and slams it shut behind him. This wakes all the junkies, and they gather at the door like zombies. The petite teenage girl tries to fight her way to the front, but she can't. She turns and runs to me.

'You got any candy for me, big man?' she pleads.

I don't respond and stare at her, and it's easy to see that she was once pretty because she still has her defined cheekbones and alluring green eyes.

'I'll suck you off, big man,' she says, and reaches for my crotch.

I parry her hand, and then I notice her belly. I focus on it to be sure, and yes, she's pregnant. I feel for the unborn child, but not for her. She reaches for my crotch again, but I step out of her reach, and this infuriates her.

'Fuck off, you fucking faggot!' she screams.

I lock eyes with her and look down to her belly, but she doesn't acknowledge. I attempt to speak, but the kitchen door opens, and she rushes towards the door. Noriega keeps his hands in his pockets as he walks past the junkies, and they reach for him like a messiah. You can tell he loves it. Suddenly, he pulls out his hands and tosses crack rocks to the centre of the room. The junkies race to the rocks. They dive, scratch, claw, and fight to get to them. A woman shoves the pregnant girl, and she crashes onto the floor, but she fights to her feet and runs to Noriega. She attempts to beg, but he shoves her onto the floor.

'I look like Santa fucking Claus to you, bitch?' Noriega scolds.

He steps over her and walks to me, and I do my best to hide the rage bubbling inside of me.

'Let's go, bruv. Plenty food, still,' he says, and walks out of the living room.

I turn towards the pregnant girl, and she stares at me. I reach for my wallet, but I stop and walk out of the room.

Noriega is in high spirits as he drives to Topper's, but I stare out the window to watch the streets. It's not that Noriega isn't talking – he hasn't stopped, and he probably won't – I'm just not paying any attention. He parks in front of a large detached house on a quiet suburban street about five minutes away from his spot. The house looks abandoned, so do the neighbouring houses, and the street is empty. Noriega pulls out a burner phone and makes a call.

'We're here,' he says and ends the call. He puts the phone away and turns to the house. 'Snowman calls it the castle. It's a fortress, bruv. Fucking reinforced doors, windows, walls, all that, yeah. Nobody can get in, not even feds.' He laughs and points to the front door. 'Unless they open the door for you.'

I nod and watch the door for what seems like an eternity as we wait for it to open. I check the time on my watch; it's 09:32. And when I turn back to the door, it opens. I step out, but Noriega doesn't, so I turn back to him.

'Snowman don't need me,' he says. 'And I got food, still. No need for re-up, you get me.'

I nod.

'You know the spot, bruv,' he says. 'I'll be there all day today pressing them boys. Make sure we ready for the new product and that. Come through when you done with bossman. Anything you want on the house, yeah.'

'Thanks,' I say, and turn to walk towards the house.

For his sake, I hope we don't meet again.

09:33

'The game never changes, brother, it just gets more fierce' 'Welcome to the castle'

I approach the open door, but I can't see anything beyond it, just darkness. I step through the door, and two muscular arms from either side of the door immediately reach across to stop me. Two large men stand at either side of the door. The taller man closes the door behind me, and the shorter man steps closer to frisk me. I remain calm but fasten my arm around my bag as his hands approach it. He stops and looks at me with a smirk. I don't acknowledge it, but I'm distracted by how good he smells – as if he bathed in perfume.

'Don't worry, I'm not checking the bag,' he says. 'Just want to know if you have anything in there you want to tell us about . . . before it's too late, you know.'

They both snigger, and I'd love to crack their heads in, but the reality is they'll do a lot more damage to me than I'll ever do to them, unarmed as I am now.

'You got anything, man?' the taller man demands.

'No,' I calmly answer.

'Okay, down the hall to the right, he's waiting for you,' the shorter man says, and steps aside.

I take a step past them into a long dark hallway, and the good smell intensifies. I walk through the hallway and study my surroundings, evaluating the threat level and my chance to survive and escape if it comes to that. I've become good and quick at the study because I've done it every day for years. Without doubt I'm paranoid, but it's saved me on occasion. I peek through an ajar door to my left and spot at least five naked women chatting in the centre of what looks like a kitchen, and then two armed men standing guard in separate corners of the room.

At the end of the hallway, a thick light-skinned black man stands in front of a closed door. His long dreadlocks flow past his waist and slightly conceal a large handgun tucked in the waistband of his baggy jeans. I approach him and attempt to speak, but he steps aside and opens the door.

I step into the room, and Topper is sitting behind a rather ostentatious desk. The room, or office if you want to call it that, is extravagantly furnished and decorated with garish portraits of fictional gangsters and Tupac Shakur. An artful painting of Tony Montana sitting on his throne hangs suggestively behind Topper. The room also smells just as good as the hallway.

'Welcome to the castle,' Topper proudly says, and smiles.

He seems genuinely happy to see me. I force a smile back and walk to the desk. Topper slowly stands, and his lavish chair looks almost identical to Tony Montana's throne in the painting. He limps around the desk and embraces me. He squeezes for longer than I appreciate before he releases the embrace.

'Sit, brother,' he says, and gestures to a chair in front of his desk.

I nod. I sit and place my bag on the desk, and he limps back to his throne.

'Hope my boys weren't too rough, frisking you and that . . . but, you understand,' he says.

'It's okay,' I say. 'I see you're doing very well for yourself.'

'Yeah, man, I'm blessed.'

'Good for you,' I say, with more than a hint of sarcasm.

'Fuck you,' he says, and we laugh. 'Truly, brother, it's all God.'

'God? Okay, whatever you say, Topper. I hear you go by Snowman now?'

'Yeah, brother, I keep the streets as cold as December every fucking day.'

'Really?' I say, oozing sarcasm.

'What, you hear something different?' he asks, suddenly furious. 'That youth Noriega running—'

'No,' I interrupt, and raise a hand to calm him. 'Noriega said nothing.'

'Now that's a fucking lie.'

I smile, and he laughs.

'Fucking youth just runs his mouth. But he does well for me . . . and he's my first cousin.'

I nod.

'Snowman?' I ask. 'C'mon, Topper, that's just stealing Young Jeezy's identity.'

He laughs loudly.

'Nah, not like that,' he says. 'I like Young Jeezy, no lie. But the name true to me, you know. I keep the streets steady cold with that caine.'

'Fair enough.'

'Thought rap was not your thing though.'

'Nothing's my thing, really. I enjoy good music. Speaking of, what happened to you rapping?'

He laughs and leans into his chair. 'Look around you, brother. I'm living the life these broke motherfucking rappers only dream about.'

I nod. That is true.

'Anyway, I'm on the clock, let's do this,' I say.

'Aright, I been watching your bag too.'

'That's okay, but I don't see any money.'

'I know you too well,' he says, and laughs. 'You see nothing till I see the bricks.'

'Okay, not like I have a choice.'

He shrugs. I unzip the bag and stack the cocaine on the desk, and he grins, revealing several gold teeth. He looks past me to the dreadlocked man at the door, and the man shouts a name I can't quite make out.

A moment later, a young woman carrying a large but light equipment case strides past me to Topper and places the case on the desk. She opens the case, but I can't see what's inside because the top blocks my view.

She picks out three test tubes and chooses a random brick. She pierces the brick with a penknife and scoops out a small amount of cocaine. She pours the cocaine as evenly as she can into the test tubes. She picks out three dropper bottles from the case – one bottle is amber so I can't discern the liquid's colour, but the other two have clear liquids in them.

She adds a drop from each bottle into one test tube, and the cocaine in one test tube immediately turns blue. There is no change in the other test tubes, and I watch them with increasing apprehension, mainly because I don't know what to expect. Then I begin to question if it's just a fucking ruse.

'Brother,' Topper says, interrupting my thought. 'You've got big balls carrying this shit across town on the fucking Tube.'

'I suppose.'

'Respect, brother.'

I nod. I'm not interested in conversation, and Topper recognises this. We both return our focus to the test tubes. Nothing happens for what seems like an eternity, and my attention soon drifts to the *scientist*.

It's clear she takes care of herself because her arms are muscular, her belly is toned, her legs are well built, and she's had work done on her breasts. She also strikes me as self-confident, which leads me to wonder what drew her into this line of work. Suddenly, she winks at me, and I realise I've been staring at her. I politely smile, and she smiles back. She turns to Topper and nods approvingly.

'What that mean, Nicole?' he asks.

'Pure. A1 Grade.'

'You're fucking with me?'

'No, boss, I don't make mistakes.'

I turn to the test tubes and the powder in one of the other test tubes is dark brown and frothing, but there is no change in the last test tube; good for me, it seems. Topper grabs the already open brick and directs Nicole to a chest of drawers beside her. She turns to it, and he gestures for the top drawer. She opens the drawer, and there's a .44 Magnum revolver, a pack of cartridges, and knife inside.

'The knife,' Topper says.

She picks the knife, shuts the drawer, and hands Topper the knife. He drives the knife into the brick and then licks the tip of the blade. He jolts and shuts his eyes. He smacks his forehead repeatedly, and I'm worried, but Nicole is unconcerned.

A few seconds later, he stops smacking his forehead and opens his eyes. His pupils have dilated, and he's excited.

'Get the girls ready to start the cook!' he says to Nicole. 'The first two batches you make fucking top quality, yeah?'

She nods and packs up her equipment.

'Step on the rest,' he says, and gestures to the bricks on the table. 'We need to make this last.'

'Sure.'

She winks at me as she leaves, and I can't help but smile.

'Colin, bring it!' Topper barks.

Colin, the dreadlocked man at the door, hurries to the desk. He turns over a black bin bag, and bundles of crisp twenty-pound notes fall onto the desk. I scan the bundles, and they don't add up to the negotiated price.

'Take the bricks to the girls,' Topper says to Colin.

Colin nods and puts the bricks into the bin bag.

'Put word on road,' Topper continues. 'New product coming fresh out Snowman's kitchen at 4 p.m., real power ting! We call it . . .' He takes a moment to think. 'Killer snowflakes.' He smirks as he delights in his creativity. 'But let the motherfuckers know they get no re-up unless they sell out the old ting, yeah? Weak or not, you see me, don't give a fuck.'

Colin nods.

'Motherfuckers can't sell crack to crackheads, and they be calling themselves pushers,' Topper says. 'Shiiit! I'm running a fucking business here.'

Topper must be playing to the gallery, which includes just me in this case, because he can't be like this all the time. He just can't, can he?

Colin nods again and walks out of the room.

'I know this don't look like what we agreed,' Topper says to me. 'But I have something for you, something really nice, brother.'

'Shut up, I want nothing but—'

'Oi, bruv!' he barks. 'Fucking calm yourself, yeah?'

He scowls at me, but I'm unfazed and glare at him.

'Still fearless, yeah?' he says, and chuckles.

He pulls open a desk drawer, picks out a furled handkerchief, and places it on the bundles of cash. He unfurls the handkerchief, and I am instantly captivated by the glistening bracelet inside. It's gold and adorned with round diamonds. It's stunning and worth a fuck ton of money, but it's not the deal.

'What the fuck's that, Topper?' I ask.

'The good shit,' he says, surprised and annoyed by my reaction.

'Okay, but what makes you think I want the good shit?'

'You were in the jewellery business back in the day. And I hear this cost an arm and a leg.'

'Right. So why give it to me? Keep it, or sell it and give me the cash we agreed.'

'I got no use for these things, and I can't sell it.'

'Why not?'

'Cos I'm Snowman. Everybody know man and they don't trust man. Or they try to cheat man cos they know man know nothing about gold and diamonds and that. But they don't know you . . . not anymore. And you know about diamonds and all that, so they can't cheat you, you know.' He smiles. 'Plus, man don't need the cash.'

'Everybody needs cash.'

'Nah, brother, I got too much cash. No more room under the mattress,' he says, and chuckles. 'You can see it a gift too, for what you done for me. You know.'

I do know. I glance at my watch; it's 10:07. I have no time for the banter. 'Whatever, I'll take it,' I say, and he grins.

I pick up the bracelet and examine it for a moment. It's more beautiful up close, and all the diamonds appear flawless.

I slot the bracelet into the inside pocket of my bag and drag the money into the bag.

'We're done, I'm off,' I say, and stand.

'Shit. You're not going chill with your brother?'

'I've got something to take care of.'

'That don't sound good.'

He forces a smile and stares at me, hoping that I fill the uncomfortable silence with an explanation of what I'm here to take care of, but I don't respond.

'Aright,' he says. 'But Nori busy, so I call you a cab.'

'Thanks.'

'Sit down, cab going take like ten minutes.'

I nod and sit.

'A cab for my brother!' he barks, and smirks. 'It feel good to be the boss, me no lie.'

'I'm sure it is. But, Topper, what the fuck is up with your grammar? I understand you didn't finish college, but last time I saw you, and I know this is more than a decade ago, you spoke relatively good English.'

He bursts into laughter, but it's still clear he's angry that I called him out.

'Anyway, what's the smell?' I ask.

'One Million,' he boasts.

'You serious?'

'What, you don't like it?' he asks, and gestures to the sealed-up windows in the room. 'All the windows in the castle shut up, you know. So the castle got its own ventilation system. I got the man fix it up with some fragrance. One Million was the only choice. I love that fragrance. We run through like ten big bottles a week, brother.'

I nod and don't speak because I won't be able to hide my disapproval. But then it is his money, and it does smell very good in here . . . his castle.

'I should buy shares in that motherfucker . . .' he says and thinks.

'Paco Rabanne?'

'Yes, that's the motherfucker, Paco,' he says, and laughs. 'Let's walk.'

We amble through the hallway to the castle's front door, and Topper speaks extensively about the state of his empire. He laments about having the territory and manpower, but not the adequate product, and is fuelled with excitement when he talks about his efforts to secure the South London connect. He hopes the top-grade cocaine I supplied him, properly stretched, will last till he secures the connect.

We stop just outside the castle's door to wait for the cab.

'So, I've got to ask, brother,' he says. 'Where you been all these years?'

'Miami . . . with Tony Montana.'

He laughs. 'Aright. You back for good, brother? I could use your name and talent on road. You help me with the Brixton mandem. I know you got shit to take care of, but I'll be here when you done with it. I'll pay you fucking well too.'

'I'm done with all that, Topper. And my name doesn't mean anything on road anymore. Been away like a century in road time, the game's changed.'

'The game never changes, brother, it just gets more fierce.'

I nod and scan the desolate street. 'I'm guessing you don't get any trouble from neighbours,' I say. 'Doesn't look like you have any.'

'Yeah. There isn't much of a neighbourhood round here. After the o-eight crisis, a lot of these houses were repossessed and abandoned. That's why I chose this location. I bought most of the houses on the street, and they stay empty till I need them. A few other houses are occupied though, but them know not to fuck with Snowman. I mind my business, cause no trouble, and they mind their business.'

'What about the police?'

'I police this fucking ends, brother. I'm the law round here.'

I nod. Huey Newton would be proud.

A Toyota Corolla parks in front of the castle.

'Your cab,' he says, and gestures to the car.

'Good seeing you again, Topper.'

'Sure. Mi casa su casa. Come back anytime, anything you want on the house.'

I chuckle; Noriega said the same thing.

'What?' he asks, confused.

'Nothing. But, speaking Spanish now? Where did the Snowman learn that?'

'College,' he retorts, and we laugh.

'And it just Snowman,' he says. 'Not the Snowman . . . you see me?'

'Sure, I can't not see you, Snowman.'

'Oi, brother, I'm on a diet!' he says, and we laugh again.

We hug, and it's another long embrace. He smacks me on the back before he releases the embrace, and I walk to the cab. I step into the passenger seat and turn back to the castle. Topper hasn't moved, and he's watching me.

'Where to?' the cab driver asks.

'The station, Kilburn station.'

10:21

'My name's not important'

The cab turns onto the high road, and I watch the rear-view mirror until we are clear of the turning to make sure we're not being followed. I open my bag and pick the bracelet from the inside pocket. I hold it inside the bag because I don't want the driver to see it. It has ten diamonds that are at least three carats and are flawless to the naked eye. It'll be a precious possession to every living soul, including me. I have to fence it sharpish because the longer I keep it, the harder it'll be to let go.

I pull out my phone and call Oleg. He answers after one ring; he always does.

'Hello?' he says in his peculiar Russian accent.

'Hello, Saviour.'

'Yes, my friend, but it is not our time yet.'

'I know, but I need your help, and it's urgent.'

'Go ahead, Oleg's listening.'

'Need to get rid of an old business item ASAP . . . got it from Topper.'

'Jewellery?'

'Yes.'

'Hmm. There's no one in that area I trust for good value.'

'What about your Persian friend in Marble Arch?'

'The Sheikh?'

'No. I think he's called Farrukh or something like that.'

'Yes, that's him. He's Sheikh Farrukh now. He's not a friend. Business associate. And I haven't done business with him in years. He's now . . . exclusive. Has his clients and isn't interested in new ones. Unless the item is special.'

'This is.'

'Okay. Farrukh is a tough appraiser though.'

'I'll be fine.'

'This is true. Okay, his shop is called Farrukh's Gold. Give me a second, I'll find you the address.'

'Okay.'

I wait a few seconds.

'You have pen and paper?' he asks.

'Don't need it, just tell me.'

He laughs and reads the address to me. I memorise it, but he repeats it, just to be sure.

'When you get in the shop, you'll first meet his son,' he says. 'Can't remember his name now, but you ask him for the Sheikh. The son is not a good businessman, doesn't have as good an eye for the merchandise. You understand?'

'I do. Thanks. I'll call you back in due time.'

'Take it easy, my friend.'

I end the call and turn to the cab driver. He hasn't said a word since he asked for my destination; I like that.

'Hey, I'm going to Marble Arch now, that okay?'

He nods, and I tell him the address.

The car has a distinct flowery scent I don't like, but I'd ignored it because the journey to the station would have been brief. I wear my sunglasses and look around the car for where the scent is coming from. I spot a Tottenham Hotspur air freshener hanging from the rear-view mirror and smile.

'You support Spurs too?' he asks, excited.

'No,' I answer, and watch his excitement fade. 'Man United.'

That sets him off. He teases me about supporting Manchester United, bemoans Chelsea's Champions League victory, which led to Tottenham losing their place in next year's Champions League, and dismisses the national team's chances at the Euros. On another day, I would have been more involved in the conversation. I'd boast about my United fandom even though I was born and raised in South London. Curse the mercenaries at City. And support Roy Hodgson. But my thoughts are on more pressing matters. George, the cab driver, doesn't seem to mind. He continues talking through my occasional nod, 'right', 'true', 'okay', 'wow', 'not really', 'shit', and the odd chuckle.

George parks in front of an unremarkable jewellery shop on a dead-end street in Marylebone. It is Farrukh's Gold, and no one would find it by chance.

'How much?' I ask.

'Fifteen pounds,' he says.

I hand him a twenty-pound note and step out of the car. I remove my sunglasses and push the shop door, but it doesn't move. I pull, but it still doesn't move. I look through the glass door to a man standing behind a counter showcase, and he hasn't noticed me. I ring the doorbell twice, and he stares at me for a short while before he unlocks the door. I step in and greet the man with a nod, and he forces a smile. He's the only one in the shop, and he wouldn't be a deterrent for anyone determined to rob the place. He's lanky and wearing thick glasses and an araqchin over his balding head.

I stroll around the small shop, and it is uninspiring, both the layout and quality of merchandise. I glance at the man, and he's lost patience, which is what I want, but I continue to browse.

'Hello, I'm Javad,' he says. 'Can I help you? You see anything you like?'

'I'd like to see the Sheikh, please,' I say.

'My father is busy at the moment. I can handle you.'

It's clear from his tone that isn't the first time he's had to say that.

'I'm not here to buy, I'm here to sell.'

'As I said, I can handle you.'

'I'm sure you can, Javad. But please, tell your father he was recommended to me. And what I'm here to sell is worth every moment of his time.'

'Can I have a look at it?' he says, with more than a hint of doubt.

'Sure.'

I pick out the bracelet and offer it to him. He's stunned by its beauty and doesn't conceal the emotion – Oleg is correct, he isn't right for this business. He takes the bracelet and briefly examines it before he hands it back. Without saying a word, he turns and walks through a door I hadn't noticed. The door closes, and I realise it's masked as a shelf. Not original, but it fooled me. Fuck, I'm rusty.

I examine the merchandise in the shop while I wait for Javad to return. The sum of it is between six to seven thousand, not worth the trouble for a professional thief. Which is why there is no security guard, I suppose. I glance at my watch, and it's been over five minutes since he left. Then I notice all the watches in the shop are two minutes behind mine. That is odd.

A couple more minutes pass before the hidden door opens. 'Right this way, sir,' he says.

Sir? Okay, then. I walk around the counter and step through the door into a small hallway. He shuts the door behind us and leads me towards a vault-like blast door.

'Wait right here, sir,' he says, and I stop a couple steps away from the door. He enters a four-digit code. 'Right this way, sir.'

I step into a room that's in sharp contrast to the shop floor. It's striking and filled with lavish jewellery, like my dream score when I was a professional. The sum of the merchandise is—

'Hello, Mr?' a deep old voice says, interrupting my thought.

I turn to the voice, and an elderly man wearing an araqchin over his full head of black hair sits behind a desk. He is Farrukh, I'm sure. I hadn't seen him earlier because he's behind a large industrial microscope. He rolls away from the microscope and squints in my direction, but he doesn't see me. He puts on his thick glasses and spots me. He must be near blind without those glasses because I'm less than five steps away.

'Mr?' he inquires.

'My name's not important,' I say, and scan the room – there is no one else but us and Javad.

'Okay, Mr, let me see what you have to sell.'

Javad gestures to a chair in front of Farrukh's desk, and I sit. Farrukh is frail, so I'm perplexed by the lack of security. If someone is determined enough to get through the blast door, what's the old man's move? There's no way he could pull a weapon, if he has one, faster than a professional. Then I spot a monitor beside Farrukh with four screens showing both rooms. I didn't notice any cameras; Farrukh knows what he's doing.

Farrukh speaks to Javad in Farsi, and Javad leaves and locks Farrukh and me in the room.

'So, may I see it,' Farrukh says.

'My apologies,' I say.

I hand Farrukh the bracelet, and he thoroughly inspects it.

'Where did you get this, sir?' he asks.

Sir again, right.

'It was a gift,' I say.

He nods and returns to inspecting the bracelet. He puts it under his microscope but doesn't focus on the diamonds. In this materialistic world, the maker's mark could mean a difference of almost fifty thousand.

He turns to me with a soft smile. 'I'll give you three hundred and fifty thousand for it,' he says.

'Sorry?' I'm surprised and almost forget to hide it – the price beats my highest estimate by over a hundred thousand.

'Three hundred and fifty . . . cash.'

I consider the price and wonder why Topper would give me something worth that much. But then, if I didn't know the bracelet's worth, Topper wouldn't. It also could be his way of balancing the ledger. He owes me his life, and he might think it worth that much. But I'm probably overthinking this.

'Sure,' I say.

'There's a tiny problem though,' he says, and smiles.

I smile back. It's never without problems, not for me.

'What problem?'

'As you must know, there is no way a man like me will have that much cash lying around. So, you will have to wait for Javad . . .'

'No,' I interrupt. 'I've got things to do.'

'Okay. So you let me have your number and when my son gets back from the bank and a couple other places where I keep my monies, I will call you. But, sir, we have come to an agreement. I'm expecting you to honour this agreement while we get the money ready.'

I don't want to give anyone my number. But for three hundred and fifty thousand in cash, I'll reconsider. Farrukh knows I'm considering and smiles to reassure me.

'All right, Farrukh, my number is—'

'Wait.' He grabs an address book and a pen. 'Okay, go ahead.'

I tell him my number, and he writes it.

'Mr?' he asks.

I smile, and he smiles back. I like the old man.

'I'll be leaving now. I'll expect your call.'

'Soon, sir.'

11:15

'I'm going to eat him'

Against my better judgement, I take the scenic route towards Marble Arch station. Marylebone station is closer, and the path is less exposed, but I want to see Marble Arch – nostalgia, I suppose. I make my way through the quiet Marylebone streets to Edgware Road and contemplate the history of the bracelet. It is bespoke, so someone is missing it; probably more than one person – whoever it was made for and whoever had it made – unless they're dead.

Edgware Road is buzzing. The pavement is crowded with pedestrians, mostly of Middle Eastern descent, and the road flows with steady traffic. The cafés, shisha bars, and restaurants that line the street are busy, and it's not even noon yet.

I walk past the Odeon cinema and reminisce. As a teenager, I brought dates here because it was away from the grind of our daily lives. This area was, and very much still is, a very different

London from where I grew up, but it's less than an hour away. I remember the cinema tickets were damn expensive too, but that was part of its appeal, and the girls appreciated it. Those days, in those moments, we both shared a life I hoped to live every day – a comfortable one.

I turn onto Marble Arch road, and it's filled with delighted tourists. I envy them, somewhat. I stop at the Arch, and it's not much to look at. I stare into Hyde Park, and several good memories fight for prominence, but I suppress them. I wonder if the thirteen-year-old me would be proud of me today . . . I hope so – I'm alive, and I'm trying my hardest, kid.

I head to the station. There's someone I need to see.

Farrukh watches his CCTV monitor as the man with the bracelet walks out of his shop, and he keeps watching for almost a minute to make sure the man is gone. He curses underneath his breath. He hoped this day would never come.

Farrukh isn't as old as he acts or sounds. He is sixty-four, but he puts a lot of work into appearing twenty years older. The ploy works a treat because he seems like your endearing grandfather. He's as tough as they come, but he's been dreading this predicament.

The bracelet has the inscription 'L Y, M, M', which stands for 'Love You, Meiling, Michael'. Michael is the man formerly known as Killer Mike, Three-Bullets Mike, Five-Bullets Mike, Teflon Mike, Money Mike, and King Mike; and now known as Councillor of East Hampstead, Michael Downing. Michael has offered half a million pounds for any jeweller or fence that brings him whoever attempts to sell the bracelet. It's been two years since the bracelet was taken. Michael has made sure people don't forget.

Farrukh couldn't care less about the money, but he's worried about his family if Michael finds out he came across the bracelet and did nothing. On the other hand, it's clear the man with the bracelet has no idea about its damned history or the grave consequence of possessing it.

Farrukh struggles with what to do, but he can't take the risk. He reaches for the telephone on his desk.

Michael Downing sits behind a desk in his large office in the Camden Council Planning and Building Development department. His suit jacket is hung on his chair, the top three buttons of his tailored shirt are unbuttoned, and his tie is loose. He has the biggest office in the building; it's a converted conference room. You'd think Michael used the stick to get this office, but politics is different – the carrot goes a much longer way, and he learnt that a long time ago. He paid over the odds for the room, just like he did to be elected councillor and chair of the planning committee.

Michael didn't mind the expense, primarily because of the opportunities to skim as the planning chair. But he quickly found out it's a lot of fucking work and red tape. He's bored of being a councillor now. His political aspirations are much higher, but he has to show up to the office somewhat regularly as he waits his turn to be a Member of Parliament. No amount of money can rush him to the top of that line, and he's tried, but his Party is a machine.

His boredom is evident in his office because there is a golf putting mat, a battered dartboard, and a mini bar. He doesn't have a television. He has no use for one, except to watch Arsenal on away days and when he can't make it to his box.

He has a computer, and that's where he's currently playing online poker with £5/£10 blinds. He folded pre-flop, but he's absorbed by the current hand. He was sure of his decision to fold considering the cards he was dealt – seven of hearts and a nine of spades. But the house cards are all lined up. Two of hearts, king of clubs, and queen of clubs on the flop. Queen of hearts on the turn. Seven of spades on the river. And after a seemingly endless bout of raising and re-raising, both players left in the hand check after the river card. The players reveal their cards; the first player has the nine and ten of clubs, and the second player has the ace of spades and jack of hearts. The second player wins the £1,035 pot ace high.

'Facking hell!' Michael screams and thumps the desk; his pair of sevens would have won the hand.

His phone rings and he snatches it off the desk, but doesn't answer at first because he doesn't recognise the number.

Farrukh considers ending the call, but then Michael answers.

'Hello, Mr Downing, this is Sheikh Farrukh,' Farrukh says.

There is no response for approaching ten seconds, and Farrukh becomes anxious.

'Hello?' Farrukh says.

'What do you want?' Michael asks.

'This is Farrukh. Sheikh Farrukh of—'

'What the fuck do you want, Sheikh Farrukh?'

'I have just seen the bracelet.'

'What! You did?' Michael exclaims.

'Yes. The man that has it just left my shop. He—'

'You let him fucking leave? Are you fucking crazy?'

'No, no . . . he will surely be back. He tried to sell it to me. I told him to come back when I have the cash ready, and he agreed.'

'I swear to God, Farrukh, if he doesn't fucking come back, you are dead. Dead, you fucking muppet!'

Farrukh takes a moment to compose himself. 'He will, I promise,' he says. 'The man does not seem to know much about the bracelet.'

'What?' Michael snaps. 'I don't give a fuck! What time is he coming back?'

'I have his number. I am to call him when I have the money, but I was simply waiting to call you.'

'Who is this fucking geezer?'

Farrukh hesitates. 'Mr Downing, I do not know,' he says.

'Mr Downing, I do not know,' Michael mimics. 'What the fuck is his name?'

'He didn't give me his name.'

'He didn't give you his name?'

'Yes.'

'Yes, he did?'

'No, no, he did not. But—'

'But what?' Michael hisses. 'You're just fucking stupid, aren't you?'

Farrukh doesn't respond.

'Aren't you?' Michael demands.

'Yes.'

'Yes, what?'

'Yes, I am stupid.'

'Fucking stupid!'

'Yes.'

'Yes, what?'

'Yes, I am fucking stupid.'

'Good! You said you have his number, yes?'

'Yes.'

'Okay, I'll call you back in a minute, and you best answer the call quick, you fucking muppet.'

Michael ends the call, and Farrukh is furious. He takes a while to calm himself. 'Bisharaf!' he mutters.

Farrukh hates getting involved with Michael, but, regardless of the reward, he knows that if Michael finds out that he'd seen the bracelet and not informed Michael, he'll be killed. And so will Javad and the grandkids.

Fury consumes Michael, but he grins. This is a bittersweet moment because he's waited over two years for a real lead on the bracelet. He calls Alan Pierce, his half-brother.

A few minutes later, Alan Pierce walks into the office. Alan is ten years younger than Michael and doesn't look or act like him. Michael is gruff, but not only is Alan inherently refined, he also works hard at it.

Alan approaches the desk, and Michael erupts from his chair.

'I'm going to fucking murder the bastard,' Michael says. 'His family. His friends. I'm going to eat him.'

'Eat him,' Alan repeats and sits on the desk. 'Try to calm down. And from what you said earlier, it shouldn't be this geezer you're after. He can't be that stupid to sell your bracelet to Farrukh. Sheikh Farrukh, for fuck's sake, if he knows the consequences. But he might know who we're after.'

Michael nods. 'Farrukh has the geezer's number,' he says. 'Think you can track it?'

Alan doesn't like that suggestion and is about to reject it out of hand, but Michael glares at him, and it's clear it wasn't a suggestion; it's an order.

11:48

'Make you feel special'

I step out of Canada Water station and enter Rebecca's address into Google Maps. It's a twenty-minute walk, but straightforward.

I arrive at the address in less than fifteen minutes. It's a new-build block of flats on a quiet street with other new-builds and freshly planted trees. I walk to the intercom by the entrance, and there is a sign above it that reads 'DOOR OPEN TO RECEPTION 8 a.m. – 6 p.m. WEEKDAYS'.

I step into the pristine reception, and the heavily moustached man behind the concierge desk doesn't acknowledge me. I head towards the lift, and he still doesn't look away from a monitor on the desk. But as I approach, he speaks.

'Excuse me! Who are you here for?'

I walk to the desk and spot a nametag above his breast pocket that reads 'Ahmed'.

'Hello, Ahmed,' I say. 'I'm here for flat 604.'

'Who?' he demands.

'Sorry?'

'Name.'

'Rebecca.'

He studies me as if assessing my worthiness to be allowed into the building. 'Sixth floor,' he says, and turns back to the monitor.

'Thanks.'

He doesn't acknowledge me. I fight back a smirk and walk to the lift.

I approach flat 604 and feel my heart skip a beat. I knock the door twice, and my excitement builds as I wait. Suddenly, Rebecca pulls the door open, and she's naked.

Ahmed watches the lift display to make sure the lift stops at the sixth floor. It does, and he pulls out his phone. He laughs to himself as he scrolls through the address book and clears his throat before he makes the call.

The call is answered, but it's voicemail. 'Drop a message,' a strong cockney voice says.

Ahmed complies. 'It's happening . . .'

Alan Pierce has made a few calls to his old Metropolitan Police colleagues. They like Alan and always make time for him. A few initially envied his meteoric rise through the ranks, but they learnt to appreciate his undeniable prowess at police work and work politics.

However, Alan wasn't a clean copper, and a closer look at his watches and shoes would have made it clear he was living beyond the means of a detective chief inspector in the Metropolitan Police; even one without a family to support. But no one bothered to take a close look, because, above all, Alan was fair. To everyone . . . criminals included. He is renowned for that.

Alan has cashed in a few big favours for Michael. On the face of it, this isn't surprising as they are brothers, but it is when you consider that Michael's actions forced Alan to retire from the police. Alan wouldn't call it retirement, though, because he didn't have a choice. Retire with a commendation and the damning facts will be buried, or get fired, give the Met a black eye, and get prosecuted.

Alan loved being police; it was his life. But he is past that now; well, so it seems. And Michael manoeuvred to put him on the council staff as head of security. He only works for Michael, though. His experience and contacts from being at Scotland Yard for over a decade are valuable to Michael and Michael's burgeoning criminal empire. And, for what it's worth, he gets paid much more in this job, so he doesn't have to appear modest.

Alan walks into Michael's office, and Michael leaps off his chair. Alan drags a chair to the desk and sits. He gestures for Michael to sit down, but Michael doesn't, so he doesn't speak. Michael curses underneath his breath and sits.

'Spoke to an old mate in counterterrorism,' Alan says. 'He can track the phone.'

'Fucking bloody hell!' Michael yells, and punches the desk, getting to his feet. 'That's what I'm talking about!'

Alan nods and waits for Michael to calm down. 'But it's going to cost you,' he says.

'Sure, money won't be an issue here. How's it going to work?'

Alan gestures for Michael to sit, and Michael immediately does. 'I'll let my mate at the Yard know when Farrukh's ready,' he says. 'My mate will call Farrukh on a secure line. Farrukh conference-calls this geezer, and my mate tracks the geezer's phone. The longer Farrukh keeps him on the phone, the better.'

'Good, good, sounds like a fucking plan.'

'Okay. Call Farrukh.'

Michael snatches his phone off the desk and calls Farrukh. It rings several times before Farrukh answers.

'Hello, Mr Downing,' Farrukh says.

'This is what's going to happen,' Michael instructs. 'Somebody will call you in a minute. You conference-call your fucking friend on the number he gave you. The copper will be tracking your friend, so keep him on the phone for as long as you can. If your friend gets spooked, it's on you, and you'll pay for that. I fucking swear, you will.'

'Copper?' Farrukh asks. 'Are you sure . . . ?' He stops, he knows it's a bad idea to question Michael.

But Michael is confused; he's sure he didn't say it was a copper, he wouldn't make such a mistake. He turns to Alan and sees the disapproving look on Alan's face, which confirms he did say it. He scowls at Alan, and Alan buries the disapproving look.

'How long am I supposed to keep him on the line?' Farrukh asks, attempting to move the conversation along.

'I don't fucking know. Just keep him on the line,' Michael says and ends the conversation.

Farrukh mutters and drops the phone. He grabs his address book and flicks to the number.

He waits for the copper's call and considers involving Javad, if only for support. But he knows it's a bad idea. Javad is soft, not cut out for this sharp end of the business. That isn't Javad's fault, though. Farrukh has shielded Javad all his life, and Farrukh won't stop now.

Farrukh bows to pray, but his phone rings, and it's a private number. He reaches for the phone and his hand trembles, but he ignores it and answers.

Making love is supposedly different from sex because the added emotion heightens pleasure. I wouldn't know because I've never made love. But then I can't imagine pleasure any more intense than when Rebecca and I have sex. I reckon it's the closest I've ever gotten to making love.

Today, Rebecca and I shared no pleasantries. We both know what we missed, and it wasn't the chat. She's said a few times that I was the best sex she'd ever had. I tend not to believe what she says, but right now, she's making me a believer. A phone rings, and I ignore it because it's not mine. No one has my number . . . oh, shit, Farrukh does. I stop and search for my jeans.

'Don't you dare,' Rebecca says and grabs my arm, but I yank my arm from her grasp and pull out. 'Are you serious?' she exclaims.

My clothes are all over the flat, but luckily my jeans are in the bedroom. I hurry to them and pick out my phone. The caller has a withheld number, but I answer anyway.

'Yes?' I say.

'Hello, sir,' Farrukh responds.

'Hello. Do you have it?'

'Straight to business, I like you. I have it? You ask me if I have it?'

'Yes.'

'Of course, I have it. And let me tell you what Javad and I had to go through to get it for you.'

'I don't need to know,' I say, and walk out of the bedroom. I don't want Rebecca hearing my end of the conversation. She's smart, and she'll put two and two together pretty quickly, which won't be good for me.

'Come on, sir,' Farrukh says. 'Javad and I went through a lot for you. It's only right you hear it. It'll make you appreciate our service even more. Make you feel special.'

Make me feel special? I chuckle to myself. I can hear slight echoes and background noise on the call, which suggests that Farrukh has me on speakerphone. I don't like it, but maybe the old man has to use the speakerphone.

'Okay, shoot,' I say.

'Shoot? Oh no, sir, we do not shoot,' he says, and laughs. 'First, Javad had to go to the bank. I bank with HSBC, but the branch around the corner from us told Javad they can't release such an amount to him without prior notification.'

'Right,' I say, and catch my reflection in a hallway mirror.

'Javad has to go to our relationship manager in the City, Fenchurch Street. He drives to Fenchurch, and the manager tells him he cannot withdraw all the money in our accounts without the other signatory of the account present. I can't drive anymore, you see, I'm too old, so I take a taxi to Fenchurch and, thank God, they give us the cash. The usual nonsense about charges and penalties, but they give us all quarter million or so in the accounts. We leave the bank, and you see we have to go to a couple other places to collect cash. But the car is clamped, you imagine this?'

Farrukh is lying. I have no time for this. 'I'm going off the phone now, Farrukh. But we'll talk all about it when I get to your shop.'

'We are friends now, eh?' he asks.

'Sorry?'

'You called me Farrukh. Only friends call me Farrukh. That's good. So, my friend, tell me your name.'

'I'm good with sir,' I say.

'Okay, sir,' he says and laughs. 'We are ready. When should we be expecting you?'

'I'll be with you in a couple hours.'

'Good. Good. So, how are you? And, err, you mind if I ask what the story is with the . . .'

A picture on the wall suddenly grabs my attention. It's a wedding portrait of Rebecca. I had no idea she's married. A stinging sensation runs through me and lingers at the tips of my fingers. I step closer to the picture and see Rebecca and Yellow – a man I know – in a loving embrace. I am shocked, and then a lot of other emotions fight for prominence. I'm hurt, and it feels worse because I didn't see it coming. I've been away for years, and, although I didn't expect her to wait for me, marriage seems a betrayal.

I study the picture. She looks beautiful in her white dress, and Yellow, to be fair, looks good in his black tuxedo. He looks even bigger than I remember. I'm sure he hasn't missed a gym session or his regular shot of steroids. I always knew he wouldn't rest till he got her, and I commend his relentless effort. Maybe she did too. I didn't think she'd be into marriage, though, it's so final. Perhaps it was just me. I salute the picture.

Rebecca hasn't said anything about her marriage. That's their bed, isn't it? The thought makes me shudder. Anyway, if she doesn't bring it up, I won't. I'm not one to spoil the mood, although I'm not sure I'm in the mood anymore. I return the phone to my ear.

'Hello . . . hello,' Farrukh says with a raised and somewhat panicked voice.

'Yes, Farrukh, I have to go. We'll talk about it when I get to you.'

'Okay, okay, bye, friend.'

'Bye.'

I end the call and put on a smile before I walk back into the bedroom.

13:19

'For your own well-being, do not fuck with him'

Rebecca is sprawled on the bed, furious. She can't believe he did that, again. His priorities have always been fucked, she thinks . . . putting business ahead of pleasure, ahead of her. Fucking idiot!

She sits in a comfortable position and spots the duffel bag. She's sure there is something important in the bag because he made sure to drag it into the bedroom even while he was getting naked.

She steps off the bed and skips to the bag. She opens it and is surprised by the cash inside. She rummages through to check if it's full of only money, and her hand grazes an item in the pocket. Curious, she unzips the pocket. She's astonished by the bracelet and picks it up to examine it. But the room is dark because the curtains are closed.

She wears a robe and hurries into the bedroom balcony, which overlooks the river. She studies the bracelet, and it's stunning. She ponders if he means to gift it to her, but she quickly dismisses the thought because that's not how he operates. He believes it tasteless for anyone to have such luxury when surrounded by people struggling to live. Fucking Robin Hood, she thinks. Then the bedroom door opens, and she hears him step in. Fuck. She has no pockets, and there's no spot in the balcony to hide the bracelet until she puts it back . . . if she puts it back. Fuck.

Farrukh is beyond scared because he doesn't know if he kept the man with the bracelet on the call for long enough. He waits a moment to make sure the man is off the line.

'I do well?' Farrukh asks the copper, who's listening in on the call.

'Yeah, just fine,' the copper responds.

'Khodaro Shokr,' Farrukh says in relief.

'What?'

'Thank God.'

'You should, old man.'

Alan is relaxed, but Michael stomps around the room. Michael hasn't stopped moving since he called Farrukh, and he's drenched in sweat.

Alan's phone rings and Michael spins to him. Alan checks the caller ID and nods, and Michael rushes over to him before he answers the call.

'Yeah?' Alan says.

'We have him. Docklands,' the copper says.

'Good.'

Michael grins.

'Obvious problem though,' the copper says.

'What's that?'

'He's in a block of flats called Cannon House. It's seven floors, lots of flats. No way we can know what flat he's in.'

'Shit, right.'

Michael's grin switches to a worried glare.

'You want me to send a couple officers there?' the copper asks.

'Thanks, but no. You've done more than enough, Pat, we'll handle it from here.'

'Okay, mate.'

'Thanks again.'

'Anytime, AP. But you owe me one. A massive one, too.'

The comment angers Alan, and he has to fight the urge to respond. He ends the call and nods to Michael.

Michael hurries behind the desk and pulls out a silver Colt Anaconda revolver hidden underneath the table. 'Let's go get this fucker!' he says.

'Why the fuck do you have that in here?' Alan chides. 'Put it away.'

'Fuck off! I'm keeping it,' Michael says, and instinctively points the gun at Alan. 'And don't fucking talk to me like that.'

'All right, calm down,' Alan says, and gestures for Michael to lower the gun.

Michael realises he is pointing the gun at Alan and lowers it.

'We won't get there in time,' Alan says. 'And you can't be anywhere near this.'

'Fuck that.'

Alan fights the urge to shake his head. 'You know we can't just kill this guy, right?' he says.

'I know. I want to punish him and then kill him.'

'First, we need to find out who he works for. Then you can kill him.'

'Yes, right.'

'As I said, we won't get there in time, but I know the right people for this. They'll get to him quick, and they'll bring him to us.'

'Who?'

'The Shetty brothers.'

'Those fucking mugs? No, this is too delicate for them.'

'Probably. But they live close enough in Peckham. And for the right price, we can make sure they act appropriately.'

'Okay, but I want Tony in this as well. He lives around there last I knew . . . in Canning Town.'

Alan raises an eyebrow; he doesn't like that idea at all. 'The chef . . . Stutter Tony?' he asks.

'Yes, Tony.'

'I know you haven't forgotten what happened last time. Tony can't work with people.'

'I trust Tony. Just make the calls, Alan. And make sure they understand how delicate the situation is.'

'Wait . . .'

'No! That's what I want. Fucking get it done already!'

Alan is furious, but he remains calm. 'Okay,' he says, and nods. 'Do we even know how this geezer looks?'

'Ah, yeah, I'll call Farrukh. Make the old man piss his pants a bit more.'

The Shetty brothers are simple thugs who'll do anything criminal you wish to delegate. Rape, assault, armed robbery, arson, murder, or rape . . . they like rape. If the price is right, they'll be on it, and that price is often lower than you'd think.

Tariq is twenty-six; he's the older brother. He does the talking, a lot of talking; thinking, as much as he can; and pricing, which depends on their level of desperation. Khalid is twenty-three and the brawn of the enterprise. He says nothing, follows his older brother's lead and does what needs doing. It seems a fair division of labour, because Khalid is 6'3" and 120 kg of some muscle but mostly fat, and Tariq is 5'10" and 65 kg of mostly hot air.

The brothers ran away from an abusive home at a young age. Their mother died giving birth to Khalid, and their father never forgave him for that. The situation got worse when Khalid grew to resemble the father's cousin, and this forced the father to recognise Tariq's resemblance to the mother's ex-boyfriend. The brothers lived on the streets of East London and in and out of homes. Their violence was groomed for survival, but it became their occupation when they realised they enjoyed it and the market for violence was always in demand.

They met Alan Pierce during Alan's early years in the Met Criminal Investigation Department. He arrested Tariq and Khalid several times for misdemeanours, and they had cultivated a cordial relationship. One day, Tariq was arrested attempting to rob a betting shop, alone. He was due a lengthy stint in prison, but he couldn't stand to leave Khalid alone on the street. Alan fixed it, and Tariq didn't spend a day in prison. After that, their relationship became transactional, although Alan has remained affable.

Alan introduced the brothers to Michael two years ago. Michael, Dead Mike as the brothers know him, is not cordial, but he pays well. He used them for everything, from murder to witness tampering, but he didn't like their style. They lack finesse, and their preferred weapon is a machete, which Michael thinks is fucking stupid. He now rarely uses them, and when he does, it's for matters of little importance. This present matter is critical, so they will be chaperoned.

The brothers are in their local chicken shop, and Tariq has been playing on the only fruit machine for approaching an hour. Khalid stands beside him, waiting his turn. Tariq's phone rings, and he takes his time to pull it out of his pocket. He recognises the number and hurries out of the shop to answer the call.

'Hello, bossman,' Tariq says.

'Hello, Tariq,' Alan says. 'Where are you?'

'My ends.'

'Good, Khalid with you?'

'Yes, boss.'

'Good. I have a quick job for you boys. You up for it?'

'Sure thing, boss.'

'It's double the regular pay because this matter is very delicate. And you'll be working with somebody.'

'Nah, I don't like that.'

'That's the way it's going to be, Tariq. Are you in?'

'Okay, we in.'

'I need you right now. You'll go pick a man up from Canada Water station. The man's name is Tony. Tony stutters. Do not mock him or laugh at him, okay?'

'He stutters?' Tariq says and laughs.

'It's not a joke, Tariq. For your own well-being, do not fuck with him. You pick him from the station and go to Cannon House – put that in your satnav, it'll take you there. No more than five minutes' drive from the station. Okay?'

'Yeah.'

'In Cannon House, you look for a black guy, about six feet, in a black jacket and carrying a black duffel bag. Don't ask me how you find him, I don't know, but you find him. He has a bracelet. We want that bracelet. But we want him too, so you can hurt him, but make sure he can talk when you bring him to us.'

'Okay.'

'Tariq, Tony knows what to do. There is no need to have a conversation with him. He won't have to say a word to you unless you boys are fucking up. Don't fuck up. Call me when it's done.'

'Sure, boss.'

'You still drive the red Honda?'

'Yeah.'

'I'll describe it to Tony. For you, Tony is a huge white man, bald and wearing a black trench coat. That's the only description you'll need.'

Alan ends the conversation, and Tariq punches the air. The brothers need the money, especially because, and unknown to Khalid, Tariq has been gambling through the money they have stashed away. Tariq even considered robbing his local Ladbrokes, and he spends most of his days in there.

Tariq hops back into the shop, and Khalid is enjoying a box of chicken wings.

'Drop that shit, fat boy,' Tariq says. 'We got a job.'

Tariq slaps the back of Khalid's head and the chicken wing Khalid is eating falls to the ground.

'What now?' Khalid asks, frustrated.

'We're talking major P.'

'Yes, I'm sure,' Khalid says, and picks up another chicken wing.

'It's for Dead Mike,' Tariq says, with a beaming smile.

Khalid drops the chicken wing and grins.

'We need to move, now,' Tariq says.

Khalid leaps to his feet and wipes his hands on his jeans as he follows Tariq out of the shop. They hurry into their red Honda, which is parked in front of the shop.

'We need to get some stuttering bastard from Canada Water station before we head to Cannon House,' Tariq says.

'What?'

'Just follow my lead, fat boy, no need to fill your empty head with the details.'

'Fuck off.'

They laugh as Tariq starts the car, and Wretch 32's 'Unorthodox' blares out of the stereo. They bump their heads to the music as Tariq drives to Canada Water station.

The red Honda arrives at Canada Water station, and a huge bald white man wearing a black trench coat waits by the entrance. It's Tony, and he is a mountain of a man at 6'5" and 135 kg of muscle.

Tony notices the Honda approach because of the music blaring out of the car. It stops in front of him, and he steps into the backseat.

Tariq can't hide a mischievous smile as he stares at Tony through the rear-view mirror. 'Are you Tony?' he asks over the loud music.

Tony ignores.

'What's your name, man?' Tariq demands.

Tony doesn't acknowledge.

Tariq switches off the stereo. 'What the fuck's your name, man?' Tariq demands with feigned anger.

Tony glares at Tariq through the rear-view mirror. 'T — T — T — To—' he stutters.

'Tony?' Tariq interrupts, and smirks.

Tony nods, and Tariq bursts into laughter. Khalid doesn't find the stutter funny but still laughs along with his brother until he glimpses Tony's glare in the rear-view mirror. Khalid stops and attempts to get Tariq's attention, but Tariq isn't paying attention to him as he cackles.

Tony struggles to control his urge to wrench off Tariq's

head. He hasn't been teased for his stutter in decades without an immediate, brutal response. One of those brutal incidents ended his career as a chef and landed him in Brixton prison on a four-year sentence for grievous bodily harm. He served two years before being supported in his parole hearing by a detective inspector he'd never met named Alan Pierce. He was granted parole, and he is forever grateful to Alan for that.

Today, Alan has implored Tony to be tolerant of the brothers, but Alan's pleas haven't always curbed Tony's violent urges. For that reason, Tony was paid a considerable amount up front, with a substantial bonus promised for his tolerance and the delivery of the man with the bracelet alive.

Tariq parks in front of Cannon House. Khalid hurries to the boot, but Tariq makes a point to bump into Tony as he saunters to the boot. Khalid picks two machetes from the boot and hands one to Tariq. They hide the machetes, and Tariq leads into the building's reception.

Ahmed notices them enter, but acts unaware of their presence, even as Tariq approaches the desk.

'Hey,' Tariq says, and leans on the desk.

'What?' Ahmed says, and turns to Tariq.

'Don't be rude, bruv, we are just looking for a friend.'

'Okay?'

'You see a black guy in a black jacket, black bag pass through here?'

'Yes, Yellow sent you?'

'Yes. Yes, Yellow sent us.'

'Okay. The man's still up there.'

'Up where?'

'Yellow's flat.'

'Right,' Tariq says, and nods. 'What's the flat number again?'

Ahmed is sceptical. He spoke to Yellow five minutes ago, and Yellow said nothing about sending people. These guys don't even know Yellow's flat number.

'Come on, bruv, we are trying to be friendly,' Tariq says, and scans the room for a camera.

'I don't know what you are talking about,' Ahmed says.

'Okay, okay,' Tariq says, and smiles.

In one swift motion, Tariq pulls out the machete and swings onto Ahmed's right hand that's set on the desk. The blade chops off four fingers and the tip of the thumb, and Ahmed screams and falls to the ground. The detached fingers remain on the desk, but the tip of the thumb rolls onto the floor. Tariq walks around the desk to Ahmed. 'You shouldn't have made me do that,' he says. 'I was trying to be friendly. This is your fault. Anyway, what the fuck is the flat number?'

Ahmed's cry becomes more frantic, and Khalid hurries to the door to check if anyone outside can hear Ahmed, but the street is empty.

'Oi, quiet!' Tariq commands Ahmed.

Ahmed stops sobbing but continues to struggle with the pain.

'All I want is the flat number,' Tariq says. 'Tell me, and I won't kill you. I promise.'

'Flat . . . 604 . . .' Ahmed says. 'Sixth floor . . .'

Tariq drives the base of the machete onto Ahmed's head, and Ahmed loses consciousness.

'That's enough, thank you,' Tariq says and turns to Khalid. 'Gimme the bag.' He throws the car's key to Khalid. 'And go get some shit to clean this blood quick.'

Khalid nods and throws the sports bag to Tariq before he runs out. Tariq turns to Tony with a smirk, but Tony is unimpressed. Tariq sniggers and picks duct tape and rope from the bag. He tapes Ahmed's mouth shut and ties Ahmed up as Khalid returns with a large kitchen roll.

Khalid cleans blood off the desk and floor, and Tariq drags Ahmed into the maintenance room behind the desk. Tariq locks the room and wraps Ahmed's fingers and the door key in a sheet of kitchen roll. He tosses the crumpled sheet into the bin and spots the tip of Ahmed's thumb on the floor. He kicks it underneath the desk and leans on the wall to watch Khalid finish his rushed clean-up.

Khalid stuffs the bloodstained sheets of kitchen roll into a plastic bag and attempts to put it into the sports bag.

'No,' Tariq says, and gestures to the bin.

Khalid is uncertain about putting the plastic bag in the bin and attempts to object, but Tariq wags a finger.

'Don't think. Just do,' Tariq says.

Tariq's condescending tone irks Khalid, but he doesn't show it and pushes the plastic bag deep into the bin.

'Fucking hell,' Tariq says. 'You find any snacks in there, fat boy?'

'Fuck off,' Khalid says, and forces a smile.

Tariq leads into the lift. He pushes the button for the sixth floor, but just before the doors close, a foot is wedged between the doors. Tariq and Khalid reach for their machetes, and Tony is alert as the doors open. But they relax when they see the Domino's Pizza deliveryman.

'Sorry, guys,' the deliveryman says and hops into the lift.

Tariq and Khalid acknowledge the deliveryman's apology with a nod, but Tony doesn't respond.

'Sixth floor, please,' the deliveryman says to Khalid, who is in the way of the control panel.

'Already done,' Tariq interjects, and grins.

The deliveryman doesn't know what to make of the broad grin, so he forces a smile and turns away.

Tariq stares at the deliveryman and wonders if they could be so lucky. He tests their luck. 'Mate, is that for flat 604?' he asks.

'Yes. Pizza for you?' the deliveryman responds.

'Yes,' Tariq says, with glee.

'Okay, you have the money?'

'Yes. How much was it again, mate?'

The deliveryman checks the price on the pizza box. 'Sixteen pounds,' he says.

'Right,' Tariq says, and sticks his hand out to Tony. Tony is confused. 'I don't have any cash, bossman.'

Tony pulls out twenty pounds and gives it to the deliveryman. The deliveryman offers Tony the pizza, but Tony ignores, and Tariq quickly takes the pizza. The deliveryman reaches into a pouch for change.

'Keep the change, mate,' Tariq says.

'Thanks, mate,' the deliveryman responds.

The lift arrives at the sixth floor, and the deliveryman steps aside for Khalid, Tariq, and Tony to step out. The three men turn to the deliveryman. Tariq grins, Khalid forces a smile, but Tony is expressionless. The deliveryman doesn't know how to react. He attempts to speak but doesn't know what to say. He nods, forces a smile, and gives two thumbs up as the lift closes.

Tariq is very pleased with himself and turns to Khalid and Tony for acknowledgement. But Khalid scans the small hallway and Tony remains expressionless. Tariq hisses and leads to flat 604.

'Let me handle this,' Tariq says, and gestures for Khalid and Tony to stay a couple steps away.

Tariq knocks at the door twice and holds up the pizza.

13:26

'Where have you been?'

I step back into the bedroom with an apologetic smile, hoping to avoid one of Rebecca's special tirades, which would be justified this time. But she's not in the bedroom. I attempt to check the bathroom, but a curtain parts and she steps back into the room. She appears calm. She approaches me, and I attempt to apologise, but she places a finger across her lips to hush me. She grabs my head and kisses me.

She bites my bottom lip and pulls it, and it hurts, but it feels so good. I missed her. She drags me into bed, and we just stare into each other's eyes for a good while.

'I missed you, baby,' she says, and grabs an iPad from a bedside table.

'Don't call me baby,' I respond.

'C'mon, baby,' she says, and smiles at me before turning

back to the iPad. 'Don't change the topic, I know you missed me too.'

I smile. 'Yeah, whatever. You're doing very fine without me.'

'What are you talking about?'

I shake my head, and she laughs. She returns the iPad and opens a drawer to pick a Silk Cut cigarette and a lighter.

'What are you doing?' I ask.

'Oh, yeah. My bad, baby,' she says, and returns the cigarette and lighter. 'I forgot you don't like me smoking around you.'

'I'd prefer you didn't smoke at all. Thought you were going to quit?'

'Please, that was ten years ago, I've quit twenty times since then.'

'Fair enough. I'm guessing Yellow doesn't much care about it.'

She shrugs. 'He wouldn't say anyway.'

'That's what you want, isn't it? A lapdog.'

'Oh, shut up. I was alone. He was there. And please, stop calling him Yellow. His name's Jamie.'

I laugh.

'What's funny?' she asks.

'Just never saw him as a Jamie. It's pretty funny.'

'Is it?' she asks, brimming with sarcasm. 'Okay.'

'Well, Jamie was always there. But to marry him?'

'What? I wanted to.'

'Right. You love him?'

'Why would you ask that?'

'I assumed that's what marriage's about.'

'Don't make that a habit, baby.'

'What?'

'Assuming.'

'Don't—'

'He's there for me.'

I nod. 'I hear you still work at the club though. And Yellow runs the place now?'

'Yes, Jamie does, with Sandy.'

'Sandy,' I say, and smile as I reminisce. 'I bet she's the only reason the club's still in business.'

'True,' she says, and laughs.

'Why do you still work there?'

'Cos I want to.'

'You do?'

She glares at me.

'All right, enough of that then,' I say.

'Where have you been?'

'Why would you ask that?'

'I understand you had to leave, baby. I do. But it's been almost ten years, and you never called. Not even a postcard. Fuck it, even an email would have done. I thought you were dead.'

'I'm . . .' I want to apologise, I should, but I don't. 'It had to be that way.'

'Then why the fuck did you come back at all?' she demands, and sits up. 'Why today? Why bother to see me?'

I want to tell her I probably wouldn't survive the day, so I've come to see her one final time . . . to say a proper goodbye. And to give her a bunch of money I know she doesn't need, but it's the only way I know to show I care. But it's not the right time, I'll tell her when it's time to leave, again.

She hisses and changes the topic. 'You want to see a movie?'

I laugh; I'm surprised by the question.

'Why are you laughing?' she asks. 'You were always into movies.'

'I still am . . . when I get a chance. But—'

'You seen *The Avengers*?' she asks, excited.

'No, haven't yet. It just came out, didn't it? You already have the DVD?'

'No, saw it at the cinema. It's—'

'With Jamie?'

'No, I went with a few of the girls. Anyway, it's awesome! Your kind of movie.'

'How's that?'

'You dragged me to see *Spider-Man* when it came out.'

'True. Although, to be honest, I really didn't care what we saw. But I enjoyed—'

'Well, of course, you did,' she says, and smirks.

'That was more of a distraction.'

'Have a sincere conversation with your dick. I think the movie was the distraction.'

We laugh.

'Oh, yeah, have you watched *The Wire*?' she asks, excited.

'That's a joke, right?'

'What? You've read the books twice or something, and you prefer the books?'

'There isn't a book.'

'Shut up, smartass, I know. But it's exactly the sort of thing you'd say.'

'True.'

'I bet you watch it all day trying to be Stringer Bell,' she says.

I laugh, and she watches me with an affectionate smile.

'He's actually my favourite character . . .' I say.

'No shit.'

'Shut up! And Omar, and Bunk.'

'Yeah, I love Bunk too. Not really a fan of Omar, though. I loved it when he—'

'Homophobe.'

'Fuck you,' she says, and we laugh. 'Anyway, I ordered a pizza for us. Pepperoni is still your favourite, right?'

'That's what you were doing on your iPad. You could've asked then.'

'Oh fuck off, I'm just being polite. I'm sure it still is. You don't change.'

'Well, I'm sure you still can't cook.'

She glares at me. 'What the fuck are you on about?'

'Relax, I'm just teasing. How did you know I was hungry anyway?'

'You weren't exactly fucking like I remember.'

'Wow!'

'When was the last time you had sex?'

'Are you actually being serious?'

'No, baby,' she says, and laughs.

'Stop calling me that.'

'Fuck off, baby. Just wondering if you're seeing someone wherever the fuck you're hiding. Maybe you even got married. Although I'd bet my life you haven't.'

'You'd lose it then.'

'What? Really? Fucking—'

'No. Fucking hell, of course not.'

'Fuck you.'

'Yeah, sure,' I say, and laugh.

'What?'

'You looked hurt as fuck.'

'Whatever. It wouldn't have mattered anyway. Cos we both know I'm the best you've ever had. You'd have come running back.'

'You can keep telling yourself that.'

She grabs my cock, and I yelp. She relaxes her grip and caresses till I'm aroused.

But then I hear a loud knock in the distance. Must be the front door.

She pulls away. 'It's the pizza, baby,' she says, and steps off the bed.

It seems like revenge to me, and it's well played.

She grabs her purse and blows me a kiss before she hurries out of the room. I'm surprised she didn't ask for money to pay for the pizza; she's certainly changed.

I can't wait for her to return, and I couldn't care less about the pizza.

Rebecca walks into the living room and stops to check for . . . but she's interrupted by two loud knocks on the door. Okay then, the delivery guy's fucking eager, she thinks. Best to sort that out first.

She opens the door, and Tariq grins; he's stunned by her beauty. She notices and initially doesn't mind, but it becomes creepy fast because he seems lost in his gaze.

'How much again?' she asks.

'For you, just a tenner,' he says.

'Sweets, I think it's sixteen.'

'Yeah? Who cares?'

She hands him a twenty-pound note, and he gives her the pizza. She forces a smile, and he pulls out his machete and places it across her neck. She is frightened but doesn't show it.

'Step back and say nothing,' Tariq whispers. 'Or I'll fucking cut you up.'

She steps back, and Tariq follows her into the living room. Khalid and Tony step in after Tariq, and Tony shuts the door behind them.

'Where is he?' Tariq whispers.

She doesn't respond, and Tariq snarls; his nostrils flare to their limits.

'Where the fuck is he?' Tariq demands.

She considers defiance, but Tariq looks crazed with rage. She nods towards the bedroom, and he gestures for her to lead.

★

I'm staring at the ceiling and still hard as nails when I hear the door open.

'You took your time,' I say, and turn to the door.

Rebecca collapses into the room, and three men – two Asians and a huge white man – burst into the room. I jump off the bed to charge at them, but the two Asian men brandish machetes, and I stop. I raise my hands to surrender because they're not here for me. Nobody knows I'm here, and I wasn't followed. But all three stare at me and with purpose. Fuck, they *are* here for me. I remain calm, nothing much else I can do now.

'Yes, she did, mate. Oh, yes,' the smaller Asian man says.

He raises his machete above his head and approaches, and my heart pounds faster than I thought possible. I can't believe I'm going to die now, like this. What a fucking li— He swings the base of the machete onto my forehead.

14:00

'What are we going to do about him?'

Sandy leads Yellow through the secluded lower ground floor of the club. Sandy's calm, but Yellow's anxious and sweating through his compression shirt, which accents his imposing physique.

'What exactly happened?' Yellow asks.

'Be patient, you'll see for yourself,' Sandy says, and gestures to a door at the end of the hallway. 'You first.'

He pushes the door open and is taken aback. A seductive young woman in lingerie relaxes on a sofa bed in the middle of the room, but a man is unconscious at the foot of the bed with blood seeping from his head.

'What the fuck is this?' Yellow demands.

'Calm down,' Sandy says. 'It wasn't her fault. He was very drunk. Right, Marina?'

'Yep,' Marina responds. 'He kept putting his sweaty hands

on me. I warned him, but he got aggressive. He said he could do whatever he wanted. He grabbed me again, and I did whatever I could to free myself.'

'Right,' Yellow says, and points to a broken bottle on the floor. 'So, you smashed his champagne bottle on his head then?'

'Yep,' Marina says.

'Are you flipping mad?'

'What?' Marina responds; she's furious.

'Calm down, Yellow,' Sandy interjects. 'Marina did what she could under the circumstances.'

'Right,' Yellow says, and wipes sweat off his bald head. 'Is he dead?'

'No, just unconscious,' Sandy says.

'Are you sure? Cos that's James Glossop, you know.'

'I know,' Sandy says.

'He's one of our biggest spenders.'

'What?' Sandy asks, and glares at him with disapproval.

'What the fuck?' Marina screams and leaps off the bed. 'Are you taking the fucking piss, Yellow? That's what you have to say? He's a big spender so he can fucking rape me, right? Fuck you!'

'Hey! That's not what I said,' Yellow says.

Marina storms towards the door, but Yellow grabs her arm.

'Don't fucking touch me!' Marina screams and pulls away. 'If it was Rebecca, you'd have the bastard killed. Fuck you!' She storms out of the room.

'What?' Yellow barks. 'You fucking stop there now!'

Yellow walks after her, but Sandy places a hand on his back, and he stops.

'Leave her, Yellow,' Sandy says. 'That was on you.'

'No.'

'Yes.'

'Whatever. She's fucking fired!'

'No, she's not.'

'Yes, she fucking is!'

'Yellow, she's not. We need her, she's our biggest draw.'

'And you think she doesn't know that? She thinks she can do whatever she wants in here. I'm not having that shit.'

'Rebecca's no different, and Marina knows that.'

'Fuck that, so what? She can't talk to me like that.'

'Yellow, that's not the issue right now.' She gestures to James's unconscious body. 'What are we going to do about him?'

Yellow walks to James and crouches to check for a pulse. 'You said he was drunk, right?' he asks, and scans the room.

'Yes. Very. He's a lowlife, drunk at this time of the day.'

'That's our business, isn't it,' Yellow retorts. 'Call an ambulance and tell 'em he slipped and fell on the bottle. He was drunk, so hopefully he won't remember anything. Who else knows about this?'

'Nobody. Marina called me immediately.'

'Okay, then that's the plan. If it doesn't work, we'll come up with something else.'

He slowly stands from his crouch. He was never the most flexible, but now in his mid-40s, his knees are stiff.

'Sounds good,' she says. 'And just so we are clear, Marina is not getting fired. And there will be no disciplinary action taken against her.'

'Sure, whatever. Get Ali to carry James out of here, though.'

Sandy nods.

'If that's all, I'll be going back to my office,' he says.

'That's all.'

Yellow stomps up the steps to the ground floor and struts through the half-full main room where women in lingerie mingle with men in booths and at the bar, and a naked woman dances on a stage. He unlocks a sturdy door in the corner of the room and plods up the stairs to his office.

Yellow slams shut his office door, and the sound is buried by the volume of the fifty-six-inch HD television hung on the wall, but the frames on the walls almost fall off. He decorated his walls with a large wedding portrait, a photograph from their honeymoon in Mexico, a painting of Rebecca, two pictures of Rebecca, one of him winning a strongman competition decades ago, a signed Thierry Henry jersey, and a signed poster of Arsenal's 2003-04 Invincibles squad.

He dumps himself on his chair and picks his mobile phone from the desk. There's a missed call, so he dials voicemail and sits back to listen to the message. He springs forward, immediately filled with rage. He switches off the TV before he calls Ahmed back, and Ahmed answers after one ring.

'Ahmed, just got your message,' Yellow says. 'This guy still there?'

'Yes,' Ahmed says.

'How long has he been there now?'

'Thirty . . . forty-five minutes maybe, I called you immediately.'

'What the fuck! I'm on my way right now. Right now. Let me know if he leaves, okay?'

'Okay.'

Yellow ends the call, grabs his car key, and charges out of his office. He leaps down the stairs and barges people out of his way as he races out of the club. He jumps into his metallic grey Range Rover parked in front of the club and pulls out in an instant.

He drives at breakneck speed, ignoring traffic lights and narrowly avoiding other vehicles. The average journey time from the club in Soho to his home is thirty minutes, but he's aiming to get there in half that time.

Yellow and Rebecca are, at first glance, not the best pairing, but he loves her, and she says she loves him. He pursued her for seven years from the moment he first saw her, and his burning desire never waned; instead, it teetered on the brink of obsession. He was a bouncer at the club, and she was the one everybody came to see. A goddess on the stage and on your lap – if you were patient and rich enough, because there was always a queue and she charged three times more than the other girls.

Yellow got into several violent altercations because of Rebecca, and most times, he was just jealous. He worked his way up to become a manager at the club and, for the first time, he felt good enough for her. But it changed nothing between them because she never cared about his position. Still, he didn't give up. And just like that, on a cold morning in January, she agreed to go for breakfast with him. He proposed six months after that breakfast, and they got married on his birthday three months later.

He is aware of her promiscuous history. It came with her job, he told himself, so he tried talking her out of dancing. She laughed that off and instead got the most flexible working hours ever because she now only works when she feels like it. He stopped her giving private dances though.

All things considered, he believes he's earned her love and faithfulness. He even has the scars to prove it. But he knows it doesn't work like that, so he's remained vigilant . . . maybe even paranoid. He struck a deal with Ahmed and Samuel, the two concierges for their building, to call him the moment a man came to visit Rebecca when he wasn't home, even if it looked like her father. He promised to pay five hundred pounds for the call. It's been two years and no call. Also, it seemed to him that she'd finally settled down . . . she seemed truly happy. And that's why he's perplexed. Why now? And who could it possibly be? Family, he hopes. Family, he prays.

Yellow is almost home. He calls Ahmed, but Ahmed doesn't answer. He redials, and still no answer. He flings the phone onto the passenger seat and climbs the pavement to speed through a red light.

He screeches to a halt in the middle of the street in front of his building. Pulls a baseball bat from underneath his seat and charges out of the car. He bursts into the reception, and Ahmed is not behind the desk.

'Ahmed! Where the fuck are ya?' he shouts, and hurries to the lift.

He calls the lift, but it's held up on the fourth floor. He waits a couple seconds and darts into the stairwell. He runs up the stairs, and his frantic pace is almost as quick as the lift. But he trips as he approaches the fifth floor and tumbles down the steps to the fourth-floor landing.

He is motionless for a moment before he screams and jumps to his feet. He runs up the stairs with more determination and even more rage. He will kill whoever it is in his house, he fucking will. He charges through the sixth floor like a raging bull and blasts through his front door.

14:30

'Dead people don't feel pain'

A hard slap wakes me, and the bastard who'd knocked me unconscious is crouched over me with his face just inches away from mine. He grins and leans away, as if allowing me to take in the full extent of my helplessness. I'm still naked, tied to a chair, with my hands tied behind me. Rebecca is unconscious beside me, and I'm relieved because it doesn't look like she's been assaulted any further. She's also tied up, though.

The bastard taps my head with his machete. 'Hey, I'm Tariq,' he says. 'What's your name, bruv?'

I wouldn't have answered, but I can't anyway because I have duct tape over my mouth.

'Oh, sorry, bruv,' he says, and laughs.

He places his machete across my neck and pulls the tape off. It hurts.

'Where is it?' he asks.

'What?' I respond.

'What?' he repeats, and chuckles. 'Really, what?'

'Yes. What?'

He scowls, but I'm not fazed.

'I'm very, very angry with you, mate,' he says. 'Not because you lied to me; it's cos I can't trust you anymore. This would have been much easier if I trusted you.' He runs his fingers along the blade of his machete. 'Now I'm going to have to get messy with you. I've been doing this years, mate, and I'll tell you this . . . when people are close to death, they always tell the truth.'

I've always wondered why that was the case. Personally, I wouldn't bother saying anything because I'm dying anyway. 'Why?' I ask him.

He's surprised by the question. 'Why what?'

'Why do they always tell the truth?'

'Hmm . . .'

He considers my question for a few seconds. 'Fear of death,' he says. 'They think the truth will help. Save their lives and that . . . end the pain.'

'Did it ever help?'

'Yes,' he says, and smirks. 'Dead people don't feel pain.'

I nod. 'Ever heard of Stokely Carmichael?'

'Who the fuck's that?'

'Don't worry about that. He once said the secret to life is to have no fear, cos that's the only way to function.'

'Mr Carmichael is a bad man, yeah?'

I shrug.

'So you have no fear then?' he asks.

'Oh, I do. Just always loved the quote.'

He laughs, and I smile.

'I've got another quote for you, if you don't mind,' I say.

'Go ahead, mate.'

'You've probably heard this before though.'

'I don't think so, mate. I can't even really read, you know.'

'Fair enough, but you must have heard it before.'

'Yeah?'

I nod.

'What is it?' he asks; he's eager.

'Go suck a fucking cock, you fucking weedy cunt,' I say, taking care to enunciate every word.

He grins and swings the base of the machete onto my mouth. The pain is excruciating, but I don't react. He's excited, and I can see in his eyes that my torture starts now. I don't know how long I can resist, but I have to because it's clear that the bracelet is the only thing keeping me alive. I glance at my bag, but it's not where I left it. I scan the room and see the other Asian guy carrying my bag as he ransacks the room.

I'm confused. What else could Tariq want? It can't be the money or the bracelet because both are in the bag that they already have. Shit! As improbable as it may be, these guys may think I'm Yellow. There's my luck. I scan the room for a picture of Yellow, and there is none. But then the room has been turned upside down. They are searching for something, something they haven't found yet.

Tariq turns to the other Asian guy. 'Khalid, take the bag to the car,' he instructs. 'Bossman said nothing about the cash, so we keeping it. Bring the hammer . . . and acid.'

'Okay,' Khalid says, and walks towards the room door, but the white guy grabs his arm.

Khalid stops and doesn't break the grip; he just turns to Tariq for instruction.

Tariq shakes his head and stands. 'What, Tony?' he asks. 'You want some of the cash?'

Tony shakes his head.

'What then?' Tariq asks, exasperated.

'N— n— nn—' Tony struggles to say.

'No?' Tariq says and grins.

Tony glares at Tariq, and Tariq grins. Tony takes a deep breath and attempts to speak, but he hesitates and doesn't. I realise Tony stammers, which is unexpected but not exactly amusing. Plus, Tony doesn't look like he should be laughed at. Especially now, because he appears overwhelmed with rage.

Nevertheless, Tariq bursts out laughing. 'So, what the fuck?' he asks Tony.

'No one le— le— le— lea— leaves this p— p— p— place till we . . . we f— f— f— fi—'

'Find?' Tariq interrupts.

'Find the b— b— b— br— bra—'

'Bracelet?' Tariq interrupts, and laughs.

Okay, they *are* here for the bracelet. But then the bracelet is in the bag, and these fuckers don't seem the type not to search the pockets of a bag. Tariq and Khalid must be trying to double-cross Tony.

Tariq laughs so hard he tears up. He attempts to speak but bursts out laughing again. Khalid can sense Tony's burning rage and tries to lock eyes with Tariq, but Tariq is consumed with laughter.

Tariq stops laughing, but he's still amused. 'Wewe?' he asks Tony and wipes tears from his eyes. 'What the fuck is that? French?' He turns to Khalid. 'Go on. You'll be back before Tony can say any more about it.' He cackles and turns to me. 'So, mate, where is the bracelet?'

I don't respond.

'What, you too, mate?' Tariq asks. 'You fucking stutter too?'

There is a sudden muffled bang, and blood spatters onto me before Tariq collapses to my feet with a hole through the back of his head. I turn to Tony, and he's pointing a large handgun with a silencer to Khalid's head. Khalid isn't paying attention to the gun, though; he's staring at Tariq's dead body, distraught.

'Do we have a p— pro— prob— blem, mate?' Tony asks Khalid.

Khalid doesn't respond.

'Do we?!' Tony demands, and jams the gun into Khalid's ear.

Khalid's distress switches to fear, and he shakes his head. I understand his fear, I'm scared too, but he has a machete and Tony has just killed his brother . . . or cousin . . . or whatever. I hope he makes a move on Tony because that'll improve my chance of surviving.

'Okay,' Tony says. 'Let's g— go search the living r— r— r— room.'

To my surprise, Khalid obeys without a fight. He walks out

of the room, and Tony follows a step behind with the gun aimed at Khalid's head.

I can't believe they left me alone in the room, regardless of being tied up. They must not know who I am. Good for me, bad for them.

I shake my hands to test the strength of the knot, but a phone rings and startles me. The phone is on Tariq, and I worry Tony and Khalid will hear it. It rings non-stop, and my heart feels like it'll explode, but then it stops. I need to hurry, and I need Rebecca.

Rebecca's hands and feet are tied, but her hands are in front of her so she might be able to untie me. I shift my weight to the side of the chair closest to Rebecca, and the chair tilts but doesn't fall. I readjust and throw my weight towards Rebecca. I crash onto the floor, inches from her head, and she wakes up with a gasp.

'It's me,' I whisper. 'Be quiet.'

She turns to me, and she's relieved.

'You okay?' I ask.

She's not sure. She checks her body and attempts to fight the rope, but she can't. She turns back to me, and she is furious.

'They didn't touch you . . . not like that,' I say.

She nods, but she's still furious.

'I need you to get to the knot around my arms,' I say. 'I need you to loosen it.'

'Who were they?' she asks.

'I don't know, but they are still here. So I need you to do it for me right now.'

She nods and crawls to the knot behind me. She pulls at the knot, and I feel it loosen. I fight to pull my hands apart as she battles the knot, and, with a burst, my hands are free. I untie my ankles and leap to my feet. I scan the room for my jeans but can't find them.

'He's fucking dead then,' she says.

I turn to her, and she is staring at Tariq's dead body. I'm surprised she's unaffected by it.

'I wanted to kill him myself,' she says.

It's clear she means it, and I don't know how to react.

There is a loud thud in the living room. We stay quiet and listen, and there is another thud, and then another, and it continues loud and frenzied, like a fight. It must be a fight. I have to act now. I untie her hands and kiss her on the forehead. I pick up Tariq's machete and hurry towards the door.

'I'll come with you,' she says, and pulls apart the rope around her ankles.

I turn to her, and she jumps to her feet. 'No,' I say.

'What do you mean, "no"?' she responds, and glares at me.

I'm shocked by the determination in her eyes. 'Please, stay here.'

'I can help.'

'I know. But I'd prefer if you were safe. Lock the bedroom door when I step out and lock yourself in the bathroom till I get back. And, please, don't call anyone until you're sure that's your only way out. But be ready to call, okay?'

She's not happy, but she nods, and I hurry out of the room.

★

Khalid walks past the open kitchen to the living area, and Tony is a step behind, holding his suppressed .45 pistol to Khalid's head.

Tony is surprised Khalid hasn't attempted to avenge his brother. Tony's looking forward to it and doesn't plan to use his gun either; he just wants a good fight. He even allowed Khalid to keep his machete, hoping that will give Khalid the confidence to fight. But Khalid stops at a sofa and trembles.

What a fucking coward, Tony thinks. Once they find the bracelet, he'll shoot Khalid in the balls and leave him to bleed out. He pushes the gun barrel into Khalid's neck. 'T— toss the blade,' he commands.

Khalid throws the machete away.

'Go on. Search f— for the b— b— br— brace— let,' Tony commands.

Khalid nods, and Tony pulls the gun away. Khalid rummages through the sofa, and Tony is disgusted with Khalid's easy compliance. Tony tucks the gun into his coat and crosses his arms to goad Khalid, but Khalid doesn't look his way. Tony scoffs and turns to the kitchen.

He noticed the kitchen design when they first entered the flat, and he likes it. He walks towards the kitchen and his phone rings. He pulls it out, and it's Alan calling. He considers not answering, but he knows that will only get Alan worried. He glances at Khalid, and Khalid is focused on the search. He walks into the kitchen and answers the call.

'Tony?' Alan says.

'Yes,' Tony replies.

'Where is Tariq?' Alan asks. 'Why isn't he answering his phone?'

Tony doesn't respond; he's admiring the kitchen. He recognises the design from the Magnet collection he had looked through when choosing a kitchen for his new flat. He wanted this but couldn't afford it.

'Tony,' Alan says, calm and authoritative.

'Tariq's gone,' Tony responds.

'Gone. What do you mean, "gone"?'

'Gone gone.'

'And Khalid?'

'Here, searching f— for the brace . . . let!'

'You haven't found it? Isn't the geezer there?'

'Yes. But—'

'Is he alive?'

'Yes. But still can't f— find the bracelet!'

'Okay, Tony, I'm on my way. I'll be there in fifteen minutes. What's the flat number?'

'Six . . . zero . . . four.'

'Okay, thank you. And, Tony, don't kill anybody else until I arrive, okay?'

Tony grunts and ends the call. He checks on Khalid, and Khalid is still searching. He shakes his head and returns to admiring the spotless kitchen.

Khalid searches an armchair close to the door. He peeks at Tony, and Tony is caressing the kitchen counter; the gun is nowhere in sight. Khalid is perplexed, but that's quickly overcome with rage. Khalid considers bursting through the door to escape, or grabbing his machete and charging at Tony, or just charging at Tony with his bare hands. He struggles to decide and becomes anxious. Tariq always said he wasn't smart enough to make real decisions, and he hated Tariq for that, but now he thinks Tariq was right.

The front door bursts open, and Khalid is bewildered and in shock as Yellow charges towards him with a baseball bat. Before he reacts, Yellow swings the bat into his jaw. His eyes roll back, blood and teeth fly out of his mouth, and he collapses like a log.

Yellow leaps over a coffee table and charges towards Tony in the kitchen. Tony pulls out his gun and takes a quick step out of the kitchen, but before he can raise the gun, Yellow swings the bat at his head. Tony blocks the bat with his arms, and the gun flies away from his grasp. Tony grabs the bat and knees Yellow in the balls, and Yellow squeals and drops the bat. Tony rams Yellow into the wall and throws a vicious uppercut, but Yellow dodges by a hair and shoves Tony. Tony staggers but quickly gathers himself, and they ram into each other.

They stand toe to toe and throw wild punches in a frenetic fist fight, but none of the punches fully connects until Yellow lands a left hook to Tony's ribs. Tony yelps and falls, but he grabs Yellow's arm and drags Yellow to the floor. They wrestle, switching top position as they roll across the living room until Yellow throws Tony into the coffee table, shattering the table and further damaging Tony's ribs. Yellow mounts Tony and drives his knee into Tony's broken ribs as he squeezes Tony's neck. Tony fights the choke with one hand, and it seems Yellow has overpowered him. But Tony reaches for Khalid's machete with his other hand. Tony is losing his breath, but with his last gasp, he grabs the machete and swings it into Yellow's head. Blood spurts from Yellow's head and he collapses onto Tony with the machete fixed to his skull.

Tony winces as he pushes Yellow's lifeless body off himself. He takes time to catch his breath but manages to struggle to his feet.

14:54

'Worth the amount you pay, I suppose'

I tiptoe towards the living room, and my heart is racing; I haven't done this in years. I approach the living room, and thuds reverberate around the flat as the fight becomes more frenetic. I hurry. I have to take advantage before it's over.

I enter the living room and spot Khalid unconscious, but to my surprise, there's a fight still going on across the room. Tony crashes into the coffee table, and Yellow pounces on him. Yellow? What the fuck is going on?

I turn back to Khalid, and he doesn't have a bullet wound. That's Yellow's work, and I don't think he will be happy to see me either. I stay back to watch the fight play out. Whoever survives will be weakened, making it a fair fight for me if it comes to that, and it probably will.

Yellow overpowers Tony and strangles him; it looks like Yellow will survive. I sneak towards Yellow's blindside, and

I step on Tony's gun – just might be a lucky day after all. I crouch to pick the gun, and I see Tony reaching for Khalid's machete. My instinct is to alert Yellow, but I don't, and in one swift motion, Tony grabs the machete and drives it into Yellow's head.

Tony pushes off Yellow's body and takes his time to catch his breath. He struggles to his feet.

I shoot him in the back of the head.

He didn't see it coming. Good for him. That's how I'd like to go.

I walk to the half-open front door and peek into the hallway; it's quiet. I close the door.

I turn around, and Rebecca is in the living room. I didn't hear her approach. She glances at Khalid across the room and walks towards Tony's dead body. She spots Yellow's gruesome lifeless body underneath Tony and bursts into tears. Oh, fuck. I hurry to her and attempt to embrace her, but she grabs my right wrist and snatches the gun with ease.

She pushes it into my forehead and glares at me.

Oh, fuck.

'You watched Jamie die. I saw you. Why?' she asks.

I recognise the rage in her eyes. I need to be careful. 'He won't have been happy to see me. Then it would have been him or me.'

'I would have handled it.'

'Sure . . .'

Suddenly, there is a noise. It's Khalid. He scrambles to his feet and charges at us.

Rebecca shifts her aim and shoots over my shoulder.

Khalid crashes to the floor by my feet. I glance at him, and there is a bullet hole in his forehead. Rebecca's fucking good with a gun.

'We had a good time, didn't we?' she asks.

I nod.

'What was it . . . six months?' she asks.

I nod.

'But for some fucking reason, you think that time, a fucking decade ago, is more important to me than the years I had with Jamie.'

'No . . .'

'Yes. Yes. Otherwise, you wouldn't have watched him die for your shit. Why did you come back anyway?'

I don't respond.

'Fucking answer me,' she demands, and jabs my forehead with the gun.

I could reach for the gun, but then one of us will surely die. Probably me, which is okay with me because she's probably going to kill me anyway. But if I get the gun, I'll have to kill her. I don't want to do that.

'You didn't come back for me,' she says. 'I would have been flattered, but we both know you'd have left empty-handed. But maybe you just came to say sorry for abandoning me. Sweet, but stupid. I don't get fucking abandoned because I don't need anyone. Either way, it's secondary to your actual reason for coming back to London today. Unfinished business, I'm sure.'

I don't respond. I don't know where Rebecca is going with

this conversation, but it's best to allow her to get there at her own time. Then she reaches into her vagina, and I'm fucking confused. I try not to react, but she pulls the bracelet out with a flourish, and I'm in awe.

'Something to do with this, I imagine,' she says and throws the bracelet at my face. 'Take it and fuck off. Don't come back, baby. Because the next time I see you, I'll kill you.' She lowers the gun. 'You have two minutes to get the fuck out of my house before I call the police.'

'I'm sorry.'

'You're not,' she says, and turns to her dead husband.

I am, but she's right. I'm not sorry I watched Yellow die, but I'm sorry it's the end of us. And I'm much sadder than I thought possible.

I pick up the bracelet. Grab my bag from underneath Khalid and gather my trainers, jeans, and jacket scattered around the living room before I walk to the bedroom.

I drop my bag, trainers, and clothes and step over Tariq into the bathroom. I clean the blood off my face and torso and hurry into the bedroom to dress up. I put the bracelet back into the side pocket of my bag and put on the bag.

I walk through the living room to the front door, and Rebecca doesn't acknowledge me. She's focused on her dead husband, and she appears more angry than sad.

I grab the door handle, but before I open the door, I'm struck by the urge to say something to Rebecca.

I don't.

I open the door and walk out of the flat.

I head straight to the stairwell and jog down the stairs, but I quietly approach the door into the reception. Ahmed knows I came to see Rebecca and he could have called Yellow, or, although far less plausible, he could be involved in my ambush. I push the door open just enough to peek into the reception, and it's empty; Ahmed isn't at the desk. I push the door open and hurry out of the building.

I step outside. Two uniformed police officers inspect a Range Rover that's parked in the middle of the street with its driver-side door wide open. The officers couldn't have arrived this quick if Rebecca called and they are more concerned with the car. But even so, when Rebecca calls, these officers would be radioed, and I need to be gone by then. The older female officer turns to me, and I force a polite smile before I turn to the pavement.

'Excuse me, sir,' the younger male officer calls.

I ignore him. I don't know what my next move is, but I won't be stopped, not by them.

'Excuse me, sir!' both officers call, but the female officer's assertive voice drowns the male officer's voice.

I turn to them. 'Me, officers?' I ask. 'I apologise, I'm still getting used to being called sir.'

'You live here?' the male officer asks, and gestures to Cannon House.

'Yes.'

'Do you know who owns this vehicle?' he asks.

'No.'

'Have you seen it around before?'

'Don't think so.'

'How long have you lived here?' the female officer asks.

'Three, four months.'

'What's it like?' she asks.

'Worth the amount you pay, I suppose.'

'Hmm . . . and how much is that?'

I smile. 'No offence, officer, but I don't know if I want you as a neighbour.'

The male officer bursts out laughing, and the female officer smiles.

'Anyway,' I say. 'Good luck with it, officers.'

'Enjoy your day,' the male officer says.

'Thanks. You too.'

I walk away.

I struggle with the urge to check if they are watching me.

A double-decker bus whizzes past and stops at the empty bus stop a few steps ahead. I recognise the bus number, and I know its route, although I've tried hard to forget it.

The exit doors open, and an elderly couple giggle as they support each other off the bus. They smile at me, and I smile back. I approach the bus entrance and the doors open, as if for me. I look into the bus, and the driver is staring at me. I step in.

15:34

'Get the artillery'

I step off the bus onto a street that's lined on both sides with brown semi-detached council houses, which all have dead, dying, or unkempt front gardens. Nothing much appears to have changed on the street. The same corner shop is at the top of the street, opposite the same decrepit church. The same trees that forever appear lifeless but somehow continue to sprout leaves. No one has cared for the houses, not even a repaint. I certainly would have repainted because I hate brown, although I figure this street is the reason I do. This here is a concrete wasteland.

The depression that I've spent years trying to bury is aroused. I should leave, but I've come this far. I walk along the pavement, head down like I used to as I counted the 112 steps. Back then, my head was down out of shame, but now, I can't afford to be recognised. The street is empty, but then there are the watchers behind the windows.

At my fortieth step, I arrive at a bump in the pavement. I smile; it used to take me about seventy steps to get here. I step on the bump and leap forward like I used to. That was fun and should take care of about four steps. But the mild pleasure disappears as I approach the telephone pole that's three steps away from the house. I rarely took the three steps though, because I was never in a rush to get to the house. I'd place one foot ahead of the other, eleven times or so, till I arrive at the house. I want to do that now to see how many feet it'll take me, but I'd look silly. I take a couple more steps, and I'm there. I turn to the house, and the depression surges.

On the side of the house there's a wide-open upstairs window. I shake my head and walk through the tall grass in the front garden. I skip over a low fence into the small alley between the houses.

I assess the window and then check if the street is clear. It is. I fasten my bag around my shoulder and take two deliberate steps back. I charge at the wall. I run up the wall for three strides, jump onto the neighbour's wall, and jump back towards the window. I grab the windowsill inside the house, and my head bumps the window.

I pull myself through and roll into the bathroom. I remain still and listen for movement in the house, but I hear nothing. I check my throbbing head for blood, but there is none.

I walk to the half-open door and hear her cackling laughter from the living room downstairs. I push the door open and step into the tight hallway, but she stops laughing, so I don't move. I listen for any sounds from the two bedrooms, but I hear nothing beyond the closed doors. She bursts out laughing again, and I tiptoe down the stairs. I stop the moment she stops laughing. I'm halfway down the stairs and can hear a television; that's good because junkies don't have TVs, at least not for long.

She starts laughing, but before I continue down the stairs, I hear movement in her bedroom. I leap back up the stairs in one stride and skip into the bathroom just before the bedroom door opens. I hide behind the door and listen as someone stomps down the stairs.

'Shut the fuck up, you cunt!' a male voice screams in a Mancunian accent that I recognise; it's him. 'I'm trying to sleep! I got work at eight!'

'Fack off, you wanker!' she responds.

I hear a scuffle, and I charge out of the bathroom and down the stairs. But they laugh, and I stop.

'I'll snap your facking tiny cock, you wanker,' she says.

'Then who'll shag your dirty cunt?' he retorts.

They laugh, and I cringe. I wish the ground would swallow me up.

'We still got any more gear?' she asks.

'I got work tonight, babes.'

'That's like in four hours. You'll be fine by then. Just construction, innit?'

'Just? Get a fucking job then!'

'You know what I mean.'

'Whatever. Yeah, we still got some.'

'Sweet,' she rejoices, and there is a moment of silence. 'That's where you kept it!'

'Think I'll let it out of my sight, you dirty junkie?' he teases, and they laugh. 'Get the artillery.'

I hear footsteps heading towards the living room door, and I leap back up the stairs into the bathroom. I close the door and wait, but I don't hear footsteps coming up the stairs. I sink to the floor and bury my head in my hands. I shouldn't have come here, I really shouldn't. I stare at mouldy tiles and struggle to hold back my desire to finish what I started years ago. In truth, it's not much of a struggle, more an exercise in patience as I allow them to get high.

Time is up. I march down the stairs and peek into the living room. Her scruffy afro is slouched on a shabby sofa and he's unconscious on a tattered beanbag. I head to the kitchen to grab a knife and walk into the living room.

I head straight for him, but as I approach, I see her. She's unconscious, haggard, and wearing a dirty hoodie and worn-out leggings. I turn back to him. It's his fault, and he'll pay for it. But she crashes to the floor with a thud, and he opens his eyes for a fleeting moment. Then he opens them wide to stare at me. He's frantic and can't believe his eyes.

'Fuck me, this is some crazy gear!' he says.

He rubs his eyes and focuses on me, but he still doesn't want to believe his eyes. He attempts to speak, but I stick the tip of the knife into his neck, and he gasps. He's terrified.

'Facking hell,' she groans.

I spin to her, and she's sprawled on her belly beside a crack pipe. She tries to push off the floor but can't, and she can't move her head either. I turn back to him, and his eyes are shut.

I should slit his throat, but they deserve each other.

I drive the knife into the beanbag just inches away from his crotch.

I walk away from the house, and I'm overcome with a thirst for vengeance. Tariq, Khalid, and Tony ambushed me and they're dead, but Topper or Farrukh set it up. I'll find out which and destroy him. I call Oleg, and he answers after a ring.

'Hello?' he says.

'Hello, Saviour.'

'What's up, my friend?'

'A fucking lot.'

'That sounds not good. What's wrong?'

'I need weapons. And, if you can, a few of your associates. I'll pay well.'

'I know you will, I know. What you want this for?'

'Just been ambushed. Not sure who's behind it, but it's either Farrukh or Topper.'

'I warned you about Topper. That man is ruthless. But Farrukh . . . Farrukh doesn't mess around. Are you sure he's involved?'

'I don't know, but I'll find out.'

'I think you will not need help for Farrukh. His place is not secure. I keep warning the old man, but he thinks I'm trying to sell him something. I am, of course, but the old man doesn't think anyone can get through his blast door. I've seen the door, it's top quality, but what happens to his son in the front, eh?' He hisses. 'Anyway, my friend, tell me about this ambush?'

'Two Asian kids . . . not kids, men . . . and a fucking huge white guy . . . looked like a bodybuilder, came for me at Rebecca's. They wanted the bracelet.'

'Ah,' he says. 'I don't know those people. But, as always, you are the last man standing. You must know more will come for you, come for this bracelet.'

'I know. They won't need to look for me, I'm going after them.'

'Okay, my friend. I'm sure it's Topper responsible for your ambush. Because from what I know of Farrukh, he doesn't consort with the type of people that came for you.'

'Consort, nicely used,' I say.

I can picture Oleg smiling. 'My friend, it's not our time yet, and I'm trying to handle some business at the moment. But I know the perfect associates to assist you with Topper. It won't cost you any money. And they will have weapons for you, lots of weapons. Good customers of mine, they are. But you should know, and I'm sure this won't be a problem for you . . . the spoils are theirs.'

'That's fine with me.'

'Good. They are professionals. The professionals for what you need.'

'That's very good for me.'

'But I must also let you know that they might be . . . trigger-happy. That's the only complaint I get anyway.' He laughs. 'So, you want them?'

'Yeah.' I glance at my watch; it's 15:51. 'I need them fast though. And how many are they?'

'Two. Just two. But better than any ten I can find you today, tomorrow . . .'

'Stop selling, Oleg.'

He laughs. 'I'm not selling. Just letting you know to thank God.'

'There's no God, Oleg. No one is orchestrating this shit. And if I'm wrong, there's a shit ton the fucker needs to account for before anyone thanks him or her or they or it.'

'Ay! You and your blasphemy. Call me back in five minutes.'

I end the conversation and turn to the church. I walked past it for more than a decade but never went inside, never had cause to. To be fair, I've never been into any other house on the street. The corner shop, though. I turn to it and reminisce. It was family-run, a happy bunch, and I was in there almost every day. An island in a sea of bleakness.

The five minutes pass and I call Oleg.

'Hello?' he answers.

'It's me.'

'I know, but say it.'

I can't help but laugh. 'Hello, Saviour.'

'Good, my friend, excellent.' He laughs. 'I got them. You need to get to Berkeley Street in Mayfair to meet them, okay?'

'Okay.'

'I give you the number to call when you get there. When they answer the call, you say "Saviour sent me", then they'll know it is you.'

'Sure.'

'I'll give you Tosin's number.'

'Tosin?'

'Yes, Tosin and Jide, they are Nigerians.'

'Hmm.'

'Why, hmm?'

'No reason.'

'All right, you ready?'

'Yes.'

I put the phone on speaker to dial the number into my phone.

'You get it?'

'Yeah, thanks.'

'It's a pleasure. May the Lord be with you,' he teases.

'Whatever.'

He laughs, and I end the call. I hurry towards the underground station. I have only three hours to seek and destroy whoever set me up.

It's early evening on an autumn day, and a bus slows to a halt at an empty bus stop in front of a corner shop. A young boy steps off the bus and plods along the pavement with his head down. He's wearing the Crystal Palace FC tracksuit with a Manchester United backpack and listening to Nas' *Illmatic* album on a Discman.

The kid is exhausted because he's just completed a gruelling training session for Crystal Palace under-fifteens academy squad. He is outstanding at football and will make the final squad, but at thirteen – 'thirteen and a half!', he'll be quick to counter – he is the youngest in the preliminary squad. He might not start on the first team though, because his right-wing position is congested – blame David Beckham for that.

He'll have a better chance to start if he moved to right full-back or centre-back. To be fair to him, he may have too much flair for centre-back, but he's 5'8", which is well above the average height of the squad, and he's sturdy for his age. The coaches keep trying to convince him those physical attributes make him perfect for centre-back. But he's not having that and would rather sit on the bench. He wants to play right-wing and wear number seven, and he knows he's good enough. The coaches know that, but they have a need at centre-back. The kid is driven, or stubborn; depends what way you look at it.

The kid isn't making much progress along the pavement because he's taking his time to count every step. He springs forward off a bump and looks back to gauge the length of his jump. He shrugs and continues, placing one foot ahead of the other till he reaches home. He turns to the decrepit semi-detached house and sighs.

He knocks the front door twice and waits for almost a minute before he pushes an ear against the door to listen for movement in the house. He hears nothing.

He thumps the door with the side of his fist. 'Jess!' he screams. 'Mu—' He stops. 'Jessica!' He thumps for five seconds before he pushes his ear against the door, but he still hears nothing. 'Fucking hell,' he mutters.

He steps back to check if the first-floor bathroom window

on the side of the house is open, and it is. He mutters to himself and climbs over the low fence into the alley between houses. He places his Discman in his bag and sets the bag on the floor. He takes off his football boots and tucks them underneath the bag.

He stares at the window as he takes three broad steps back and bounces on his toes for a couple seconds before he charges at the wall. He runs up the wall for three strides, jumps onto the neighbour's wall, and leaps towards the open window.

He climbs into the bathroom and takes a moment to catch his breath before he charges out. He runs towards Jessica's bedroom but stops the moment he hears loud sex in the room. He knows the man with Jessica is a stranger because he doesn't recognise the man's pleasured groan, and he imagines bursting through the door and driving a knife into the stranger's chest. He closes his eyes and counts down from ten to calm down. He opens his eyes and skips down the stairs.

He collects his backpack and football boots from the alley and heads into the messy kitchen. He dumps his boots and picks his folded training jersey from his bag. He carefully unfurls the jersey and slides four eggs and half a tomato wrapped in cling film onto the counter. He pulls a half-full bag of Frosties from his bag and places it on the counter.

He opens the fridge, and there are just two cans of beer, a tub of expired butter, and several sachets of McDonald's ketchup inside. He pulls a half-full bottle of milk from his bag and places it in the fridge. The milk is the last of the items he took – stole will be more accurate, but accuracy isn't always essential – from the training facility's kitchen. He picks out the butter and shuts the fridge.

He wipes a large area of the counter with his jersey and pulls a cook's knife from a knife block to dice the tomato. He looks through the sink, full of days-old dirty dishes, and picks out the frying pan. He rinses the pan with hot water and wipes it dry with his jersey. He places the pan on the only burner with its knob intact and switches on the heat. He digs out bits of the butter that don't look rancid, and he's startled by footsteps racing down the stairs.

Jessica was once a talented singer-songwriter; she had a record deal at just sixteen years old. But today she's a thirty-one-year-old do-anything-for-a-hit junkie. Luckily for her, she has good genes, and that masks the extent of her addiction. Right now, she's not high, but she looks crazed as she chases the chubby stranger down the stairs with no clothes on. He's dressed in a work suit, but he's struggling to buckle his belt around his large gut as he hurries towards the door.

'What the fuck?' she screams, and grabs his arm.

'Leave me alone!' he screams, and brushes her off.

'No! This is fifty!' She waves the money in his face.

'What? That's the price!'

'On the fucking street, it is! But you're in my house, you fat fuck!'

'Fat fuck? Fuck you and your loose cunt!'

She slaps him with all her might, and he staggers backwards. He's perplexed by her fearlessness because he's almost double her size. But fuck that, if you want to fight, she's up for it, and she couldn't give a fuck about your size, your gender, or your age. She's not scared of beatings either. She's used to them, and she knows she'll fuck your shit up before she goes unconscious or dies. But then again, she's not worried about death; she believes it can't be worse than the life she's living.

'Come on, you limp-cock fuck!' she screams.

He raises a clenched fist to strike her, but the kitchen door opens, and he stops.

The kid steps out of the kitchen and walks past them into the living room. He closes the door and puts his ear against it to listen. The front door opens and slams shut, and Jessica runs up the stairs. He closes his eyes to count down from ten, but he suddenly charges out of the room.

He runs straight to the frying pan with melted butter burning and reduces the heat. He breaks the eggs into the pan, two at a time, and tosses in the tomatoes. He stirs the eggs as they fry, and he's at peace.

Jessica walks into the kitchen wearing just a vest and no underwear, and she's on the phone. 'It wasn't my fault!' she screams into the phone. 'I tried . . .' She rolls her eyes. 'What the fuck did you want me to do?'

. . .

'I . . .'

. . .

'Well, where the fuck were you?'

. . .

'Fuck you too, wasteman!' she screams, and ends the call.

He watches her and waits for any acknowledgement of his

presence, but she doesn't even look his way. She opens the fridge and reaches for a beer but sees the bottle of milk. She grabs the milk and drinks it.

'Don't, that's for breakfast tomorrow!' he pleads.

She doesn't respond.

'At least don't finish it!' he pleads.

She finishes the milk and tosses the empty container towards the overflowing bin; it bounces off to the floor.

'Sorry,' she says, but there is no emotion in her voice, and she still doesn't look his way.

She picks out a beer and strolls towards the door.

'Are you hungry? I'm making scrambled eggs,' he says.

'Sure, whatever.'

'Jess, are you all right?'

She ignores him and walks out of the room.

'Mum!' he shouts.

She stops but doesn't turn to him. 'I told you not to call me that again,' she says. 'I meant it.'

She walks up the stairs, and he stares at the empty doorway. He appears calm, but he's far from that. He's learnt to internalise . . . to keep his emotions hidden. Big boys don't cry, he was told. He was lied to.

The eggs are ready, so he rinses two plates and splits the eggs. He grabs a plate and walks to the hallway.

'Jess!' he calls and waits for a response, but there is none. 'The eggs are ready. There's a plate for you in the kitchen!'

He waits again for a response, but there is none.

Jessica doesn't much care for the kid, but she keeps him

around because he provides, and he always has. Whether it's the child benefit cheques or his innate ability to get stuff, which is also called stealing. But she doesn't ask him to get things anymore; she learnt quick not to ask.

When he was ten, she noticed his talent. He'd stopped asking for the pittance of allowance she begrudgingly provided, but he wasn't starving. He had new Jordan trainers, not one or two, he had enough, and he had a Game Boy Colour too. She started to work him.

She started with small things – a watch, a wallet, a phone – but then she asked for a TV, and he dragged home a brand-new state-of-the-art TV less than twenty-four hours later. But then the kid wanted something back, he expected it, but it was something she couldn't or wouldn't provide. Her affection. She stopped asking, but he didn't stop getting things, because he knew he had to provide, to survive and to sustain her habit.

Anyway, the kid dumps himself on a worn sofa in the living room. He looks at the empty TV stand; there was a TV there yesterday, it didn't last a week. He shakes his head and pulls out his Discman. Five minutes later, he's devoured the eggs and is rapping along to 'It Ain't Hard to Tell', when a loud bang on the front door startles him.

Jessica pulls it open.

Rod, her lanky boyfriend, pimp, and enabler, shoves her to the floor.

He marches into the house and glares at her with blood-red eyes; he's high, and as opposed to her solely opiate addiction, he's high off crack cocaine.

'Wasteman?' he screams and kicks the door shut behind him. 'Fucking wasteman? I'll show you wasteman!'

He grabs her thick afro and drags her through the hallway. She screams and fights, but she can't break his grip.

The kid steps into the hallway and watches Rod drag Jessica up the stairs. He wants to charge after them and mutilate Rod, but he walks back to the sofa to grab his phone. He calls 999.

'My mother is being attacked by her boyfriend,' he says. 'And it's not the first time.'

. . .

'I'm fine.'

. . .

'In her room upstairs.'

. . .

'I'm downstairs, and I said I'm fine.'

. . .

'Yes, 98 Nimrod Street.'

. . .

'Thank you.'

He ends the call and tucks the phone to his pocket. He picks up his plate and walks to the kitchen. He heads to the sink and opens the tap to the max, hoping to drown out her desperate screams. But he can still hear her as he washes his plate. He stops and closes his eyes to count down from ten, but her screams are distracting.

'Eight,' he counts out loud. 'Seven . . . six . . . five . . .

four . . .' He stops and opens his eyes. His eyes are calm, but he's full of rage.

Rod is naked on top of Jess as he fucks her. She screams in pain, but he pushes her head to the floor and whips her with his belt. They are on the floor of her chaotic bedroom because he doesn't want to fuck her on the same bed she just fucked a punter.

The door bursts open, and Rod spins towards it as the kid walks in.

Rod is shocked. 'Fuck off!' he screams at the kid.

'Get off her,' the kid says.

'What?' Rod screams.

Rod pulls out of Jessica and shoves her aside. 'Are you fucking mental?' he roars and stands.

The kid shrugs.

'You think you can take me?' Rod asks.

'You think I can't?' the kid retorts.

Rod charges at the kid, but the kid pulls the cooking knife from his sleeve and slashes Rod's chest.

Rod yelps and rams the kid through the bedroom door.

The knife flies away from the kid's grasp as they stumble towards the staircase. Rod shoves him down the stairs, then glares down at him. He struggles to his feet and stares back.

Rod marches down the stairs, and Jessica scurries out of the bedroom to watch.

The kid watches Rod approach, and he's not afraid. Rod throws a punch and he tries to duck, but it catches him on the temple, and he stumbles towards the kitchen.

Rod chases after him and punches him in the nose.

He crashes to the floor.

Rod lifts and slams him onto the pile of dishes in the sink.

He slides off the broken dishes and falls to the floor. He coughs out blood and grimaces in pain; his nose and ribs are broken, and his left arm is dislocated.

Rod stands over him, but he looks past Rod to Jess who is watching from the doorway. Suddenly, he drives his head into Rod's testicles.

Rod screams and clutches his testicles, and Jess gasps in horror.

The kid stands and smashes Jess's plate of eggs on Rod's head. Rod falls and curls up to protect himself, and the kid limps to the knife block on the counter.

'Stop it!' Jess screams at the kid. 'What are you doing?'

The kid pulls out a carving knife.

Just before Jess sets off to stop him, a loud bang on the front door startles her.

'It's the police! Open up!'

Jess screams and runs to open the door.

The kid is not fazed. He swings the knife across Rod's back, and it cuts deep.

Rod screams and turns around to protect himself with his arms, but the kid slashes his forearms deeper and deeper with each swing.

The kid stops to wipe the blood from his eyes and then he raises the knife above his head to drive into Rod's stomach.

'Stop!' the officer commands.

The kid stops.

'Drop the knife!'

The kid doesn't respond.

'I said, drop it, boy!'

The kid watches Rod cry and doesn't respond.

'Kid, please drop the knife,' another male officer says with a soothing voice. 'It's over. He's done.'

The kid drops the knife and turns around. There are two police officers about two steps away from him, and Jess is behind them, weeping. A young Alan Pierce is one of the officers, and he's calm, but the other officer brandishes a baton and glares at the kid.

The other officer takes a step towards the kid, but Alan stops him. 'I'll deal with him, Paul,' Alan whispers. 'Call for the ambulance.'

Paul nods and radios for an urgent ambulance.

Alan pulls out a handkerchief and walks to the kid. He wipes the blood around the kid's cold eyes. 'You okay?' he asks the kid.

The kid nods.

'What did he do to deserve this?' Alan asks and gestures at Rod.

'He did nothing!' Jess screams and runs towards them, but Paul grabs her. 'He just attacked him!'

'Him?' Paul asks Jess and points at the kid.

'Yes! He attacked my boyfriend!' she responds.

Her reply confuses Alan and Paul, especially considering the dispatch call and the striking resemblance between Jess and the kid.

'Your boyfriend?' Alan asks Jess, and gestures to Rod.

She nods.

'And he is?' Alan asks and gestures to the kid.

'HE attacked my boyfriend!'

'And who did that to you?' Alan asks and points to her bruises.

She hesitates. 'Did what?' she screams.

Paul shakes his head in amusement, but Alan struggles to hide his anger.

Alan turns to the kid. 'Let's go, kid,' he says.

The kid turns to Jess, and she looks away. He turns back to Alan and nods. Alan pats him on the shoulder and leads him out of the kitchen.

'What are you doing?' she asks Alan.

'Taking him into custody,' Alan responds.

'You're arresting him, good! But where are the fucking handcuffs?'

Alan wants to scream at her, but he takes a moment to calm down. 'He doesn't pose a danger to us,' he says. 'Does he, Paul?'

'Not one bit,' Paul responds.

She is enraged and points to Rod, who is whimpering in a pool of his blood. She opens her mouth to speak.

'Don't!' Alan commands. 'If you say one more word, I'll arrest you and cuff you so tight you won't feel your hands for a week.'

She glares at Alan but doesn't speak.

'You'll take care of that?' Alan asks Paul and gestures to Rod.

Paul nods.

'Thank you,' Alan says. 'We'll be in the car.'

Alan leads the kid out of the house.

16:00

'I'm Jide, and the ugly bastard's Tosin'

I walk out of Green Park station, and Piccadilly is bustling. I head straight to Berkeley Street.

Berkeley Street is quintessential Mayfair. It's lined on both sides with lavish restaurants, cafés, galleries, and showrooms, and every other car on the street is luxury. People walking the streets are affluent, and none are in a rush. I enjoy watching people. On another day, I would've sat by a window in one of these cafés, drinking green tea.

I stop by the junction opposite Nobu Restaurant, which I imagine is a good landmark. But before I call, I consider their names – Tosin and Jide. I've never worked with Nigerians, and they don't exactly have a trustworthy reputation. But I'm sure Oleg knows what he's doing . . . right? For a fleeting moment, I consider if it could be Oleg that set me up, and that makes me smile. Sometimes the extent of my paranoia amuses me. I call.

'Saviour sent me,' I say.

'Right, you here?' the man on the other end asks.

'Yes. I'm by Nobu.'

'Okay. We'll be there in five minutes. In a black car.'

He ends the conversation. He didn't sound Nigerian, not even African. He has an American accent, and that has me worried. But then again, no one will try anything stupid in broad daylight on Berkeley Street, not even Americans.

Precisely five minutes later, a black Mercedes E-Class Saloon parks in front of me. There are two black guys in their mid-twenties in the front seats, but they're wearing flash sunglasses and look straight out of *Miami Vice*. Plus, the car is conspicuous. I look away, and the driver lowers his window.

'Please, take your time,' he says to me.

I recognise his voice from the call. I nod and step into the back seat of the car. The driver focuses on the road as he sets off, and the passenger turns to me. He's eating a cup of Ben & Jerry's ice cream; looks like cookie dough, good choice.

'I'm Jide, and the ugly bastard's Tosin,' the passenger says.

'Baba eh,' Tosin responds. 'Don't know about you but I'm handsome,' he sings.

'Iya eh,' Jide says, and they laugh. He turns back to me. 'Oleg told us you have problems with 'em Kilburn boys. We do too. Makes us friends for the day.'

'Cool,' I say.

'He said you need to make a stop at Marble Arch as well,' Tosin says and glances at me through the rear-view mirror. 'You want to head there first?' He turns to Jide and points to the cup of ice cream. 'You better not stain the seat, cos I swear . . .'

'Fuck off, it's finished,' Jide says, and tosses the empty cup out the window.

'Fucking idiot,' Tosin teases, and glances at me through the rear-view mirror. 'So?'

'Yes, we'll head there first,' I say. 'You guys have weapons, right?'

They burst out laughing.

'Wo dude yii oh, o béèrè foolish things,' Tosin says.

'Weapons abi? Ti o ba ri boot, oun yoo ku,' Jide says.

Although I don't understand, it's clear they are teasing me.

'Mo like jacket rẹ, sha,' Tosin says.

Jide turns to study my jacket and turns back to Tosin. 'Me too,' Jide says. 'Mo ro pe mo rii ninu Selfridges.'

I don't mind being teased, but I hate not knowing what's been said. Tosin mentioned jacket and Jide turned to stare at mine, but they can't be teasing my jacket. It is old, but it doesn't look old, and it's a simple leather bomber.

'Yeah, we got weapons,' Jide says.

'All sorts, dude,' Tosin says.

'Shut up and drive. I'm talking here,' Jide says to Tosin.

'Fuck your mother,' Tosin responds.

'My mother?' Jide says, and feigns being offended. 'She's not an ashewo like your mother.'

Tosin laughs. 'Are you sure? You don't even know your mother,' he says.

'Fuck off,' Jide says.

They laugh, and Jide turns back to me. 'Ehen, fresh guy,' he says. 'We have everything you'll possibly need. Oleg supplies us on the regs.'

'Okay, cool,' I say.

'Dude, you aren't saying much,' Tosin says. 'What's with "cool", "cool", "okay", "cool"?'

I don't know how to respond, but he smiles, and Jide laughs. They're teasing again. I don't understand their banter, but they seem to find each other hilarious.

I force a smile. 'My bad,' I say. 'How did you guys meet Oleg then?'

Jide attempts to speak, but his phone rings. He pulls it out and answers immediately. 'Hey, baby.' His American accent returns, but his smile disappears. 'What you mean by that?'

. . .

'I'll come later, seriously, something came up, baby.'

. . .

'C'mon, don't talk like that, you come first.'

. . .

'Okay.'

. . .

'Okay.'

. . .

'Okay.'

. . .

'Wait, don't be like that.'

He listens and becomes dejected; it's clear he's getting a

scolding. Thirty seconds later, he places his phone on the dashboard.

Tosin bursts out laughing. 'Flora?' he asks.

Jide nods.

'Pussyboy,' Tosin teases.

'Your father,' Jide says and cracks a smile.

'You never brap am, abi,' Tosin says.

'Nah, not yet, but it's not even about that.'

'Really?' Tosin asks and laughs. 'Eat the pussy then. You never know, she just might like it.'

'I don't do that.'

'Fucking liar.'

'Fuck off. I'm serious, I told you she's a virgin.'

'I didn't believe you then, and I still don't.'

'Shut up,' Jide says, and turns to me. 'Fresh guy, this is your fault.'

I thought it was. He probably had to change plans with Flora last minute because of our sudden business.

'I apologise,' I say.

'We are at Marble Arch,' Tosin says. 'Where to from here?'

I should have said Farrukh's Gold is more Marylebone than Marble Arch, but we're here now. I tell Tosin the address, and we head towards Farrukh's Gold.

It ought to be straightforward to get past the blast door to Farrukh if he's genuinely expecting me. But if he's responsible for my ambush, shit will hit the fan the moment I ring the doorbell. I'll have to break in and make Javad open the blast door. If Farrukh fucks with the likes of Tariq and Tony, he wouldn't want to involve the police. Plus, most of the merchandise in the back room is stolen property. Farrukh will call other goons or whoever he pays for protection, but they won't get there in time.

'We're here,' Jide says.

Tosin parks a few metres away from Farrukh's Gold. A grey BMW parked in front of Farrukh's Gold is the only other vehicle on the street. Someone needs to remain in the car to be on the lookout, and in case we need a quick getaway, and I don't want to pick.

'I need only one of you for this,' I say.

'Really?' Tosin asks, and they both smirk.

They stare at me, and I can see my reflection in their sunglasses. I don't speak and wait for them to decide, but they're not going to, and I don't enjoy staring at my reflection. Well, Tosin's already at the wheel, so that's the decision made for me.

'All right, Jide, let's go,' I say.

Jide laughs, and Tosin shakes his head. 'Why him?' Tosin asks.

'Cos you are fucking ugly,' Jide says, and turns to me. 'Abi, fresh guy?'

'You're already at the wheel, Tosin, and we just might need a quick getaway.'

'Yeah, whatever, dude,' Tosin says.

'Don't mind him, my guy, let's go,' Jide says to me and turns to Tosin. 'Wahala, abeg open boot.'

Jide and I step out of the car, and beyond Jide's silk collarless shirt, he's dressed in black trousers and black Oxford brogues.

He looks rich, but he'd look less *Miami Vice* if he just tucked the shirt in and took off the sunglasses.

'Could you do me a favour?' I ask.

'Yeah,' he says, with more than a hint of doubt.

'Tuck your shirt in and take off your sunglasses.'

He raises an eyebrow over the frame of his sunglasses and turns to Tosin. 'Tosin, can you imagine my guy wants me to tuck in—'

'Shut up! Good for you,' Tosin says.

Jide turns back to me. 'So, you are my daddy now,' he teases.

I smile. 'There are a lot of expensive items in there. In a back room that we can only get in through a blast door. I don't look like I can afford anything in that room. But you do. And you can make that look effortless if you just do what I ask.'

'Sure, why not,' he says. He tucks in his shirt and removes his glasses. 'How do I look?' he asks.

'Wealthy.'

'My man,' he says, and smacks me on the shoulder.

He leads to the open boot, and there are two black pullover hoodies, two pairs of black trainers, two baseball bats, and a single baseball inside. He rolls up the carpet, and there's a hidden compartment underneath.

'Open it,' Jide says to Tosin.

The compartment slides open to reveal a mobile arsenal. There are six handguns, two assault rifles, two assault shotguns, countless ammunition, and weapon attachments such as sights, suppressors, and grips. There are also two bulletproof vests.

'You asked if we had weapons,' Jide says, and smiles.

'I sure did,' I say, and nod.

'Which do we need?'

'Handguns, silenced.'

He nods and pulls out two M9 pistols and two suppressors. He chambers a round on each M9 before he attaches a suppressor. He hands me an M9 and reaches for extra magazines.

'We won't need them,' I say. 'It's only two guys in there.'

He considers my reasoning for a moment and nods. He closes the compartment, rolls down the carpet, closes the boot.

'Just follow my lead,' I say.

'Okay, I got your back,' he says with conviction.

I tuck my gun into my waistband and lead to Farrukh's Gold.

I ring the doorbell and watch Javad through the glass. He turns to us and smiles when he recognises me. He unlocks the door, and Jide and I walk in. I do my best to appear calm, but I'm anxious and prepared to shove my gun into Javad's mouth the moment he looks at me the wrong way. Javad seems pleased to see me though; like he was expecting me.

'Hello, sir,' Javad says. 'Welcome back, and who is your friend?'

'Hello, Javad,' I say, and gesture to Jide. 'He's the buyer Farrukh and I spoke about.'

I study Javad as he turns to Jide. He forces a smile and stares at Jide, and it's clear he is dubious about Jide.

'I saw a couple pieces in the back room I think my friend would like,' I say. 'I spoke to Farrukh about it when he called to tell me the money for the bracelet was ready. He said to bring my friend along.'

I wait for a response, but Javad just stares at Jide, unsure. Jide is calm and maintains eye contact with Javad.

'Are we good, Javad?' I ask.

'Yes,' he says, and turns to me. 'Yes, sir. Please follow me.'

Although Javad tries to hide it, it's clear he has no idea what I'm talking about. Still, he leads us through the secret door.

'Thanks for everything,' I say.

'You are welcome, sir,' he says.

'I hope it wasn't too much of a hassle getting the Beamer unclamped?'

'Clamped? It must not have been mine, sir. I've never gotten clamped, and we've paid for the parking space, it comes with the rent.'

'Oh, my bad, it looked like yours.'

Farrukh lied. I thought so, but now it's confirmed. Doesn't mean he's behind the ambush, but the old man better have a plausible explanation.

Like earlier, Javad gestures for Jide and me to wait a couple steps behind. Jide turns to me with a raised eyebrow, and I motion for him to wait. Javad enters the door code, and I swing the base of the gun into the back of his head. He collapses in a heap.

Jide and I burst into the room, and Farrukh is at his desk, analysing a necklace with his microscope. I raise my gun and hurry towards the desk, while Jide flanks it. Jide's movement is impeccable; he's probably ex-special forces. I wouldn't want to be at the end of his gun.

Farrukh hears me approach and turns to me. He's startled, but I can't tell if he's surprised to see me alive or it's the gun.

'Is Javad okay?' he asks.

His head jolts, and blood spatters over the desk.

I turn to Jide, and smoke oozes out of his gun barrel. I'm angry, but then it's my fault. I should've told Jide I wanted to question Farrukh before we killed him, if we killed him. But he agreed to follow my lead, and I didn't shoot. Oleg warned me he and Tosin were trigger-happy, but this is a frail old man, there is no thrill in that kill. Especially if Farrukh is innocent.

'Here,' he says, and beckons.

I walk to him, and he points to a red button underneath Farrukh's desk.

'I've seen that a few times lately,' he says. 'In places like this that need top-grade security and want nothing to do with the police. It's a silent alarm straight to a private security firm that'll be very close, and they'll come in hot. The old man was bout to push the button with his knee.'

'Fuck me.'

'I don't do guys. I know you're fresh and all, and I told you I got your back, but I didn't mean it like that.' He smiles.

I smile back. 'I needed to ask him some questions.'

He shrugs, and we walk to the desk. He crouches to a black box by Farrukh's feet, and I search the table for anything that can help answer my questions. I have no idea what to look for and don't find anything anyway. But Jide stands and shows me a flashcard.

'Storage for the security cameras,' he says and drops the flashcard into his pocket.

He shoots the black box, and the monitor switches off.

'Let's get out of here,' I say.

He nods and follows me to the door. To my surprise, he isn't interested in any of the valuable merchandise we walk past. I skip over Javad, who is still unconscious by the blast door, but Jide shoots him twice in the head. Fuck. I'd hoped Jide would deem it unnecessary. Especially because I'm certain Javad isn't involved. But Jide's a professional, no room for sentiments or witnesses. My choice. My fault.

We step out of Farrukh's Gold and stroll to the car, which Tosin has turned around for a quick getaway.

'Boot,' Jide says as we approach the car.

'Kilo ṣẹlẹ,' Tosin says, and leans out of the car towards us.

The boot opens, and Jide quickly rolls up the carpet. 'Open it,' he says, and pulls out his gun.

I hand him my gun as the compartment opens, and he replaces them. He closes the compartment, rolls down the carpet, and shuts the boot, and we enter the car.

'Kilo ṣẹlẹ,' Tosin says again to Jide.

Jide wears his seatbelt. 'Two kills; had to be done,' he says without emotion.

Tosin nods and drives. 'You okay?' he asks and glances at me through the rear-view mirror.

'Yeah,' I say. 'We're on to Kilburn.'

Tosin and Jide nod.

17:26

'Surprise is our best ally'

After a brief period of silence, Jide and Tosin are back bantering. But I'm deep in thought, trying to devise a plan to attack Topper's castle. And it seems the castle is the fortress Noriega claims it is because every plan I think up has flaws that'll get at least one of us killed before we even get in. And I have a good feeling that if one of Jide and Tosin gets killed because of my flawed plans, the other will kill me.

I focus on the street, hoping to calm my chaotic thoughts. And I remember Noriega took me to his spot. He said he'd be there all day. 'Come through . . . anything you want on the house,' he said.

I'll do that.

'Tosin,' I say, and he glances at me through the rear-view mirror. 'Head for Shoot-Up Hill. I've got a plan.'

'Sure,' Tosin responds, and stops at a red light. 'What's the plan?'

'One of Topper's guys—'

'Who's Topper?'

'Sorry, Tyrone—'

'Snowman,' Jide interjects.

'Yeah,' I say, and nod. 'One of his guys has a spot around there. He'll get us into Snowman's place.'

'Snowman's guy,' Tosin says, and drives. 'Is his name Noriega by any chance?'

'Yeah, that's him,' I say, astonished that they know Noriega.

Tosin smirks and Jide laughs.

'Dude is Tosin's bitch,' Jide says.

'Behave,' Tosin says to Jide. 'The skinny fool and some of Snowman's other boys tried me at a private casino in Hampstead. Supposedly, I was rude to him. I was playing blackjack . . . was up big too, so I was buzzing. But he just kept hollering and being a general dick on the roulette table beside me. Everyone else was scared of him and his boys; even the host just left him to it. I had enough, so I politely asked him to be quiet. He and his boys didn't take it well. I tried to talk them down. Seriously, I did. I even almost apologised. But they weren't interested. Plus, they thought I was alone, so light work for them.' He gestures to Jide. 'This fucking guy was with Flora. Doing whatever it is couples do when not fucking or eating pussy.'

'Shut up,' Jide says.

'Speaking of,' Tosin says, and glances at me through the rear-view mirror. 'You seem like a real man. You eat pussy?'

I don't want to engage with that, but then I don't want to seem condescending.

'Depends on the pussy,' I say.

Jide laughs, and Tosin shakes his head.

'Dude, I don't know what sort of girls you're fucking with,' Tosin says.

'No, no,' I protest. 'Yeah, I do, sometimes.'

'Fucking hell!' Jide says.

'Dude, I'm not asking if you eat pussy for breakfast,' Tosin says, and laughs. He turns to Jide. 'I told you, real men eat pussy.'

'Whatever,' Jide responds.

'As I was saying,' Tosin says. 'I was not alone. I had a little friend with me, and we sorted them out easy . . . light work for me. The casino is one of my favourite spots to play blackjack, and there were witnesses, so I didn't kill any of them. Fucked 'em up though. I'm sure you've seen the scar across Noriega's lips.'

'Yeah,' I say. 'Can't miss it.'

'That's me with my very sharp little friend,' Tosin says. 'Clean slice across his lips, so he never forgets to be quiet. It is simple courtesy.'

'If Noriega sees Tosin, I swear he'll pee his pants,' Jide says.

'That's good,' I say. 'Might come in handy.'

'We're on Shoot-Up Hill,' Tosin says. 'Where we headed?'

I recognise a tower block; I know the way from here. I direct Tosin to a quiet street around the corner from Noriega's spot. He parks, but keeps the engine running.

I shift to the centre of the back seat and lean forward between them. 'Okay, here is what I'm thinking,' I say. 'We need to get into Snowman's place, but he's done a fucking good job to make it difficult to get in.'

'How did you get in earlier?' Tosin asks.

'I was with Noriega. He parked in front of the building and called somebody. About a minute later, the door opened.'

'Right, so we use him again,' Jide says.

'That's what I'm thinking. But it can't be that easy, right?'

They nod. 'Any other ideas?' Jide asks.

'Nah, that's it,' I say.

'Okay, we'll make that work then,' Jide says, and turns to Tosin. 'Abi, Tosin?'

Tosin nods and drums his fingers on the steering wheel, and Jide stares at the dashboard. They're pondering.

I give them a couple minutes with their thoughts. 'All right,' I say. 'In a minute, I'll go convince Noriega to take me back to Snowman's place.'

They both turn to check my confidence for the task, and they nod.

'You guys should wait here,' I say. 'Cos if . . . when I convince Noriega, he'll drive us past this street on the way to the castle. And you guys tail us. He drives a black Mercedes—'

'I know his car,' Tosin says.

'Oh, good,' I say. 'Once Noriega and I get to Snowman's place, I expect the same routine – he'll call, and about a minute later, the front door will open. If possible, I'd like you guys close to the building when it opens. All the windows are boarded up, and there are no cameras outside, so there's a good chance no one will see you approach. Don't worry about Noriega seeing you from the car cos I'll take care of him soon as he makes the call.'

'Okay, we're good with that,' Tosin says. He turns to Jide for a reaction, but Jide is deep in thought. He turns back to me. 'I was looking forward to finishing Noriega myself.'

'I can imagine,' I say. 'But it has to be done this way.'

Tosin nods.

'I'll need a silenced gun to take care of Noriega,' I say. 'I think it's best we remain as quiet as possible for as long as possible. Surprise is our best ally.'

'I'm with you there,' Tosin says.

'Inside, there are two armed guards on either side of the front door. Soon as I step in, both guards will focus on me, and one of them might even search me for a weapon. That's the best time for you guys to step in and subdue them.'

'Subdue? You mean kill, right?' Tosin asks, but it's not a question; he's scolding me.

'Yes, I do.'

'Say it then.'

'You kill them.'

He nods.

'After that,' I continue, 'we get loud. Assault weapons will be best at this point.'

Tosin smiles.

'I can't carry an assault weapon to Noriega's, so I'd like one of you to bring me one.'

'Sure.'

'Surprise should give us the upper hand. And then loud gunfire should scare any half-brave idiots in the house. I want us to keep the body count to a minimum.'

Tosin approves with a nod. I glance at Jide for a response, but he's still deep in thought.

'There is a problem though,' I say. 'I have the ground floor covered in terms of layout, and I have a good idea of the level of resistance we'll meet. But I have no idea what's going on upstairs.'

'That's the problem?'

I hesitate because it doesn't seem like a question; seems he's scolding me, again. 'Yes,' I answer.

They smile at each other.

'I don't know what you know about us,' Tosin says. 'But that's not a problem for us. That's what we do.'

It was a clear reprimand, but I'm not going to acknowledge it.

'Tell us about the ground floor,' Jide says.

'There are three doors along the hallway. The first door is on the right just after the stairs; that's the toilet. The next one is on the left. That's the kitchen, a big one too . . . looks like where Snowman gets his product street-ready. There were a few women in there waiting to get it done . . . I counted five, but there are more. Two armed men also; positioned in corners of the room, and again, I'm sure there are more.

'The last door is on the right at the end of the hallway. I'll take care of that room, Topper is inside. He has an armed guard in front of the door though, and he'll see us soon as we—'

'We'll take care of him,' Jide says.

'I'll handle upstairs,' Tosin says. 'Jide will handle the ground floor with you.'

Jide nods in agreement. They don't seem fazed at all, and that eases my anxiety, a little.

'We good?' I ask.

'Pretty good,' Tosin says.

'Good,' Jide says. 'And don't worry, we've been in much tighter spots.'

I'm sure they have. Jide was impressive at Farrukh's Gold . . . maybe even too impressive. If Tosin is similarly skilled, our chances to survive aren't half bad. I want to look in their eyes because I know that'll fill me with more confidence, but they are still wearing sunglasses; Jide put his back on after leaving Farrukh's. I fight back a smile. They are fucking unique.

'It's been good fucking with you guys,' I say.

'Wow, what's up with that?' Jide quips.

'Behave yourself,' Tosin says to Jide, and turns to me. 'Relax, we'll be all right.'

'We got your back,' Jide says.

Their conviction is assuring.

'I'll need a silenced handgun now,' I say. 'Preferably the one I used earlier.'

'You know what to do,' Jide says.

'Okay.'

They trust me enough to access their arsenal myself, and

that's also assuring. I step out of the car and walk to the boot, and it pops open as I approach. I roll the carpet.

'Tosin,' I call.

'Ahn ahn,' he grumbles, but in jest. 'I'm now your errand boy too, abi?'

The compartment opens, and I spot the M9s Jide and I used at Farrukh's Gold because they still have suppressors attached. But then I'm intrigued by the other weapons and wonder which they'd bring for me. I dismiss the thought, pick one of the M9s, and tuck it into my waistband. I close the compartment, roll down the carpet, and shut the boot.

I head for Noriega's spot. It's on me now.

18:01

'Did your mother name you that?'

I turn into the street I remember Noriega's spot to be, and his Mercedes is parked in front of the crack house. He's still there. I walk past two kids leaning on a wall, and they follow a step behind me.

'Oi, blad, what you want?' one of the kids demands.

I ignore, and a large group of kids hurry towards me. All the kids, besides the one holding the pitbull, tuck their hands underneath their hoodies as if to grab weapons. I stop, and the two kids following me join the group in front of me to create a barrier between me and the crack house. The pitbull barks at me, but I ignore the dog and focus on the kids. They are all wired, so I'll have to be careful. I don't want to hurt them.

'Blad! This isn't your ends! I don't know you! What the fuck you want!' the kid holding the pitbull demands.

'Noriega,' I say.

'Yeah?' he says, and sneers.

He passes the pitbull to another kid and walks to me, and he's so close that I feel him breathing. He's big for his age, but he only reaches my chest, and I don't look down to him.

'What the fuck you want Noriega for, blad?' he demands.

'Just get him, he knows,' I say.

'What's your fucking name, man?' another kid in the wall demands.

They're annoying me, so I look away and scan the run-down street to calm myself.

'Ey, bruv, what you doing 'ere?' Noriega shouts.

I turn to the crack house, and Noriega is outside the front door.

'Skinnyblack, let the man pass,' Noriega says, and struts to his car. 'He Snowman's brethren with the new ting.'

Skinnyblack, the kid in front of me, steps aside, and the kids behind separate. I walk past the kids, and one reaches for me.

'Are you fucking crazy?' I snap. 'Don't touch me.'

'Ay ay, Shadow! No need to search the man, yeah,' Noriega shouts.

Shadow steps back but glares at me. If I didn't know better, I'd be scared. I fight back a smirk and walk towards Noriega.

'Nori, your man shouldn't move to me like that, yeah . . . I'll end him,' Shadow says from behind me.

I turn to Shadow and smirk, and he, Skinnyblack, and another kid lift their jumpers to show their handguns. My smile disappears; I didn't expect the kids to have guns. I underestimated them, and that would have cost me my life. I continue to Noriega and force a smile as I approach. But the smile is half-hearted because I'm angry with myself for underestimating the kids.

'Everything okay, bruv?' Noriega asks.

'Yeah,' I say, and we bump fists.

'My bad for that, these are my youth. Like my security, you know.'

He breaks out his peculiar smile, and it enrages me so much I want to snap his neck. But his time will come . . . soon.

'It's all good,' I say.

'Good. So, wagwan, bruv? You come check me?'

'Yeah, was headed to Snowman's place to follow up the earlier meet. Decided to check on you . . . see how the top man gets shit done, you know.'

'Yes, bruv. You like what you see, yeah?'

'Well, you're doing all right.'

He laughs. 'Just all right, yeah?'

I shrug, and he laughs again. 'I have no more time to chill though,' I say. 'It took me forever to find this place. And your youth didn't help.'

'Ah, that's the point, like . . . keep it safe and that. I could give you a ride to Snowman's, you know.'

'Sure?'

'Sure, bruv.'

'Thanks, man.'

It's difficult to keep a straight face because I can't believe how easy that was. We enter the car, and Noriega shouts instructions to the kids before he drives off.

'You know why we call my youth Skinnyblack, yeah?' Noriega asks.

'Cos he's fat and white.'

He bursts out laughing. 'Yes, bruv!'

'Very original,' I say, brimming with sarcasm.

'Original?' he asks, failing to pick up on my tone of voice.

'The name, it's very original.'

'Yes, you like my name, yeah?'

He makes a sharp turn, and I'm distracted by how fast he's driving through residential streets. 'What?' I ask.

'My name, Noriega.'

'Did your mother name you that?'

'No. I name myself after the great Manuel Noriega.'

'The great? Really?'

'Yes, bruv, the great drug lord.'

I stare at Noriega, and his scar is more striking now that I know how it happened. 'I think you mean Pablo Escobar.'

'What?' he asks, and turns into the street where I'd left Tosin and Jide.

'The great drug dealer you're talking about, that's Pablo Escobar . . . not Noriega.'

I glance at the spot Tosin parked, but the car is not there. 'Noriega was a military leader of Panama.' I scan the street, but the car is nowhere in sight. 'He dabbled in trafficking. Cocaine, guns, money . . . but mostly for Escobar and the other Colombian cartels.'

'What you talking about?'

'Forget it.' I'm anxious because I didn't see Tosin's car. But

I compel myself to relax. Tosin and Jide know what they are doing. 'What did your mum name you?'

'John.'

'What was wrong with John? Not bad enough, eh?'

'It's okay.'

He smiles, but he's not amused; he's reminiscing. I take the opportunity to check the mirrors for Tosin's car, but there is no car behind us. I try to convince myself that if I can see them following us, Noriega can too, and Tosin would avoid that . . . But I'm a paranoid fucker.

'You see my youth, Shadow?' Noriega asks.

'The kid that tried to frisk me?'

He laughs. 'Yes, bruv, the youth's a killer.'

'Killer?' I ask with a raised eyebrow.

'Yes, the youth fearless. Heart of stone and that.'

I nod. 'How much you pay those kids?'

'I pay them enough. I got money.'

He cracks his peculiar smile and parks. And like earlier, he parks right in front of the castle. He pulls out his phone and makes the call.

'We in here,' he says, and ends the call.

I check the mirrors, but I don't see them or the car. Fuck it. Noriega turns to me, and I point behind him. 'What the fuck's that?' I ask.

He looks over his shoulder, and I shoot him twice in the chest.

I grab Noriega's lifeless body before it slumps through the seat belt and prop him up. I turn to the building, and Jide and Tosin are crouched on either side of the front door. Wow. How the fuck did that happen so fast. I don't react and focus on the door, and we wait for it to open.

The door opens a few seconds later, and I step out of the car. I walk to the door, and as I approach, I notice Jide is watching me, and Tosin is watching the door. I stop in the doorway, and the same two guards are at either side of the door. The guard who searched me takes a step to me, and I make eye contact with Jide. He and Tosin step in and shoot the guards twice in the head.

The guards collapse, and Tosin and Jide aim into the hallway, but it's empty.

They holster their handguns, and Tosin hands me a semi-automatic shotgun.

Jide pulls off his bulletproof vest and puts it on me. He adjusts it to fit my torso and secures it.

Tosin points to the shotgun and signals five fingers and then two. I understand and nod.

They ready their assault rifles and turn to me, and I pump the shotgun. They charge into the castle, and I follow.

18:02

'Our guy can take care of himself'

Tosin and Jide were born in Nigeria and moved to America in their early teens. Tosin grew up in Chicago and Jide in Atlanta. When they were nineteen, they were recruited by the Navy SEALs and trained for a covert unit funded by the US but independently operated by the Nigerian government. The unit's sole purpose was to eradicate a fast-rising terrorist organisation in Northern Nigeria funded by Al-Qaeda.

Tosin and Jide have been inseparable since they met at the training base. They were the youngest recruits and bonded over their very similar upbringing, cultural preferences, and sense of humour. Also, they were – and still are – physically identical, so everyone on the base referred to them as twins, and soon they regarded themselves as twins.

After fifteen gruelling months, the unit was ready – nine toughened recruits and a tough captain. The unit moved to

Northern Nigeria and operated successfully, by any measure, for two years – until their success became a problem. The rivalry between Nigerian intelligence and armed forces for credit, coupled with corruption and tribalism in the government, led to the eradication of the unit.

All members of the unit are believed to be dead, but three survive. Tosin and Jide, not their real names, and the captain. The captain is lying low in northern Cameroon as he recovers from life-changing injuries suffered from the car bomb believed to have killed him. Tosin and Jide are ghosts in plain sight, utilising their unique set of skills to become mercenaries.

Today is their umpteenth mission, but it is unique because they have a history with the target and are working with someone else for the first time. They watch their ally disappear into the distance.

'O like plan yẹn?' Jide asks in their peculiar mixture of American English and Yoruba.

Tosin nods. 'You think one of us should go watch my guy's back?' he asks, referring to their ally.

'Your guy, eh?'

They laugh. 'Fuck off. Our guy.'

'Our guy can take care of himself.'

'Sure? Cos awọn kids pẹlu Noriega don't fuck about.'

'Ma worry.'

'You should call Flora. This thing can go wrong.'

'It won't.'

Tosin smiles.

'You know what I'm thinking?' Jide asks.

'No, what are you thinking?'

'Seeing as we have no information on the top floor . . .'

'I'll be fine,' Tosin interrupts. 'I scouted the house after that bullshit at the casino. I have a good idea of what to expect.'

'Okay, but I think you should take some flash grenades.'

'Yeah, I like that. You take some as well, cos the room downstairs definitely has more guards than he saw.'

'I will. Guns?'

'M4s.'

'Yeah.'

'I think the Benelli will be good for our guy . . . easiest to handle.'

'You don't think he can handle an assault rifle?'

'I dunno, I don't think he has any training.'

'I think he'll be fine. But I agree, the Benelli.'

'How many flash grenades do we have with us?'

'Six.'

'We split them.'

'Tactical belts then.'

'Yeah, extra ammo, and vests.'

'I'll be fine without one . . .'

'This is no time to be brave.'

'I know, but we both know our guy will need it more than I will. We're not losing anyone.'

'Fair.'

They focus on the street to watch for Noriega's car, and Tosin's hands are clamped to the steering wheel, ready to set off.

A few minutes pass before Jide checks the time on his phone. 'How long has he been gone for?' he asks.

'Dunno, but that's what I was saying. Should we check on him?'

'No. He'll get it done,' Jide says, and smiles. 'And I know you just want to go kill Noriega.'

'Nah,' Tosin denies, and they laugh. 'I'm looking out for our guy.'

'We'll see them soon. Trust me. Anyway, what if there is no money in the house?'

'Now you trust me, there is money there. After that bullshit, I wanted to wipe them out. I scouted Snowman's entire operation for ten nights and seven days.'

'You love your reconnaissance, sha.'

'Fuck. It was drilled into me, it's in my blood now. Anyway, each night the same four dudes in random pairs leave the house at 2300 hrs to collect the day's takings from all of Snowman's spots. They bring all that money back to the house, and I never saw it leave.'

'It could've been moved since then.'

'Sure. But I watched them for a couple weeks. If they move the money, they wait till it reaches an amount that they can't keep in the house. So if we catch 'em right, they'll be a ton of it. And my educated guess is the money is kept upstairs, so it'll be more secure. Soon as you're done downstairs, come up.'

Jide nods and sends a text, and Tosin focuses on the street. Tosin spots Noriega's car turn into the street and sets off well ahead of the car.

'What happened?' Jide asks.

'That's them in the Mercedes,' Tosin says, and gestures to the rear-view mirror.

Jide looks into the mirror and spots Noriega's car in the distance. 'You circling to tail 'em?' he asks.

'No. I know where the house is.'

'Oh, yeah.'

'I know the perfect spot close to the house to get ready.'

'Okay.'

A couple minutes later, Tosin parks in the corner of a desolate street. 'The house is just around the block,' he says. 'We'll see them drive past.'

They take off their sunglasses and Jide places them in the glove compartment before he steps out of the car. He hurries to the boot, and it opens as he approaches. He sets the hoodies and trainers on the floor and rolls up the carpet, and like clockwork, the compartment opens. Tosin joins him behind the boot, and they switch their shoes to trainers and wear the hoodies. They put on the bulletproof vests, and Tosin secures his, but Jide leaves his unstrapped.

They wear tactical belts, and Jide slots the suppressed M9 into his thigh holster. Tosin attaches a suppressor to a Beretta 92 handgun and chambers a round before he slots the gun into his thigh holster. They attach slings to M4A1 assault rifles and wear the rifles across their backs. Tosin attaches a sling to a semi-automatic shotgun and wears it. They clip three flash grenades each to their belts and put extra ammunition into a pouch on the belt. They close the compartment, roll down the carpet, and place their shoes in the boot before they shut it.

They embrace and pray under their breath. 'With the strength of our fallen brothers. You are never forgotten. In your names, we pray,' Tosin says to conclude.

'Amen,' Jide responds.

'Now let's work,' Tosin says.

They pull out their handguns and run in a crouched position to the top of the street. They hide behind a car to watch the adjacent street, and Noriega's car whizzes past.

'Them, right?' Jide asks.

Tosin nods. 'Snowman's place is a bit further down,' he says. 'I'll lead. We use the cars parked on the street as cover. We get close enough and wait. You watch the house, and I'll watch Noriega's car. I'll signal when our guy takes care of Noriega and then you signal when it's clear to advance to the door. Good?'

'Good.'

'Ready?'

'Ready.'

Tosin leads through the desolate street, and they stop behind a car a short distance away from Noriega's Mercedes, which is parked in front of the castle.

'Can you see them?' Jide whispers.

Tosin is about to respond, but an elderly black lady stops her electric mobility beside them. They both aim for her head but don't shoot because she doesn't turn to them.

She rummages through her handbag. 'You here for Tyrone?' she asks with an assertive Caribbean accent.

They don't respond.

'One of you boys speak already. I try not to look your way.'

'Yes, ma'am,' Tosin says.

'Okay,' she says. 'I'm going bingo now. You boys make sure you murder the rassclaat very good before I come back, you hear me?'

'Sure, ma'am,' Tosin says.

'That be very well 'ppreciated round here,' she says, and drives away.

They turn to each other and shrug. Tosin places a hand on Jide's shoulder and watches the car, and Jide watches the house. Tosin sees their guy shoot Noriega, and he taps Jide's shoulder twice. Jide nods, and they dart to the front door. They hide at either side of the door, and Tosin signals that he'll watch the door and Jide watch their guy.

The door opens, and they don't move an inch. Their guy steps out of the car, and Jide watches him approach. He stops in the doorway and makes eye contact with Jide, and Jide signals Tosin. They spin into the house and fire two shots into the guards' heads. The guards collapse, and they scan the hallway, but it's empty.

Tosin hands their guy the shotgun, and Jide secures the vest on him. Tosin signals that the shotgun has seven shots, and their guy nods. They pull their assault rifles, and Tosin sets his rifle to fully automatic fire, and Jide sets his to semi-automatic fire. Their guy pumps the shotgun, and they charge into the house.

18:36

'What you waiting for?'

Tosin leaps up the stairs and Jide leads me through the hallway. We stop by the half-open toilet door, and he peeks in; it's empty. He signals for me to proceed, and I run ahead to Topper's office. I attempt to open the door, but it's locked.

'Who that?' Colin asks from inside the room.

I hear Colin approach the door, and I kick it in. The door smacks Colin in the face, and he stumbles backwards. He reaches for his gun and I shoot. The shotgun blast drives him onto Topper's desk, and the recoil thumps me in the shoulder. The desk crashes into Topper just as he pulls his revolver and the gun flies away. I charge into the room and Topper scurries towards the revolver.

I aim for Topper, but I don't shoot because I need answers. 'Stop!' I shout.

Topper doesn't listen, he reaches for the revolver and I have no choice but to shoot. The blast drives him into the wall and the recoil sends a jolt through my body. He collapses, and I hurry to him. Ah fuck, he's dead. He's bleeding from holes in every limb, and a mix of blood and brain tissue oozes from a large hole in his head. I swallow saliva in disgust and hear a faint bang, then a louder bang, and then ear-splitting gunfire around the castle. I realise my ears have been ringing since the jolt from the shotgun.

The intense gunfire around the house stops, but there are spurts of gunfire in the room above me. I dart towards the stairs and the kitchen is silent as I run past. I'm halfway up the stairs when the shooting stops, and the house is dead quiet.

I tiptoe up the stairs, and there are three dead bodies in the hallway. I peek into the bathroom – it's empty, so I advance to the next room. I lean on the wall by the open door and listen for movement inside, but I hear nothing. I spin into the room with the shotgun raised and I'm shocked by the carnage. Everyone in the room is dead, the walls and overturned furniture are covered with blood splatter, and there's a heap of blood-soaked cash on the floor. Someone grabs my shoulder.

Their guy runs to Topper's office and Jide slides across the hallway to the kitchen door. Jide pulls the pin out of two flash grenades and kicks the door open. He throws the grenades in opposite directions of the room and spins out before they detonate.

He steps back into the room, and a man with a gun tucked in his waistband stumbles towards the door. He shoots the man twice in the head and runs along the wall to a lifeless man with third-degree burns across his face. He shoots the man between the eyes to confirm the kill and hurdles a couple of frantic naked women to a man crawling to a handgun. He stomps the man's head to the floor and shoots it twice.

A gunshot whizzes past Jide into the wall and he spins to a clothed woman covered head to toe in cocaine. She supports herself on a kitchen counter and struggles to aim because her vision is impaired. He shoots her in the chest and the bullet pierces through her heart, killing her instantly.

He scans the room as he walks to her body, and there is no more resistance, just naked women in distress. He rolls the dead woman over with his foot and glares at her; she's the first person to get the drop on him.

He leaps up the stairs and charges towards the gunfight in the room at the end of the hallway. He slides into the room and spots Tosin poised in the centre. Tosin spins to a man crawling over a broken stool towards a gun, and he and Jide shoot the man in the head in unison.

They scan the room. Everyone else is dead with one bullet wound in the head. That's Tosin – clinical as always.

'You good?' Tosin asks.

'Yeah,' Jide responds, and they bump fists.

'How's our guy?'

'Good too.'

'You sure?'

Jide nods.

'Good,' Tosin says, and walks to a black bin bag that's full to the brim. He rummages through; it's filled with clean twenty-pound notes. 'Check what's in there,' he says, and points to a half-full white bin bag close to Jide. 'It's all twenties in here.'

Jide checks, and the bag is three-quarters full of clean ten-pound notes. 'Tenners,' he says.

Tosin walks to a blue bin bag and checks; it's a third full of clean fifty-pound notes. 'Fifties here,' he says.

'Must be fives in the green then,' Jide says, and walks to a check a full green bin bag; he's correct. He gestures to an industrial washer-dryer washing cash. 'Why the fuck are they washing the money?'

'Makes it easier to count, I suppose. And much easier to package and transport.'

Jide shrugs.

Tosin picks the blue bin bag and hands it to Jide. 'Put these in with the tenners and carry that. I'll carry the twenties, it's full enough. We'll leave the fivers. Unless our guy wants it.'

Jide pours all the fifties into the white bag. 'Don't think he's here for that,' he says.

Tosin nods and ties up the black bag, and Jade ties the white bag. They carry the bags over their shoulders and hurry out of the room.

'Let's go!' Jide says.

I turn around, and he and Tosin are smiling. They seem happy to see me. But then they're carrying bin bags that appear full of money; that's probably why they're happy.

'What you waiting for? Let's get outta here,' Tosin says, and they run towards the stairs.

I follow them out of the castle. I didn't think we left anyone alive, but I hear screams from the ground floor as we run to the street. I follow their lead to the Mercedes, and Tosin hops into the driver's seat as Jide and I race to the boot.

Jide opens the compartment and replaces our weapons. Tosin joins us behind the boot as I remove the bulletproof vest, and Jide replaces Tosin's weapons and the vests. Jide closes the compartment and rolls the carpet, and Tosin and I drop in the bin bags. They lay their hoodies over the bags, and we rush into the car. The engine is running, so Tosin speeds off like a shot.

18:45

'My man'

Tosin speeds away from the castle, and Jide watches the mirrors to check if we are being followed. We turn onto Kilburn High Road and Tosin blends into the traffic. But Jide continues to watch the mirrors until we are a couple minutes away from the castle. They bump fists and turn to me; I nod. We're clear. Topper's dead, we're all back in the car in one piece, and Tosin and Jide have substantial loot. On the face of it, that's complete success, but it doesn't feel like that at all because I'm still not sure who set up my ambush.

'Where to now?' Tosin asks.

I hadn't even begun to think about that. I check my watch; it's 18:45. I'm still on time. 'I need to meet Oleg,' I say. 'Just drop me at the next station.'

'Where you going to meet him?' Tosin asks.

'Paddington.'

'That's close. Where in Paddington?'

'He'll pick me up from the station.'

'Okay, I'll take you there.'

'Thanks, mate.'

'It's all good.'

Tosin heads towards Paddington, and the car is silent. We won't be discussing what we just did, and that's good with me because I'm struggling with it; with the savagery of it. They don't seem affected though. I guess they are numb to it, like I thought I was, but now know I'm not.

'You okay back there, my guy?' Tosin asks.

I look at him through the rear-view mirror. 'Yeah, I'm okay,' I say with as much conviction as I can muster.

'Good. I'll play you some good Nigerian music,' Tosin says, and a little screen descends from the ceiling in front of me.

'Oya!' Jide says.

The video of a song titled 'Dami Duro' by Davido plays on the screen. The song starts off pretty well and only gets better to the extent that I catch myself bumping along to it. I don't know what I expected, but the song exceeds that by a mile. The video is fun as well, but then something in the video's flamboyance reminds me of Topper. I turn to them, but Jide is texting and Tosin is focused on the road. I guess it's just me, my thoughts, and good Nigerian music.

So, which of Topper or Farrukh set me up? Farrukh's motive is easy – greed. He wanted the bracelet and didn't want to pay for it. And his odyssey to get my money was a blatant lie. But my main problem with Farrukh being the one responsible is that he doesn't strike me as the sort to have Tariq's number on speed dial. Maybe I'm underestimating him.

Topper's motive is just as easy – revenge for an incident in our past. I'm adamant I saved his life that night, but he probably doesn't see it that way. Another motive is greed. He wanted his money and bracelet back. But he didn't need to pay me. He could've just killed me soon as I stepped into his castle. Or handed me over to the police, which would've been a smart move on his part because it would've earned him a lot of goodwill with them. It's been ten years, but I know I'm still at the top of their most wanted list.

It's also possible that Topper and Farrukh set me up together. But my rationale for that is convoluted and contradicts Occam's razor, a principle I abide by. Even more perplexing is pondering how the fuck Tariq, Khalid, and Tony found me. Is there a tracker on the bracelet? No, because Farrukh and/or Topper would've known I was coming.

Fucking hell, I don't know. And it's also become clear someone other than Topper or Farrukh could be behind my ambush. And this person has considerable resources, which explains why Topper didn't want to sell the bracelet himself. If that's the case, I'll continue to be hunted long as I have the bracelet. But that's fine with me because that's been my life for a decade. The fucker should join the queue and act accordingly.

And if this fucker does exist, that means I'm responsible for countless pointless murders. I want to convince myself they were all in the game, Farrukh included, and they knew the risks. And I will in time. But not Javad. He wasn't in the game, even if he thought he was. And he sure as shit didn't know the risks.

A song titled 'Oliver Twist' by D'banj begins, and Jide and Tosin erupt into a rapturous singalong. Jide also does his best to replicate the dance in the video while seated. I watch them, and I'm entertained until I notice that we're in Maida Vale. I should call Oleg because we're close to Paddington, but I won't stop them enjoying their song. They are a lot of fun, which I imagine is unusual for savage mercenaries.

The song lasts the rest of the drive to Paddington station, and Jide switches it off as Tosin parks beside the station.

I lean forward between them. 'Thank you,' I say.

'Our pleasure,' Jide says.

'Give me a moment,' I say. 'Need to call Oleg.'

Jide puts his phone to his ear and strikes a peculiar grandiose pose. 'My man,' he says with a funny attempt at a Russian accent.

We all laugh because the pose is Oleg's and so is the phrase. I imagine it's Oleg's most used phrase, and I've never seen the humour in it, but it sure sounds funny coming from Jide.

I call Oleg, and it rings just once. 'Hello?' he answers.

'Hello, Saviour,' I respond.

'My man.'

I smile; Jide's imitation was good.

'Everything okay?' Oleg asks.

'Yep.'

'Very good.'

'Where are you? I'm here.'

'Ah, sorry, my friend, I'm on my way. Ten minutes. I know, I know, I'm late, I'm always late, but you are always early.'

'I know. I'll call you back in fifteen.'

'Okay.'

I end the call and laugh. 'He actually said "my man", and Jide sounded almost like him,' I say.

They laugh.

'Seriously?' Tosin asks.

'Yep.'

'Of course, he did!' Jide says. 'I know my guy too well.'

'He's still a bit away,' I say. 'He says like ten minutes, but I know that's like twenty minutes.'

'Yeah, that's Oleg,' Tosin says. 'We can wait.'

'At all, oh,' Jide says. 'I text Flora that I'll be at hers in fifteen minutes . . . and that was ten minutes ago. I don't want any more trouble, and I need some loving tonight.' He turns to Tosin. 'No, I'm not interested in your love tonight.'

'Your daddy,' Tosin says.

We laugh. Although late to it, I get their sense of humour. Also, I appreciate Jide's position, and I'm hungry. I scan the street and spot a steakhouse. I don't really like steaks, but it'll do.

'It's cool,' I say. 'I'm hungry anyway, so I'll go get some food.'

We've reached the end of our time together. More than anything, I've felt safe with them. I'd go into battle with them any day, but they probably won't need me. And I hope I never need them again. I reach out for a handshake and Jide is first to shake my hand, and then Tosin does.

'Be safe, dudes,' I say.

'Ah ahn, are you my daddy?' Jide teases.

'Behave,' Tosin says to Jide and turns to me. 'Be safe too, dude. It was a pleasure doing business with you.'

I nod at them, step out of the car, and walk to the steakhouse.

19:30

'I gave him my word'

I'm sitting by the window in the half-empty steakhouse, waiting for Oleg and my steak. I didn't bother with the menu because when it comes to steaks, I always order the same thing – rib-eye cooked medium well with peppercorn sauce and fries. I watch the entrance to Paddington station to occupy my mind, hoping to impede the impulse to think about Rebecca. And it's working, somewhat, because I'm intrigued by the diversity of the people entering and exiting the station.

I notice my waitress approach with my meal.

My steak arrives, and I check my watch; it's 19:33, Oleg is running later than usual. I call him, and it rings once before he answers.

'I'm here,' he says. 'Where are you?'

'You are?' I ask, surprised. 'Thought you were taking your time, like always.'

'I've been here walking around the station, you know I don't know your number.'

'Oh, yeah, sorry. I'm in the steakhouse opposite the station.'

'All right, I'll be with you in a minute.'

'You want me to order something for you?'

'I ate a whole chicken about an hour ago, I'm very okay.'

'Okay, see you in a bit.'

I end the call and tuck into my steak. After a couple slices, I conclude it doesn't taste good. I add a little salt and a lot of pepper before I eat the next slice, and maybe it tastes better.

I'm about halfway through the steak when I hear Oleg's cheerful voice at the entrance. I look over and see him being directed to me. I smile as our eyes meet, and he smiles back, baring all his teeth. He's grown a beard, lost most of his thick black hair, and gained a lot of weight but he hasn't let that affect his swagger as he strides towards me. It's nice to see a friendly face, especially his, especially today. I stand as he approaches.

'My man,' he says, and we hug.

'What's up with the belly, Oleg?' I say, and gesture to his sizeable belly. 'You don't go to the gym anymore?'

'My friend, it's a sign of good living.'

We laugh.

'I'm guessing the other sign is hair loss,' I tease.

'Oh yes, it starts with that,' he says, and gestures to my shaved head. 'You should know all about it.'

'Hey, I'm a young man, just like the clean look.'

'We all do, my friend.'

We laugh and sit.

'Don't worry, I'll be done in a bit,' I say, and gesture to my half-eaten meal.

'Take your time,' he says and leans onto his chair with a grandiose pose. 'I just spoke to Tosin, he told me how it went. You deserve to rest a little.'

I nod.

'They made a lot of money,' he says. 'So I'm expecting serious business from them.'

'Good for you. Where did you find them anyway? They are fucking good . . . fucking savage too.'

'I know. It's an exciting line of work. I meet the best of the best, the best of the worst, and the worst of the worst. They found me. Needed things only Oleg could provide. You like the upgrades in their car?'

I nod. 'They have serious firepower, that's for sure.'

'That's all Oleg, my friend,' he says, with pride. 'Tosin had a lot of good things to say about you.'

'Really?'

'Calm down. Don't get too excited.'

'Fuck you.'

'I feel like matchmaker,' he says, and laughs. 'Next, you ask if he likes you too.'

'Fuck yourself, Oleg.'

'No no no,' he says, and wags his thick index finger. 'I got lots of ladies that want to fuck Oleg.'

'Right.' I take a moment to eat the last piece of meat. 'How is Anastasiya?'

'Very beautiful. Looking more and more like her grandmother every day. You met my mother, yes?'

'No, we met just after she passed away.'

'Yes, yes, I remember. Aleha ha-shalom.'

I nod to show respect. 'And Katerina?'

'Ha!' he exclaims and smacks the table. 'That bitch! She's trying to increase maintenance, you know. Trying to blackmail me. Oleg Jogovich? Never!'

'Really?'

'Yes,' he says, and smirks. 'But I'll sort it out.'

'Don't do anything stupid.'

'How can I? Anastasiya loves her mother, and she means the world to me.'

'I know.'

'Anyway, I have something good just for you.'

I eat a bunch of fries and wash them down with a gulp of water. 'You must know how much trouble that sort of talk has gotten me into today. I don't want anything that we haven't already discussed.'

'I know, I know, but it's me. I would never fuck with you. I ever give you anything that bring you trouble?'

I smile. 'No.'

'You see.'

'All right, I'll have a look.'

'Good,' he says, and glances at the time on his phone. 'Rest time is finished now. We need to go.'

'I know. Waiting for the waitress so I can get the bill.'

He scans the restaurant, and there is no waitress in sight. 'You can pay at the front desk.'

'Oh, yeah.'

I head to the desk, and the hostess smiles as I approach. I glance at her nametag – 'Camilla'.

'Camilla, I'm in a rush, so I'm here to pay my bill,' I say with a voice I don't recognise because I'm instinctively attempting to sound cheerful.

'Hello, you know who served you?' she asks with a raspy but even more cheerful voice.

I try to remember my waitress's name.

'Don't worry, I know your table.'

'You do?'

'Yes, I do.'

'I guess you were watching me then.'

'It's my job,' she says. 'But . . . maybe.'

I smile. I consider asking for her number, but I also know she deserves better, much better than me.

'Twenty-eight pounds, please,' she says.

'Okay.'

I hand her forty pounds and smile one more time before I walk back to my table.

'We're ready?' Oleg asks.

'Yeah,' I say and grab my bag.

Daylight fades, but streetlights illuminate the busy street as Oleg leads the way to his car.

'You sure you want to do this?' he asks.

'Yes.'

'You don't have to.'

'I gave him my word.'

He shakes his head with disapproval. 'Okay, then. But why does it have to be today?'

'Cos I want to do it today.'

He wants to object but doesn't and shrugs. 'Oh, yes, how is Rebecca?' he asks, concerned.

'She's okay.'

'Good! I was worried she didn't survive the ambush. Cos you haven't mentioned her.'

'Well, she's promised to kill me next time we meet.'

He turns to me with a raised eyebrow. 'What exactly happened in there?'

I don't know where to begin, but before I can respond, he pushes a button on his key fob and the headlights on a new silver Range Rover parked in front of us flicker. I smile; *crime does pay*.

'I see you like the car,' he says, and smirks. 'I just got it back, upgraded it in the same place I did Tosin's. You'll see what I mean very soon.'

'What I see is a reason Katerina asks for more maintenance.'

'You think? She drives a Cadillac CTS Coupe, what else does she want?'

We step into the front seats of the Range Rover. 'I imagine her premium's crazy. Especially cos I'm sure you don't declare most of your income.'

'She turned the shop into a salon, and it's doing well.'

'That's good.'

I glance at the footwell because there isn't as much legroom as I expect in a Range Rover, unless I sprouted overnight. It's comfortable enough, though. He starts the car and a DMX song from his first album *It's Dark and Hell is Hot* blasts out of the stereo. I love the song, but I can't immediately remember its name.

'Still like DMX?' I ask over the loud music.

'Of course, my friend, I love this album . . . timeless,' he says, and lowers the volume of the stereo.

I nod; it's good to know some things haven't changed.

'So,' he says, and starts to drive. 'What happened at Rebecca's?'

'I'm still not sure, Oleg.'

'Just tell me everything.'

'Sure. Rebecca and I were chilling at hers . . .'

'Chilling? What? You see her for the first time in many years and what you do is chill?'

'You know what I mean, Oleg.'

'No, I do not.'

'You do.'

'So you know what I know now, my friend?'

'Okay. We were . . . you know.'

He laughs. 'Were what? If you fuck her, you say you fuck her.'

'I did say she's promised to kill me, right?'

'Okay . . . sorry about that.'

'I don't need sympathy.'

'Yes, you do, my friend.'

'I don't. And why did you lie about Jessica?'

He doesn't respond for a few seconds as he focuses on a roundabout. 'Yes, I lied. And I'll do it again. You didn't need to know the truth. It would have affected you, like it always does.'

'It doesn't.'

'Your mother is lost. But you've always known this, and still, you asked me to check on her . . . to give her money. And I did, every two months for fourteen months. The fourth time I did I left a note with a phone number in the envelope, expecting her to call . . . show some gratitude or even some interest in where the money is coming from. But no call, no text. She must know it was you and she did not care. And I'm sure you saw that the money only helped her and her partner fall deeper into that hole. So, eventually I stopped and told you what you wanted to hear.'

I know he's right, although only to an extent. But I know he believes he's absolutely right.

'I tried to stop you going to that house today,' he continues. 'I told you she moved, but you never asked me where to. I knew it wasn't because you didn't care . . . it was because you knew I was lying, for your own good.'

I change the subject and tell him what happened at Rebecca's apartment. He's never heard of Tariq and Khalid, nor of a stuttering Tony. But when I mention Yellow, he interrupts.

'Yellow? How did he come into this?' he asks.

'I really don't know. But he's Rebecca's husband. You know that?'

'Yes.'

I shake my head.

'What?' he asks. 'You didn't need to know this.'

I tell him the rest of what happened at the apartment, and he's just as astonished and confused as I was with Rebecca and the bracelet.

'C'mon,' he says, and turns to me.

'Serious. And eyes back on the road.'

'That's fucking crazy, my friend,' he says, and turns back to the road.

'I know. And she's fucking serious about killing me the next time we meet.'

'I always liked her, but I like her more now.'

'Fuck off.'

He laughs. 'You know, my friend, if you make it to the end of today alive, you should write a book about your life. Make serious money.'

'Who the fuck's going to read that?'

'You'd be surprised. This is what Katerina's friends are reading. They have book club, and they love it. True crime, they call it. But make sure you change my name in the book, yes? But keep me smooth and beautiful Russian Jew.'

The song 'Stop Being Greedy' starts and I think about the days I had this album on repeat for months.

'You're thinking about the book, yes?' he asks.

'Absolutely. I'm thinking about how stupid an idea it is.'

He laughs and turns into a derelict driveway that leads to an abandoned warehouse. He drives into the dark warehouse and parks but leaves the headlights on.

'Who do you think sent those men after you?' he asks.

'I don't know, I couldn't get a word out of Topper or Farrukh.'

'I think Topper.'

'Of course, you do.'

He chuckles.

'We're here,' he says. 'Let's see what I have for you.'

'Yeah, let's do that.'

20:13

'The preacher's wife is ecstatic . . .'

Oleg and I step out of the Range Rover onto the warehouse's dusty concrete floor. The warehouse is vast and pitch-black, apart from the area lit by the car's lights.

'Come to this side,' Oleg says.

I walk around the car, and he grins as I approach. He turns to look at the car, and after a couple seconds, I also stare at it, but there is nothing out of the ordinary.

'What now, Oleg? This one of your silly jokes?' I ask. 'Cos I don't get it, nothing's happening. And you should know by now that you aren't funny.'

'Oh, yes.' He turns to me, excited. 'I have a good joke for you. Your kind of joke.'

'What the fuck does that mean?'

'Just listen,' he says, and raises a hand to urge my silence. 'The preacher's wife is ecstatic. After all her hard work in missionary, Jesus is finally coming . . . but he pulls out too soon.'

I don't want to give him the pleasure of laughing. But I can't hold back for long, and I burst into laughter. He's right. It is my kind of joke.

'Did you come up with that?' I ask.

'You never know, my friend, you never know.'

He turns back to the car and pushes a button on the key fob three times. He waits for two seconds and pushes another button on the key fob. 'Step back, my friend,' he says, and takes a wide step away from the car.

I step back, and a compartment hidden underneath the car slowly emerges. It's impressive.

He grins. 'You like it, eh?' he asks.

I nod.

'Very expensive,' he says. 'Same place I had Tosin's Mercedes done. I got this back three weeks ago.'

'Tosin's is different. This is some high-tech shit.'

'I know. The chassis of a Rover sits up high from the road, so the engineers had more space to work with. And more importantly, I was willing to spend more money than Tosin.'

The top of the compartment slides back underneath the car and reveals sturdy combination-lock cases of different sizes. He crouches to a case and blocks my view as he unlocks it. He picks something out and turns to me with a grin as he presents a golden Desert Eagle Mark XIX with a suppressor attached.

'Wow!' I exclaim, and accept the gun.

'I told you I'll get anything you want,' he says, and beams with pride.

I examine the gun from every angle. 'I wasn't serious when I asked for this, you know.'

He shrugs.

The moment I played *GoldenEye 007* on my Nintendo 64, I wanted a golden gun. But I was fifteen years old, and I grew up to believe it only existed in fiction. But here it is . . . and it's mine.

'Thank you, Oleg,' I say.

'It's my pleasure. Happy birthday, my friend.'

'It's not my birthday.'

'I don't believe you. I know you well. You want to do this thing today because you believe your birthday is a good day to die.'

I chuckle. 'No, today's just a good day to kill.'

I don't know how he worked it out, but he's correct. Today is my birthday, which does make it a good day to die. I guess I'm not as difficult to read as I think. He doesn't need to know he's correct though.

'Thank you so much for this,' I say, and gesture to the gun.

'It's okay. I have something else just for you.'

He opens another case, picks out an item, and offers it to me. It's a fucking grenade.

'What the fuck is that?' I ask.

He breaks out an expression I recognise from the many times I've witnessed it over the years. It's his expression when he's about to start his hard sell, which has a reasonable conversion rate because he is fucking relentless, and I want him to stop.

'It's a grenade,' he says, and lifts the grenade closer my eyes.

'Well, I'm not blind, Oleg. I was just really hoping . . .'

'A timed grenade,' he interrupts, and points to the grenade's pin. 'You see this?'

'Yeah, really, I'm not blind.'

'You turn this to the time you want the grenade to explode.' He points to a dial. 'You see the numbers? Zero to sixty seconds . . . one to five minutes. You set time, drop grenade, and escape long before it explodes.'

'Okay. That's impressive. And I bet when it explodes, it's really quiet too, right?'

He glares at me, and I laugh. 'C'mon, what's wrong with you?' he asks.

'What's wrong with you? I asked for a handgun with a suppressor, and you offer me a grenade with it. I'm trying to get shit done quietly.'

'I know, I know, but you never know when you might need it.'

I chuckle. 'I could shoot you in the foot right now.'

'No, you cannot, no bullets. I'll get you cartridge.' He picks out an extended gold-plated cartridge and hands it to me. 'I had it made for you. .44 Magnum extended cartridge. Fourteen rounds of hollow-points.'

'You really are taking care of me.'

'I always do. So you should trust me when I offer you the grenade.'

'Oleg, Oleg,' I say, and shake my head. 'All right, tell me the truth. You had a buyer lined up for the grenades, but the deal fell through. I'm sure like me they thought it as useful as golden bullets.'

He laughs. 'They didn't show up for the meet. They must be dead or something, cos they seriously wanted them. Now I have to get rid, but I don't know anyone in this town that wants grenades, timer or not. And the little shits cost me a lot of money.'

'And you thought I might be interested?'

'Doesn't hurt to try.'

'I suppose.'

'You can have one for free. Try it out, you never know.'

'Try out a grenade? In London?'

He laughs. 'You don't know how things happen tonight. You might need it.'

'Right.' He's still selling, and he won't stop. I better take one to shut him up. 'I'll have one.'

'Really? That's my man!'

He puts the grenade into a pouch and places the pouch in a handgun case. He hands me the case, and I set the golden gun and cartridge inside. I'll throw the grenade into the Thames the first chance I get, and hopefully it won't explode. He pushes a button on his key fob, and the compartment returns to its hidden position underneath the car.

'All right, back in the car,' he says.

We step into the car, and he reaches across me to pick a brown envelope from the glove compartment.

'So, this is it,' he says, and waves the envelope. 'Are you sure . . .'

'What the fuck, Oleg? How many times are you going to ask that?'

'Okay, all right, calm down,' he says, and laughs. 'This is all the information the investigator provided. It's not much, but it's enough. Pictures of Lucas and his whore, you need to look at them.'

'He looks different now?'

'No. You'll need it for the whore.'

'Right.'

'So, as we spoke about, Bob – the investigator – tells me Lucas is not a man of routine.' He waves the envelope. 'This is the only thing Lucas has done routinely in four months, but Bob says Lucas can change just like that.' He snaps his fingers. 'Lucas has no home. Doesn't even sleep in the same place for two nights. He is a paranoid man, and he should be. He's a grass. And from what I hear, he is very good at this. He's put many people in prison, so he's a very wanted man. But the police like him very much because of this work, and your mutual friend Chief Superintendent Moore makes sure his boys provide Lucas with a sort of *lak-eds-cal*—'

'*Lack-a-dai-si-cal.*'

'Yes . . . *lack-adas-ical* police protection,' he says, and grins. 'I learnt that word from Bob.'

'I noticed. You used it; when you said all this before.'

'No harm in repeating it; it's your life, my friend. So I say again, try not to be too disappointed if Lucas doesn't show today. Also, and I know I didn't say this before – Lucas doesn't have a particular time that he shows up; Bob says anytime from 9 p.m.'

I nod and check the clock on the dashboard; it's 20:27.

He pulls two A4-sized photographs from the envelope and hands them to me. 'He drives a green Nissan Primera, remember the plate number.'

I study both photographs to sear the image of the beat-up car into my mind. He pulls out several more images and hands them to me. All of them are of a black girl, probably in her mid-twenties, sitting in the same spot in front of a closed clothing store. She smokes in one picture, eats from a box of chicken in a couple others, and is asleep on the ground in the rest. She's dressed differently in each photograph, and you can tell the chronology because her physical deterioration is clear.

'This girlfriend of his,' I say. 'Or whore, dealer, whatever you want to call her . . . she sits in this same spot all night waiting for Lucas to show up?'

'Yes, the same spot, same street, Albert Road. And she brings the drugs. They get high in the car, some days they fuck too . . . in the car.'

He pulls out another group of photographs and hands them to me. They are of Lucas and the girl having sex.

'Seems like Bob had a nice time,' I say.

'With what I pa— what you paid him, he better.'

'Seems worth it so far.'

'I suggest you wait for them to get high before you make your move.'

I focus on the girl in the photographs, and it's evident she was once, not too long ago, an attractive young woman. I wonder how she got stuck in Lucas's web.

'What do we know about the girl?' I ask.

'Her name is Cookies.'

I raise an eyebrow, and he laughs.

'She's a working girl. That's what they call her on the streets,' he says.

'Her real name?'

'Oh, err . . . S-A-D-E.'

'Sade. It's Nigerian.'

He shrugs. 'Are you sure this has to be done?'

'Again, Oleg?' I ask, and glare at him.

'Are you sure?' he asks and glares back. 'You know DCS Moore is just keeping Lucas alive as bait for you. And the Russians too . . . they have a very long memory.'

I nod; I know.

'So, you are sure you have to do it? Because look at him.' He jabs a finger at the photographs. 'Death is better than the life he lives now.'

It's a reasonable point, but yes, it has to be done. 'Yes, I'm sure,' I say. 'Even criminals ought to have honour.'

He nods. 'Criminals ought to have money too. And you're spending all of yours hunting him.'

'That's fair. Speaking of money.' I pour all the money in my bag onto his lap. 'For everything you've done for me.'

'Ah, this is too much.'

'Behave. We both know nothing's too much for all you've

done for me. I was going to give a bunch of that to Rebecca. But then again, Topper didn't give me everything we negotiated in cash. Anyway, buy something for Anastasiya from me, okay? If she still remembers me.'

'I will. Anything for Jess?'

'No. But there is a corner shop on that street. If you can, find out if it's the same family that has owned it for the past twenty years. If it is, send them ten.'

'Sure.'

'Also, and I know you don't want to hear this, but if I die tonight, I want to be cremated.'

'Stop this.'

'No, listen.'

'C'mon.'

'Seriously, just listen. I don't want to be buried; I want to be cremated.'

'No one will listen to me.'

'I know. Tell Jess and make sure she does it. It all comes down to money with her, so give her just enough to make sure she does it . . . not a penny more.'

'Okay.'

'Thank you.'

He hides the money underneath his seat, and I put the gun case into my empty bag.

'Let's go do this,' I say.

'Yes. You'll be right on time. It's thirty minutes from here.'

He switches on the stereo, plays the first track from the *It's Dark and Hell is Hot* album, and increases the volume to a near-deafening level. He knows we won't be talking for a while because I need to get myself in the right state of mind to kill Lucas. I can't fail. My peace and honour are at stake.

20:32

'London is no city for old men'

I study the photographs, mostly to get Sade's face fixed in my mind; Lucas's face is already forever etched in it. I can't look at the photographs of them having sex for more than a brief glance though, because although they don't try to hide, the photographs still seem intrusive.

I slot the photographs into the envelope and put the envelope back into the glove compartment. I immerse myself in the music, but then 'I Can Feel It' – a track with a heavy Phil Collins 'In The Air Tonight' sample – begins, and I switch the stereo off. Oleg turns to me, puzzled, but he doesn't speak and turns back to the road.

'London's different, isn't it?' I ask, attempting to spark a conversation.

'What you say?'

'London's very different.'

He nods in agreement but doesn't speak. And a few moments pass before he glances at me and reads that I want a conversation. 'I know, it's very dangerous,' he says. 'The young kids nowadays are lost. Watch too much TV, you know.' He shakes his head in disgust. 'They just go round shooting and stabbing themselves. And for what? Nothing!' He hisses. 'Stupid gangs all over the place too. They don't know that the gangs that came before them, the ones they are trying to copy . . . they had a purpose, they had values . . . and only to survive hard times. These kids have it easy. What are they fighting for, eh? Money? Territory? Pride? Girls? Not to survive . . . not to better the next man's life.'

I nod and allow a moment to make sure he's finished. I hadn't expected such a response from him. 'You feel strongly about this,' I say. 'I'm surprised, especially considering you're an arms dealer.'

He smirks. 'If you see what I have seen, you won't be surprised.'

I nod. 'Speaking of TV. Saw on the BBC two weeks ago that the reason for the riots last summer and the general youth unrest is that these kids feel socially excluded, affected by the spending cuts . . .'

He glares at me, and I fight back a smirk. I was pushing his buttons, and his reaction never fails to amuse me.

'Okay, Oleg, easy, I'm just relaying a different opinion.'

He shakes his head. 'They dress like fools. Act like fools. Even speak like fools. I speak better English, and I came to this country when I was twenty-seven!'

I chuckle. 'So, it's the *kids* making it dangerous?'

'Yes, and idiots like Topper who indulge them with the money, the guns, and the drugs. London is no city for old men.'

'Shit, okay. I suppose you don't sell to them?'

'They can't afford Oleg. And even if they could, I wouldn't do business with them.'

'You always had principles.'

'So do you. So please don't die, there are very few of you left around.'

'I won't, Oleg. I can't, not with you taking care of me the way you do.'

He laughs and pats me on the shoulder.

I spot a young woman pushing a buggy along the street, and she looks no older than sixteen. 'I've seen a lot of teenagers pushing buggies today,' I say. 'This new? Or I just didn't notice before.'

'It's the TV and the Internet. These kids are exposed to sex very early, and they want it now . . . can't wait. They don't think about the consequences.'

'To be fair, I couldn't wait either. But there are always condoms and pills and patches and all other stuff if you don't want to use a condom.'

'You go tell them. I'm already talking to Anastasiya about it.'

'Really? Good.'

'Plus, you must have noticed that most of the people walking these streets are us.'

'Us?'

'Yes, us . . . the immigrants.'

'Oh, right,' I say. 'I'm London all the way through though. Born and bred here, and so was Jess . . . probably my dad too, but who knows about that fucker, eh?'

We laugh.

'The English with money don't live in the city anymore,' he says. 'They work here, but live out in the home counties. Most of my English clients live out there now.'

'Fair enough.'

We stop at a red light and he connects an iPod to the stereo. He selects a song just before the traffic light changes to green and drives as the synthesised electronic beat of the song begins. I like it. I check the title, and it's La Roux's 'In for the Kill' (Skream's 'Let's Get Ravey' Remix). I smile and Oleg smiles as well; the pertinence of the title is not lost on us.

'Since when do you listen to dubstep?' I ask.

'It's Meggy's iPod. She left it in the car when I dropped her at work this morning.'

'Meggy . . . that's your girlfriend, right?' I ask, although I know it is.

He nods and blushes.

'She likes dubstep, cool,' I say. 'How old is she?'

He hesitates. 'Nineteen.'

We are silent for a moment.

'Oleg, that's young.'

'Whatever!'

'Wow.'

'Fuck off. She's very mature.'

'I'm sure, and beautiful too.'

'No, no, it's not that. She's a wonderful person. She's been very good for me. Makes me happy. And Anastasiya likes her very much.'

I smile because his defence of her worth is touching. I'm happy for him.

He glances at me. 'Why you smiling?' he asks.

'Congratulations, Oleg.'

'What?'

'I think you're in love again.'

'Stop it,' he says, and waves me off.

A few minutes later, Oleg parks in front of a closed corner shop on a poorly lit residential street. I check the time and it's 21:07.

'Albert Road is around the corner,' he says, and gestures ahead. 'Turn right at the end of this street. You'll recognise it from the pictures. Cookies should be there.'

I nod.

'You have a plan?' he asks.

'Not really, but don't worry about it.'

'I've learnt not to worry about you. But . . . good luck, my friend.'

'Good luck?'

He laughs. 'I don't know what to say. Okay, what do you want me to do with your ashes?'

'I'd be dead anyway, so what do I care.'

'You care not to be buried.'

'Fair. I don't want to bother you when I'm dead . . . cos I know you'll go fucking crazy on the casket and the stone and visit with flowers every fucking year.'

He laughs.

'I know you will,' I say. 'I don't want it. Do whatever you think best with the ashes, but don't fucking keep them.'

He smiles and nods. 'Okay, off you go, you sad bastard. Get the fuck out of my car.'

'How do I get out of this place anyway?'

'Oh, yes.'

'If I don't die, you know.'

We laugh.

'Where's the closest tube station?' I ask.

'Tube station?' he asks. 'You want to—'

'Yep. Actually, don't worry, I'll check on my phone.'

'No, I'll direct you. We passed it on our way. It's like five minutes' walk from here.'

'Ah, that one. I'll be okay then.'

'No. You asked. Let me answer, no?'

I laugh, and he gives me the directions.

'It could be dangerous at this time of the night, my friend, this area is not safe,' he says.

I chuckle. 'And that's what I'll be worried about, I'm sure.'

I step out the car and shut the door behind me. I don't look back to him because I'm awful at goodbyes, and this one could mean a lot more than I'd want. I know he'll understand; he knows me well enough. I walk towards Albert Road, and I hear the car drive off. Oleg's gone.

I turn onto Albert Road and recognise the bleak street. I search for Sade and spot her sitting on the pavement in front of the closed clothing store about fifty metres ahead. My impulse is to turn and hide, but she might have noticed me already. Lucas is paranoid and could've convinced her to be just as paranoid.

I walk down the other side of the street from her and try not to get her attention, but she raises her head as I walk past. I look at her, and she's staring at me. I scan her body for a weapon and she grins at me. I force a smile and look away. I turn onto the next street and soon as I'm sure she can't hear me, I run and circle back to Albert Road.

I hide in the darkness behind a building on the corner of Albert Road and watch Sade.

21:15

'I've got needs'

Sade sits in her usual spot on Albert Road, and she appears homeless in a ragged oversized hoodie. She's waited for Lucas for over an hour and has been scratching her right calf every second of it. But the itch hasn't stopped. She yanks out the large hair clip that's holding up her braided hair and uses it to scratch herself.

Sade's always anxious about these meetings, but she's much more anxious today because she's convinced herself to do what she's known for months needs to be done. She is no murderer, but Lucas has to die, and she will kill him today. He relentlessly sexually, physically, and verbally abuses her. But more enraging for her is that he's coerced her into becoming an addict, which is something she fought against for years.

Sade believes prostitution is the hand she was dealt. She was orphaned as a child and dropped out of school in Year 9 with minimal life skills. That didn't leave her with many choices to earn a living, she believes. But she made a point to never indulge in the other vices associated with her work, especially the drugs.

Sade had seen Lucas on several occasions because he was a regular with Amy, one of the girls she worked with. He always tried to have a word with her, but she wasn't interested. She had more than enough clients, and she knew he was an addict that had to be on something to feel any pleasure. But then her world turned upside down when she ran into him at Paddington police station.

She had grown tired of Eddy, her pimp/landlord, smacking her and the other girls around for no reason other than he was high. So she decided, without consulting the other girls, to report Eddy's second business to the police. It was a small-time drug business that mostly catered to the girls' clients, and Eddy operated it out of a council flat on the same street as the house the girls worked. Eddy's younger brother Freddy handled the day-to-day, and Lucas, as you'd expect, was a regular customer.

When she was leaving the police station, she was consumed with a sense of release and forgot to leave as she came in – with her hoodie over her head hiding her face. She remembers as she approaches the exit, but it's too late because she locks eyes with Lucas who's been watching her since she stepped into the reception. He is dishevelled but wearing a fresh baseball cap he only wears to cover his face when making the monthly trip to report at the station.

She stops, and he grins, brandishing his new dentures – his real teeth are scattered in gutters somewhere in Brixton. She wants to scream . . . run back into the station to report Lucas for anything she can think of, fact or fiction. But no, she won't let Lucas scare her. She looks away from him and struts out of the room.

Eight days after the interview, specialist firearms officers raid Eddy's drug flat. The story goes that Freddy was high, as he is 24/7, and pulled out his shiny Smith & Wesson pistol. But he was killed before firing a shot. Freddy never got to fire the gun, although he'd tell you differently if he were still alive to tell his many tales. Eddy was distraught and, even though he was in cuffs, he had to be restrained by four officers to be carried into a police van.

In the raid's aftermath, Paul, Eddy's cousin, took control over what was left of the drug business. Paul also became a custodian of the girls and the whorehouse. He was soft with the girls and didn't seem the type to hit women. All he demanded was the prompt payment of rent every Thursday before 9 p.m.

In contrast to Paul's treatment of the girls, he is notorious for his extreme response to anyone that crosses him – all men as of yet. He and Eddy, who's on remand, are adamant there's a grass, but neither has a clue who it might be. So Paul's primary task, besides resurrecting the drug business, is a violent search for the grass before Eddy's trial begins. But they don't suspect any of the girls because they don't think the girls have the balls.

A week after the raid, Sade and a few other girls are smoking outside their whorehouse when a green Nissan Primera pulls up in front of them. Amy jogs to the car because it's one of her regulars but doesn't get in. Instead, her conversation with the driver becomes heated.

Amy turns to Sade. 'Cookies!' she calls. 'Get your skinny cunt over here, you bitch.'

Sade is furious but doesn't respond because Amy resolves all her disputes with fists. Amy is the oldest of the girls, and seemingly as a result, she has the fewest regulars by a considerable margin. She does everything possible to keep her regulars and gets incensed if any of the other girls as much as smiles at them.

Sade walks to the Primera, and Amy walks off as she approaches. Sade looks into the car, and her heart sinks. It's Lucas, and he has the same teeth-brandishing grin from the police station.

'Get in, sweetness,' Lucas says. 'I think we have a lot to talk about.'

She gets into the car but doesn't look at him; she just stares ahead into the dark street as he leers at her.

'So, you heard what happened to Freddy?' he asks. 'Huge loss, don't you think? Was a stand-up lad.'

'Yeah,' she says.

'Yeah, and you hear Eddy's looking at ten to fifteen years?'

'Yeah.'

'Fucking sad shit. He and Paul really think there's a grass, but I told Paul no one around here would be stupid enough to grass 'em up.'

'Okay.'

'Yeah, but then I remembered.' He pauses for effect. 'Just

a few days before the raid I saw you in Paddington . . . the police station.'

She glares at him. 'What the fuck are you chatting, mate? Calling me a grass?'

'Not at all. But Paul might see it different from me. I'm an understanding lad, but Paul? No. Geezer's crazy. You hear he broke all Shauny's limbs the other night? Just cos someone told him that a friend heard that Shauny's the grass.'

'I don't know any fucking Shauny, and I don't give a fuck what you say to Paul.'

'You can't be serious, sweetness, he'll kill you . . . and your little niece too.'

'What?' she screams, and fights the urge to strangle him till his eyes pop out. 'Don't you dare mention her again!'

'Ay, take it easy. I've been watching you for a while now. I asked one of the girls about you. It's a good thing you're doing, taking care of your little niece after your sister had one too many.' He grins. 'I'm proud of—'

'Shut the fuck up, okay?' She closes her eyes and fights tears for almost ten seconds before she opens her eyes. 'What do you want?'

He smirks. 'Now we are talking. I like you. You have such nice lips that'll fit perfectly around little Lucas.' He feigns a shiver.

'You know the price.'

'No, sweetness, it's going to be free. You'll fuck me as well . . . free, and you'll get me some of Paul's finest product as well.'

'Free?' she asks, and laughs to herself. 'I don't do charity, and I definitely don't do drugs.'

He laughs. 'Stop acting like you have a choice. Anyway, we can't do this here in your place. Paul will snap both our necks if he finds out you're fucking me for free. I know a quiet corner, so just let me know what day you're free, and we'll make it a weekly thing.'

'Weekly?'

'Yeah, sweetness, I've got needs.'

'Whatever.'

He strokes her shoulder. 'Good girl, so give me your number. I'll call you.'

'Ask Amy, she fucking knows it!'

Sade steps out the car and slams the door. She walks towards the house but is overcome with emotion and runs off into the night.

Today, Sade's meeting Lucas for the tenth time and his erratic behaviour has worsened each time. She's tried killing him once before. The third time they met, she had a knife with her, but she was too afraid to do it. Today, she has a gun, and the fear will be her drive.

She hates what his drugs are doing to her. Especially because she fears she'll come to the same fate as her older sister, Tope, who raised her after their parents died in a house fire. Sade was twelve at the time of the fateful fire and was away on a weekend school trip. Tope was eighteen and in Liverpool studying veterinary science. Both dropped out of school after the fire. Tope chose to drop out to raise Sade, but Sade was forced to drop out the next year because no school could or was willing to contain her burning rage. Tope died five years ago from a heroin overdose, and since then Sade has raised Tope's nine-year-old daughter Oyinda. But Oyinda is now the source of Sade's greatest pain because Oyinda knows Sade's become an addict, just like her mother.

Sade has waited for Lucas for over an hour and, as always, there's no activity on the street. She considers having a nap, but a man turns into the street. She watches him walk along the other side of the street and it seems he's checking her out. This hasn't happened to her in quite some time, but she still knows to work it. She tries to strike a pose, and she runs her fingers through her hair, but he looks away. She watches him turn into the next street without even a peek back at her.

She tries to brush off her humiliation, but she can't because he looked interested in her. She ponders if her pose came across too eager. Especially because she reckons the man is not from around here, considering how carefree he's walking about with such an expensive bag.

She sighs and considers having a nap again, but she's too anxious to sleep, and when she sleeps, she can't stop dreaming about killing Lucas. She battles her anxiety for several more minutes before she gives in to exhaustion. She takes off her hoodie and folds it into a makeshift pillow on the floor beside her. She lays her head on it and falls asleep.

An hour into her nap, Lucas parks in front of her. He looks at her with a grin and pushes the horn to wake her. 'Hello, sweetness,' he says. 'Sorry I'm late, had some business.'

She doesn't acknowledge him. She puts her hoodie on and steps into the passenger seat but still doesn't look at him.

'Sweet Cookies,' he says. 'How are ya?'

'Good.'

'How's the week going?'

'Good.'

'C'mon, Cookies, talk to me, I've missed you.'

'Right.'

'C'mon, bitch, talk,' he barks. 'I'm fucking bored here.'

She doesn't respond.

'I'm fucking tired of your skinny cunt,' he says.

'Really?' she asks, and smiles.

'Yes, bitch.'

'Okay. But if my cunt's so skinny, why don't I ever feel you inside me?'

He slaps her across the face, but she shows no pain. 'Fucking bitch, where's my shit?' he demands.

She reaches into her hoodie for the angel dust and her fingers brush the gun. She becomes tense, but he isn't paying any attention to her as he reaches for a metal plate underneath his seat. She pulls out the angel dust wrapped in foil, and he hands her the plate.

She wipes the plate on her hoodie and pours the dust. She uses an expired gym card to make six lines of the brown powder. As always, he goes first. He sniffs a line and closes his eyes to savour the intense hit. She considers shooting him, but he opens his eyes, and she sniffs a line.

A few minutes later, the angel dust is finished – he had four lines, and she had two – and they're floating on the peak of their high. He cackles like a maniac, and she fights through mild hallucinations.

'Suck it, bitch,' he says.

22:10

'As long as I'm breathing, I strive to keep my word'

I've been hiding behind the wall approaching an hour. I watched Sade at first, but she soon fell asleep. Deep sleep too, without care for any ill-intentioned passer-by. But then no one has walked through the street, and I imagine she expected that based on her experience. With Sade asleep and the lack of activity on the street, I'm left to watch the sporadic traffic for Lucas's car.

I need to pee, but I don't want to miss anything. I check the time like I've done almost every five minutes for the past half hour, and it's 22:10. No car has driven past in ten minutes. I decide not to hold it any longer and dart to the other corner of the building to pee. I hurry back behind the wall and peek at Sade, and she's still asleep.

I always thought that when I found Lucas, killing him would

be simple. Just a bullet between the eyes. But I fear that in the past half hour I have over-considered it . . . and I'm still undecided. Fuck. I check on Sade and wish I could nap as well, even if only for a minute because I am exhausted. But I can't, I've waited too long for the approaching moment to sleep through it. I sit on the floor to rest my tired legs and check the time; it's 22:12.

I open my eyes and yawn; it feels like I've just woken from a nap. But I haven't. I couldn't have. I check the time, and it's 22:45. My heart sinks, and I turn to Sade. She's not there, and I become frantic. I leap to my feet to scan the street. Fucking hell. How the fuck could I have slept through . . . I spot Lucas's car parked by the pavement. She's in the passenger's seat and he's in the driver's seat. I relax, but I'm still mad at myself. I'll wait for the perfect moment to strike, but then he slaps her, and I'm triggered to act right away. But she doesn't react.

I watch them get high, and then I gaze into the serene night sky to clear my mind. I'm ready. I turn to them, and she's sucking his cock – perfect moment to strike. I pick the golden gun from my bag, insert the cartridge, and chamber a round. I run to the car, and he's too absorbed in pleasure to hear me approach. I stop by his window and aim for his head. I should kill him right now, but I need to talk to him.

'Lucas, put your fucking hands where I can see them!' I demand.

He turns to me and is overcome with fear. He attempts to force laughter, but he can't and raises his hands to surrender.

'Sade!' I call.

She raises her head to me and appears out of it.

'Run, Sade. Run away, far away, and don't look back!'

She stares at me and doesn't react, and I worry she might do something drastic. But she smiles, and it's the happiest smile I've seen in years. 'Oh, my angel,' she slurs. 'I knew you'd come back for me.'

The horrified look on Lucas's face makes me smile.

'Leave now, Sade,' I say. 'You don't want to be here for this.'

'You know him?' Lucas asks her.

She ignores him, and stumbles out of the car.

'You fucking bitch!' he screams.

'Shut up, Lucas,' I say.

She walks towards me, but I glare at her, and she runs away. I smirk at Lucas, and he becomes even more horrified. I keep the gun aimed for his head and walk to the open passenger door, and his eyes follow me. I step into the car and swing the gun into the back of his head; it bounces off the window.

'Don't hit women,' I say.

He appears lifeless, but I know he's not dead or unconscious.

'Lucas, don't fuck with me or I'll end your life right now,' I say, and push the gun into his ear, but he still doesn't respond. 'Lucas, I'm going to count from ten. If you really are unconscious, or dead, you wouldn't mind me putting a hollow-point through your ears.' He doesn't respond. 'Ten . . . nine . . . eight . . . seven . . . six . . . five . . . four . . .'

I shoot his right knee, and he screams in pain.

'What the fuck, mate!' he wails, and clutches his knee.

'Shut up! Hands back up,' I say, and push the gun back into his ear.

'My fucking knee,' he cries, and raises his hands just above his shoulders.

'You seem surprised to see me, Lucas. I told you I was coming, and you know me – as long as I'm breathing, I strive to keep my word.' I gesture to his limp cock sticking out of his open zipper. 'I should just shoot your cock off right now.' He reaches for his cock, but I push the gun harder into his ear. 'Keep your hands up.'

'Okay, okay,' he says, his voice trembling.

I scan him, and he's so dishevelled; I even recognise his worn-out jeans. 'Why did you do it?' I ask.

'Do what, mate?' he asks, and glances at my gun. 'Love the gun! You always did have panache.'

'Don't fuck with me.'

'Really, mate, what the fuck? I'm fucking bleeding here.'

'I'll shoot your other knee if you don't answer.'

'Is Cookies your sister or something?'

I shoot his other knee, and he howls in pain. He reaches for the knee, but I jam the gun back into his ear. 'Don't fuck with me, Lucas,' I say. 'Keep your hands up.'

He grimaces as he raises his hands. 'Shit, mate, I'm fucking hurting bad,' he cries.

'I know, but you are going to die in a minute anyway, so try not to worry about it and answer my question . . . why did you do it?'

'Were you blind, stupid, or what? Sean and I were lovers, and you came and fucked it all up!'

I stare at him for a moment before I respond; he must think I'm stupid. 'Right,' I say. 'Guess it didn't matter that Sean wasn't gay and you're a fucking homophobe.'

'Whatever,' he says, and giggles. 'Bet I had you on the hook for a bit though.'

I swing the gun onto his crotch, and he groans.

'Shit!' he screams. 'Fuck! Shit! What do you want?'

'The truth.'

'What the fuck does that matter now?'

I don't respond, and he curses underneath his breath.

'I'd been working for that Yankee fucker for years,' he says. 'Taking all his shit! And then you show up, and he's all about *Pretty fucking Boy*! Shit! You couldn't do anything wrong. You took my spot and didn't even leave me any fucking scraps. You took food off my table and didn't give a fuck. Actually, you thought it was fucking hilarious, didn't you? I had worked too fucking hard too fucking long for that shit!'

'So, you go with them Russians?'

'Fuck, yes! Better them than you selfish cunts.'

'You're one dumb bastard, you know that?'

'Oh, I know. And I never met my old man either. Bet he was a dumb cunt too.'

'Why did you get them coppers involved?'

'Them bent fuckers? They weren't with me. They worked for the Russian. And they were going to fucking kill me.'

'No shit, Sherlock.'

'I don't need that fucking tone, you ass-fucker! Just kill me already. I'd rather be dead than a cripple.'

He appears resigned to his fate. He's also quivering and struggling to keep his arms up.

'Put your hands down,' I say. 'But keep them where I can see them.'

He lowers his hands to his knees and tries to stop the bleeding, but he can't. 'Just kill me, mate,' he says.

'No rush, we'll get to that soon enough. You're working with coppers now though, aren't you?'

'What? Cookies told you that? That's a fucking—'

'Stop. Jack Moore. I know he is alive. I haven't been under a fucking rock.'

'Well, I had no choice with Jack. He'd been keeping me alive hoping you'd come back. But then you never showed up, so I had to start earning my keep with his officers. And how else am I supposed to fucking eat? Nobody wants to work with me.'

'Still, there are rules—'

'What?' he shouts, and shakes his head. 'You think I give a fuck about fucking rules? Whose rules? Yours? How's that worked out for you? All that righteous shit you have going on won't get you anywhere. We are criminals. We break the rules. That's what we do! We take what we want, when we want, by any means, at any cost. That's the only way to make it in this bullshit.' He takes a deep breath. 'I was tired of being nobody. I had put the years in. It was my time, and I was going to make it happen.'

He glances at me, and I can see all the pain in his eyes.

'I went all in,' he continues. 'Stacked the deck as much as I could cos I knew you wouldn't die easy. I'd tried before. I know you know I set up the Brixton thing.'

I nod; I know.

'But you fucking refused to die, *again*,' he says, and chuckles. 'I lost Cherie. I lost everything. All the bridges burnt to the ground. I've got no fucking friends. I regret that night more than you—'

'Shut up,' I snap. 'I lost my life that night. Lost my peace of mind. You can't fathom how many hours, days, nights, weeks, fucking years that I've lost seething, contemplating vengeance. I've killed you thousands of times, thousands of ways in my mind . . . none of them satisfying. But the worst part is that the moment is finally here, and it's utterly fucking unsatisfying as well.'

'Maybe don't do it, then?' he quips, and we laugh. 'And you sure use some fucking big words.'

We laugh again for a few seconds.

'You used *panache*,' I say. 'That's big. Started reading then?'

'Got a lot of free time, mate. And the lads' mags aren't what they used to be.'

He laughs, but I don't react.

'I don't know where you've been all these years,' he says. 'But I suggest you go back soon as you can. Cos them Russians have spared no expense looking for you.'

'For their sake, I hope they don't find me.'

He scoffs and shakes his head; *he still underestimates me*. I should shoot him through his ears and end his misery, but

I can't bring myself to do it. I just can't. This is not what I expected vengeance to feel like. But he has to die. If only to bury the past. And for Sade as well, cos he'll probably kill her if I let him live. I know what to do, but it's going to be messy. I reach into my bag with my left hand and feel for the grenade.

'If you're going to do me, do me already!' he demands.

'All right, but you're going to count to the moment I put the bullet through your head. Start from ten.'

'What! Fuck you! That's just fucking wrong!'

I shove the gun into his crotch, and he howls. 'That's the point,' I say. 'Start. Now.'

'Okay! Okay! Fucking hell,' he says, and struggles to hold back tears. 'Ten . . .' He looks at me with eyes full of tears and sorrow, but there is no empathy in my eyes, so he looks away. 'Nine . . .'

He counts, and I raise the gun back to his head. I push the pin on the grenade just a little, and I have no idea the time I've set to detonate, but I'm sure it's less than the maximum five minutes. I pull the grenade out of the bag and glance at the dial. Shit. The time I set is in the seconds. I drop the grenade and step out of the car with my gun still aimed at his head.

He stops counting and looks at me, perplexed, as I backpedal away from the car. I nod at him and put the gun in my bag, and he's relieved. I turn to run away, but the grenade detonates. It's a powerful explosion, louder than anything I've ever heard, and it lifts me off the ground. Everything slows as I fly through the air. I feel my heart beat and blood jet through my arteries. A jolt runs through my body, and my vision becomes almost panoramic. Suddenly, I'm outside my body, watching myself crash to the ground, and I shut my eyes.

I open my eyes, and I'm on the floor, back inside my body, but I can't feel anything. I watch Lucas's demolished car burn as I fight to stay conscious, but I've got no . . . fi . . .

Lucas is beyond confused as he watches *Pretty Boy* step out of the car and backpedal. Pretty Boy puts his gun away, and Lucas pulls out his cell phone. Lucas quickly scrolls through his recent calls to Jack Regan – his nickname for DCS Jack Moore, who's consumed by vengeance and has been hunting Pretty Boy for a decade. But just before Lucas pushes the call button, an explosion erupts from his feet and obliterates him.

Lucas is dead. He really couldn't be any more dead.

The heightening sounds of approaching sirens wake me. I try to stand, but I can't feel my legs. I try to push off the ground, but I can't feel my hands either. I try to look at my arms, but I can't feel my neck. Fuck, I can't feel anything. I close my eyes and concentrate on moving my fingers and toes, but the sirens are distracting. I scream as panic overwhelms me, and adrenaline charges through my body. I feel my limbs.

I leap to my feet, grab my charred bag, and attempt to run, but my legs are unsteady, and every step is excruciating. I power through the pain and limp as fast as I can away from the sirens.

I round the corner to the street Oleg dropped me off and hesitate to recall Oleg's directions to the station. I'm not sure about my recollection, but I hurry in the direction I remember anyway. I stumble into the high street and see the underground station two hundred metres ahead. I'm relieved. I reduce my pace to a steady walk and do my best to be unnoticed.

I enter the station and head to the tube map on the wall to trace the route to Waterloo. I check my watch for the time. The glass is cracked, but the time ought to be correct because the second hand ticks along; it's 23:24. I need to be in Waterloo sharpish. I walk to the barrier and place my Oyster card on the card reader, but the barrier doesn't open. I glance at the station entrance, and the sirens seem at their loudest. I fight back panic and place the Oyster card on the reader, but still no response. I glance at the female station attendant sitting behind the ticket office window, and our eyes meet; she's watching me.

'Try the other one,' she says, with a cheery voice, and points to the barrier next to me.

I nod and step to the barrier. I place my Oyster card on the reader, and the barrier opens. I skip through and hurry down the stairs, feeling every step.

21:00

'I don't scare easy'

Rebecca is alone in a police interview room, glaring ahead at nothing. She's dressed in an oversized jumper and track bottoms the police provided after taking her clothes for forensic testing.

A female detective walks into the room with a uniformed female police officer, and Rebecca relaxes her glare.

'Ms Pepper, we have the things you wanted from your home,' the detective says, and the uniformed officer places a gym bag by Rebecca's feet.

'Thank you,' Rebecca says.

'Thank you,' the detective responds. 'I appreciate you taking the time to make a statement right now. I promise to let you know soon as we are finished at your home. And when your husband's body is ready.'

Rebecca nods.

'Do you have a place to stay till we are done at your home?'

Rebecca nods again.

'Okay. Can I have the address?'

Rebecca hesitates.

'It's routine,' the detective says. 'We just want to be able to reach you if we have more questions.'

'You have my number.'

'Yes, we do. But it's standard for us to have an address as well.'

'The Regency Hotel in Soho. I'll let you know the room number when I do.'

'Thank you. Also, I strongly advise that you let us know if you move from the hotel. And we advise against travelling outside the United Kingdom until the investigation is complete.'

'Sure.'

'Again, thank you.' The detective gestures to the uniformed officer. 'PC Shannon here will drive you to the Regency.'

Rebecca nods.

Rebecca is in the back seat of a police car as PC Shannon drives towards the Regency, and the car is silent.

PC Shannon's mobile phone vibrates, and it surprises her. She ignores the call, but the vibration continues for almost a minute before it stops. Less than a moment later, the phone vibrates again.

PC Shannon slows to a stop at a red light. 'Sorry,' she says over her shoulder and pulls out her phone. 'Must be important . . .' She stares at the caller ID, perplexed. 'I'll just make a quick stop.'

PC Shannon parks in the nearest space and answers the call. 'Yes, sir,' she says, anxious.

. . .

'Sorry? I don't . . .'

. . .

'Sir, I'm not . . . I don't . . .'

. . .

'I'm not sure about this, sir.'

. . .

'Sir, I don't.'

. . .

'Okay, sir.'

PC Shannon ends the call and drives on, but she's nervous. Rebecca can sense this, and thinks she knows why. PC Shannon makes a turn into a side street, away from the route to the hotel, and confirms Rebecca's thoughts.

'Is everything okay?' Rebecca asks, and watches PC Shannon in the rear-view mirror.

'I'm sorry,' PC Shannon mutters.

'It's okay.'

'It's not.'

'I'll be fine.'

'I'll wait around the corner.'

'No. Do as you were told, okay? Please?'

PC Shannon makes eye contact with Rebecca through the rear-view mirror, and Rebecca nods to reassure her.

'Okay,' PC Shannon says, and parks in the middle of a dark and empty side street. 'This is where I'm to drop you.'

'Okay,' Rebecca says, and steps out of the car.

Rebecca watches the police car drive off and takes her electric toothbrush from her gym bag. She takes off the brush head, holds the toothbrush by the exposed sharp end, and pulls her jumper's cuff over her hand.

A black Jaguar saloon parks in front of Rebecca, and its back door opens. Rebecca looks into the car, and Alan Pierce is in the back seat. A tall and formidable woman in her late twenties with cropped ice-blonde hair is the driver, and the only one else in the car.

Rebecca steps into the car and closes the door. The driver locks the doors.

'Hello, Rebecca Pepper,' Alan says. 'Forgive me, but I'll get straight to it because I've got somewhere to be. I read your statement. It's bloody good. Very believable and covers all the bases, really. But someone is missing from it. I need to know who he is and how to find him.'

'I don't know what the fuck you're talking about.'

'Okay. I'll give you this to consider. Ahmed Khan, your building's concierge . . . I hear he's getting better rather quick and he'll be ready to make a statement soon. What do you think is going to happen to you when the police find out your version of events is very different from his? And that you just forgot to mention this mysterious man in a leather jacket?'

'You sent those fuckers, didn't you?'

'I can help you with Ahmed. I just need you to call your friend.'

'Sure,' Rebecca says, and points the sharp end of the toothbrush at Alan's neck.

Alan is calm, and the driver doesn't even react – because she's been pointing a pistol at Rebecca through her seat.

'Franka, don't shoot,' Alan says to the driver, and she nods. He turns to Rebecca. 'Put that away. You're not going to hurt me, and I don't intend to hurt you. Not here. Not now. Because then I'd have to hurt the righteous PC Shannon. That'd be disappointing . . . and foolish. And I don't do foolish. Unless I'm forced to.'

'I know you're not going to do shit to me,' Rebecca says, and pulls the toothbrush away. 'I know who you are. I know your mob. But you don't know me. I just wanted to give you a quick taste. So you know who you're dealing with. And that I don't scare easy. Then we can have a proper conversation.'

'Fair.'

'Your mysterious man is no friend of mine. He got my husband killed for whatever shit you guys are into. And I don't have his number . . .'

'That's okay. I do.'

'Good for you. But I'm not sure he'll be eager to speak to me. I promised him I'll kill him the next time I see him. That's why his name is not in my statement. He's mine to deal with. Which brings me to you and your mob . . . stay the fuck out of my way.'

Alan laughs. He nods at Franka, and Franka unlocks the doors. 'Okay, Rebecca,' he says. 'Enjoy your hunt.'

Rebecca steps out of the car, and Alan waves at her before the car drives off.

She pulls out her phone and makes a call.

'Hello,' a woman answers with a hint of a Russian accent.

'I'd like to speak to Oleg, please.'

'Hmm. You called the shop, yes?'

'Yes. Hendon Off-licence.'

'Well, this is Katerina. The shop has not existed for years. It is my salon now, but it's late, so your call was forwarded to my cell. You can leave a message, and I'll make sure Oleg gets it.'

'It's urgent.'

'I'm sure it is.'

'Tell him it's Rebecca, and this is about our mutual friend.'

'Ah. Hold on, Rebecca.'

There is a minute of silence.

'Hello, Rebecca,' Oleg says. 'Last I heard you were not happy with our friend.'

'I'm not. But I need you to pass on an urgent message.'

'Okay?'

'I've just run into Michael Downing's brother, and they are looking for our friend. They are the ones that sent those men to my home. They have his number, and I think they are going to use it to track him. He needs to ditch it.'

'Ah. I see. That is a problem. I don't have that number, and I just drove past where I left him. It's a fucking mess. Police everywhere, but he is not there. I know where he is heading though. And I'm sure they will soon.'

'He's going to need our help.'

'*Our* help?'

'Yes.'

'Okay, Rebecca. But I must warn you. If you look at our friend the wrong way, I will kill you.'

'I understand.'

'Where are you? I'll pick you up.'

'Come pick me up too,' Katerina adds. 'I owe him.'

'Okay,' Oleg says. 'I'll bring the toys.'

23:45

I check the time as I walk up the escalator leading from Waterloo underground station to the rail station; it's 23:45. I hurry into the concourse and scan the departures board for the next and probably last train to my destination. It departs at 23:47 from platform thirteen.

I hurry to the platform and leap onto the first carriage of the train. I dump myself on a seat as the train doors close and watch the train leave the station. I place my bag on the table and rest my head on it. I'm exhausted, and every part of my body hurts, but it's over, and I'm alive. I close my eyes and relax.

An hour later, although semi-conscious, I hear the recorded voice call out arrival at my destination. Still, it takes a couple seconds for my tired mind to comprehend. I spring to my feet, grab my bag, and run off the train just before the doors close.

I limp into the long-stay car park beside the station, and my Land Rover is the only car parked inside. I step into the car and start the engine, but before I drive, I reflect on my return to London. I killed Lucas, so it's mission accomplished, but as always, things didn't go as planned and many more people died because of that . . . because of me. I sigh and rest my head on the steering wheel to ease the piercing pain in my neck.

ABOUT TEN AND A HALF YEARS AGO

'The fatman is dead'

Jake is on all fours in the middle of his bakery shop; his left eye is swollen, blood streams from his broken nose, and his tattered t-shirt is covered with his blood. He crawls to Sean Pounds, who is sat at a table enjoying a sizeable piece of toffee cheese-cake, and he begs for mercy, but Sean ignores him.

Sean Pounds is not his real name, but the name he chose to start a new life in London two years ago. He's from Chicago, but he killed an associate during one of his frequent alcohol-fuelled outbursts. The customary punishment is death, but he was well respected so they spared his life. Instead, he was banished, and his right pinky finger that wore the ring signifying his high rank in a major Chicago criminal organisation was cut off.

Sean is in his early forties and already greying, but he loves his salt and pepper hair because he thinks it makes him resemble

George Clooney. To be fair, he isn't that far off – he looks like George Clooney's hardened younger brother. Sean also enjoys dressing to the nines, and today, he's covered up in a lavish fur-collar coat. Lucas stands behind Jake, and despite wielding a bloodied cricket bat, he looks neat; he's even wearing a silk scarf around his neck.

'Mr Pounds, I swear to God I'll get your money,' Jake pleads. 'Just business is very slow this time of the year.'

'C'mon, fatties eat cake whatever the weather,' Sean says with a deep-voiced Chicago accent. 'Either way, you should have considered that before you asked me to stake you ten grand. I warned you too . . . gambling isn't for everyone.'

'No, Mr Pounds, it's not that—'

'Shut up, fatman,' Sean says. 'You don't pay me my money in a week . . . that's bad, but I might overlook it because, you know, shit happens, especially with stupid fucks like you. Two weeks . . . that's fucking with my patience. Three weeks . . . that's liberties. But a month . . . that's, as you English say, taking the fucking piss.' He turns to Lucas. 'Sort this place out. Fatman here got to learn some shit.'

Lucas nods and shatters a glass showcase with the bat.

'Please, Mr Pounds, stop,' Jake pleads. 'I swear I'll get the money.'

Sean doesn't respond for a few seconds as he watches Lucas batter the cash register. 'I know you will. You've got to,' he says. 'This is just for wasting my time. Making me come all this way. It's damn cold outside, and I'm getting old.'

Lucas shatters another showcase and pounds the cakes inside.

'Lucas!' Sean calls, and Lucas turns to him. 'Leave the cheesecake. I love it.'

'All right, mate,' Lucas says.

Lucas sidesteps the cheesecake and takes a deep breath before he continues pounding.

'Stop!' Jake shouts. 'Please, stop! I have something for you!'

Sean doesn't respond and eats a forkful of cheesecake.

'Please, Sean, I do,' Jake pleads.

'Lucas, take a break,' Sean says.

Lucas swings one more time before he stops; his face is beet red.

'What you got?' Sean asks Jake.

'My mother's engagement ring,' Jake responds.

'Okay?'

'She left it to me when she—'

'Shut up. Fuck do I care about that? What's it worth?'

'Last I knew . . . seven thousand.'

'Shut up, mate,' Lucas says. 'No man would give your mother anything worth that much, and certainly not your old—'

'Shut the fuck up,' Sean interrupts, and glares at Lucas. He turns to Jake. 'Okay, fatman, let's see it, go get it.' He turns back to Lucas. 'Accompany his fat ass.'

Jake limps into the back room, and Lucas follows a step behind. Sean enjoys the last forkfuls of his cheesecake before they return. Jake limps to Sean, and Lucas eats a fresh croissant as he follows. Jake places a velvet ring box on the table and steps back.

'Fuck you going?' Sean asks. 'Open it!'

Jake wipes his sweaty fingers on his trousers and opens the box. He picks out a ring with three diamond stones, and his fingers tremble as he hands it to Sean.

Sean examines the diamonds. 'Hmm . . . I like it,' he says. 'I know just the whore to give it to.'

'My pleasure, Mr Pounds,' Jake says.

'Shove your pleasure up your fat ass. This ring only waves five grand and gives you another week. We'll be back for the balance, plus whatever interest I deem necessary.' He gestures to an unconscious young man by the front door. 'And your son who thinks he's Superman . . . I'll kill him. Don't make me do it.'

Jake nods.

'Okay, pack me up the rest of the cheesecake,' Sean says. 'And make it snappy too.'

'Yeah, mate, pack me a few of these as well,' Lucas says, and eats the last piece of his croissant.

Jake glances at Lucas with a forced smile and waits for Sean to approve Lucas's request.

'Mate, are you waiting for Sean's permission?' Lucas asks Jake and stomps towards him. 'You fucking cunt!'

'Lucas, stop!' Sean says, and laughs as he turns to Jake. 'You stupid, fatman? Get him whatever he wants. Don't you see he's the one with the bat?'

Lucas seethes, and Jake gives him a wide berth as he limps towards the cheesecake. Jake packs it up and limps into the back room for the croissants.

Sean stands and grabs a soft drink through the shattered fridge door. 'Lucas, you want a drink?' he asks.

'Coke,' Lucas replies.

Sean tosses a can of Coke to Lucas and gulps down his soft drink on the spot before he sits.

Jake returns with two paper bags and he stares at Lucas.

'Oh, I'm sorry,' Lucas says, brimming with sarcasm. 'I got permission for the Coke from Mr Pounds. You don't mind, do you, Jake?'

Sean laughs. 'Be nice to the man, Lucas,' he says, and stands. 'Get the stuff and let's go.'

Lucas drops the half-empty can of Coke onto the floor and snatches the bags. Sean leads Lucas to the door, and they step over Jake's son's unconscious body to exit the bakery.

They walk out into the chilly November night, and Lucas hurries past Sean to the driver's side of a black Range Rover parked across the street. Lucas struggles to get the car key from his pocket because he's holding the pastry bags and cricket bat. He pulls the key out as Sean approaches the car, but it drops to the floor.

'Take your time, fire crotch,' Sean says. 'Maybe you're not cold, but I am.'

Lucas grabs the key and unlocks the doors, and Sean steps into the passenger's seat. Lucas places the pastry bags on the back seat and shoves the bat underneath the driver's seat before he jumps in. He starts the engine and turns up the heat before he sets off.

Lucas stops at a red light and turns to Sean. 'What are you going to do with the ring?' he asks.

'Said I was going to give it out. Fucking deaf?'

'All right, but before you do, we should make sure it's worth what the fatman says.'

Sean smirks. 'You don't trust him? C'mon, Lucas, he can't fuck with me like that . . . no fucking way.'

'Still.'

'Hmm . . . all right then, but I don't trust the pawnshops in this fucking town.'

'I know someone.'

'Who?'

The light turns green, and Lucas drives. 'The kid I used to work with . . . the jewel thief.'

'Sure, I've always wanted to meet the kid. But do I got to pay him too?'

'No, I'll have a chat with him.'

'All right, let's go see the kid then.'

'I'll call him.'

Lucas parks in the first available space and makes the call. 'Oi, geezer,' he says into his phone. 'Jeez, relax!'

. . .

'C'mon, no, I'm not. I just need a favour.'

. . .

'Fucking relax, I just need you to look at something.'

. . .

'A diamond ring.'

. . .

'It's urgent.'

. . .

'It's not mine, it's for a friend,' he says, and laughs. 'You didn't even say hello. I know you miss me.'

. . .

'Fuck you!'

. . .

'Where are you?'

. . .

'I know it.'

. . .

'Yes, I'm coming now.'

. . .

'Like right now, I'm on my way.'

. . .

'All right,' he says, and laughs to himself as he puts his phone away.

'Good?' Sean asks.

'Yeah, he's good. He's close too. About fifteen minutes away.'

'Good.'

Fifteen minutes later, Lucas parks across the street from Sports Café on Haymarket. He lowers the car stereo blaring Bob Dylan's 'Hurricane' and calls the kid.

'Mate, we're outside,' Lucas says into the phone. 'How long?'

. . .

'Don't keep me waiting,' he says, and puts the phone away.

Lucas watches the Sports Café entrance and turns up the stereo for Sean to enjoy his Bob Dylan compilation CD.

A few minutes later, the kid walks out of Sports Café. 'That's him,' Lucas says, and points at the kid.

Sean turns to the kid and is impressed by his style. The kid is wearing a red Adidas track top underneath a fitted leather jacket, and red retro Air Jordan trainers. 'Hmm . . . he looks very different from what I expected,' Sean says. 'He's a pretty boy.'

Lucas raises an eyebrow and scans his old friend, the supposed pretty boy. Lucas will concede the kid is handsome and somewhat strapping, but pretty is a fucking stretch. The kid wouldn't appreciate being called pretty either, or boy, or even kid for that matter. He's nineteen, and a fully fledged man in his estimation.

'I'm going to have a chat with the *Pretty Boy*,' Lucas says.

'Wait,' Sean says, and hands Lucas the ring box. 'I'm not paying for shit, okay?'

Lucas nods and steps out of the car. He walks to his old friend and reaches out for a hug.

'Fuck off, Lucas, don't touch me,' the Pretty Boy says.

Lucas chuckles. 'Mate, you still not over that?'

'I don't know what you're on about, and I don't give a shit. Let's get to it. I'm watching a game . . . the second quarter will start soon.'

'You still watch that NFL? Tried it the other night . . . don't get it at all. Love my rugby union.'

'I know you know that I know you know I don't care about that.'

Lucas takes a moment to understand what Pretty Boy said. 'Wait,' he says. 'You could have just said "I know you know".'

'I know. But now you have a slight understanding of how it feels to have your time wasted on trivial shit.'

Lucas rolls his eyes and hands Pretty Boy the box. Pretty Boy opens the box and scans the ring for two seconds before he closes it. 'Seven hundred, at most,' he says, and offers Lucas the box.

'Seven hundred!' Lucas shouts, and refuses the box. 'What?'

'Yep.'

'Hey, don't rush it. It can't be seven hundred.'

'You seem to be an expert now, so why come to me?'

'No, seriously, mate, you sure it's just seven hundred fucking quid?'

'Yes, Lucas,' Pretty Boy says, and gestures to the ring box in his outstretched hand. 'I'd like to get back to my game now. And lose my number.'

'Just wait a second,' Lucas says, and jogs to the Range Rover. Sean lowers his window and Lucas leans in. 'Sean, you won't believe this,' Lucas says. 'The ring is worth seven hundred quid.'

'What?' Sean roars, and turns off the stereo. 'You not fucking with me, are you?'

Lucas shakes his head, and Sean shoves the door open. Sean barges Lucas out of his way and marches across the street to Pretty Boy.

'Hey! You sure the ring cost seven hundred?' Sean asks Pretty Boy.

Pretty Boy smiles. 'I suppose you think if you – with your Barry White voice, ten-grand watch and Burberry coat – ask me the same question Lucas did three times, my answer will change,' he says. 'It won't.'

Sean forces a smile and turns to Lucas. 'You got yourself a witty friend, Lucas,' he says.

'We aren't friends,' Pretty Boy says.

'Yes, we are,' Lucas says.

'Whatever!' Sean barks, and turns back to Pretty Boy. 'A friend of mine told me the ring cost about seven grand.'

Pretty Boy laughs, and this angers Sean.

'Okay, I see you're not amused,' Pretty Boy says, and opens the ring box. 'The stones on the ring are not diamonds, they're gemstones, and they'll cost tops five hundred together. The band is an alloy . . . cost you a hundred at most. Then the other hundred for the Swarovski workmanship and brand.'

'Swarovski?' Lucas asks.

'Yep. If you want to confirm it, go to one of their stores tomorrow. They don't sell this ring anymore, it's fairly old, but they'll surely recognise it, cos I do.'

'The fatman is dead,' Sean roars.

'Terrible for *the fatman*,' Pretty Boy says and tosses the box to Lucas. 'I'm going back to the game now. Lucas, lose my number.'

'Fuck you!' Lucas says.

'Hey, wait,' Sean implores Pretty Boy. 'Come with us? I'll make it worth your time.'

Lucas is shocked and hopes Pretty Boy doesn't accept, but Pretty Boy takes a moment to consider.

'Where to and how much?' Pretty Boy asks.

'We are going to pay a visit to my *friend*,' Sean says. 'And the price is whatever you think you deserve for us interrupting the game.'

Lucas struggles to hide his anger. He can sense what is happening and its inevitable consequence for him, but he is powerless to stop it.

'Fair enough,' Pretty Boy says.

Lucas curses underneath his breath and Pretty Boy notices. But Sean doesn't even look Lucas's way before he stomps towards the Range Rover.

Lucas buries his anger and hurries past Sean to the car, and Pretty Boy follows. They enter the car, and Lucas sets off to Jake's bakery.

'You better drive fast, fire crotch,' Sean says to Lucas.

Pretty Boy watches Lucas through the rear-view mirror because he expects a response to Sean's gratuitous insult, but Lucas doesn't respond. Instead, he drives faster. Pretty Boy is angry for Lucas, and with Lucas for the meekness. He turns to Sean, and it's clear from Sean's demeanour that he has no concern or respect for Lucas.

Pretty Boy smiles; he understands the state of affairs between Sean and Lucas.

'DON'T CALL ME A KID'

Lucas parks the Range Rover in front of Jake's bakery, and Sean charges to the boot. Lucas pulls the cricket bat from underneath his seat and hurries to Sean, but Pretty Boy doesn't rush; he steps out and scans the street before he walks to the boot. Sean pulls two golf clubs from a golf bag and hands one to Pretty Boy. Sean and Lucas stride towards the bakery, and Pretty Boy strolls after them.

Sean kicks open the bakery door. 'You are dead, fatman!' he roars.

Jake's son is mopping blood off the floor by the door. He spins to Sean, and Sean swings the golf club into his head. He collapses to the floor beside his girlfriend, who's sweeping shattered glass, and she is frozen with terror. Sean marches past her like she doesn't exist and points his bloody golf club at Jake, who is standing behind a shattered showcase.

'You best not move, fatman!' Sean roars.

'What's wrong, Mr Pounds?' Jake pleads.

Lucas approaches Jake's son's girlfriend with a grin, but Pretty Boy steps in front of him and grabs her shoulders.

'Look at me,' Pretty Boy says, and she turns to him. 'Leave now. Do not call the police, or we'll find you. And you know what happens when we do.'

He releases her, and she scurries out of the bakery.

'Come here!' Sean says to Jake.

Jake considers running, but he knows he won't get far. He limps to Sean, and Sean swings the golf club into his right knee. Jake howls and falls, and Sean tosses the ring box at his head.

'Shut the fuck up!' Sean screams, and Jake stops howling. 'How much you say that shit cost again?'

'Seven thousand,' Jake says. 'I swear!'

'You swear?'

'Yes . . . on my daughter's life!' Jake pleads, and sits on the floor to nurse his busted knee.

'Jake, just fucking stop, I hear it cost seven hundred.'

'No, no way, Mr Pounds,' Jake says, and shakes his head. 'They must be trying to cheat you.'

'Really? You're still . . . okay . . . shit . . . okay then,' Sean says, and turns to Pretty Boy. 'Please. Talk to the fat fuck.'

Pretty Boy nods and walks to Jake. 'Mate, honestly, I admire your attempt at hustling them,' he says, and gestures at the wrecked bakery. 'I imagine you were desperate. And you probably would have gotten away with it too . . . until I got involved. Unfortunately for you, I've been in the jewellery business for a while now, and I know that ring.'

'A while? You're a kid! You know nothing!' Jake screams and cries.

Pretty Boy watches Jake cry and feels nothing. 'Don't call me a kid,' he says. 'And we both know I'm telling the truth.'

'Tell him!' Sean shouts.

'Fuck off! Kid!' Jake shouts.

'Okay,' Pretty Boy says, and sighs. 'I'm going to count from ten. Before I get to zero, I strongly suggest you just tell the truth.'

'Fuck off, kid!'

'Oh no,' Lucas goads. 'You're fucked, fatman. You don't want him counting.'

'Ten,' Pretty Boy counts. 'Nine . . . eight . . . seven . . . six . . . five . . . four . . .' He swings the club into Jake's crotch.

Jake squeals and grabs his crotch with both hands, and Pretty Boy smashes his shoulders. Jake's arms fall to the ground, and he tries to move them but can't because the pain is excruciating. Pretty Boy traps Jake's left leg and taps Jake's crotch with the golf club, increasing impact with every swing.

Jake fights to move his arms to protect his crotch, but he can't. He tries to move his legs, but he can't.

'Okay! Okay!' he screams, and turns to Sean. 'I'm sorry, Mr Pounds. I'm so sorry. I didn't know what else to do. I was going to tell you when I got your money, I swear. I just needed time.'

Sean shoves Pretty Boy aside and swings his club into Jake's head. Blood spurts from Jake's mouth and Pretty Boy leaps back to avoid it. Jake collapses, and Sean pummels him with the club. Pretty Boy is surprised by Sean's rage because it's clear Jake is dead, but Sean continues to pummel his lifeless body.

Sean stops, but only because he is out of breath and has Jake's blood in his eyes. He brushes past Pretty Boy and hands Lucas his crooked and bloodied golf club. He grabs Lucas's scarf to wipe the blood off his face, and Lucas is furious but does nothing. Sean wraps the bloodstained scarf around Lucas's neck and marches towards the door. Lucas curses underneath and follows Sean, and Pretty Boy shakes his head in disgust.

Sean stops at Jake's son's unconscious body and snatches Lucas's cricket bat. Lucas hops back as Sean raises the bat above his head, but Pretty Boy grabs Sean's arms mid-swing. Sean glares at Pretty Boy, and Pretty Boy glares back at him. They glare at each other for several tense seconds, and Sean is impressed by Pretty Boy's fearlessness. Sean nods, and Pretty Boy releases his arms. Sean hands Lucas the bat and strides out of the bakery, and Lucas follows. Pretty Boy scans the bakery for a camera, but there isn't one. He walks out.

They enter the car, and Lucas hides the golf clubs, cricket bat, and his bloodstained scarf under his seat before he turns to Sean for instructions.

'To the club,' Sean says, and gestures to Pretty Boy. 'I need to get him his money, and a nice gift too.'

'I THINK YOU'LL LIKE HER'

No one speaks during the drive to Diamonds, a strip club in the heart of Soho that Sean bought with a substantial portion of the money he received from selling his Chicago assets. Lucas parks right in front of the club, and Sean leads to the entrance.

The two large doormen in overcoats step aside. 'Sup, boss,' they greet Sean, but he ignores them and walks into the club. Lucas greets them with a nod, and they nod back, but Pretty Boy doesn't acknowledge them and follows Lucas into the club.

'What the fuck?' the younger doorman asks with a strong Essex accent.

'What?' the older doorman responds.

'Fucking guy can't greet?'

'Who, Sean?'

'No, the new guy.'

'Leave it.'

'Yeah, whatever.'

'Kid looked sharp, though.'

'Yeah . . . but fuck him,' the younger doorman says, and they laugh.

Sean leads Lucas and Pretty Boy through the crowded main room to the stunning bar, which Sean had painstakingly remodelled to resemble his favourite uptown Chicago bar. The bar is busy, but a bartender notices Sean and rushes over.

'The usual to my office!' Sean orders over the deafening dance music. 'And get me Sandy, now!'

The bartender nods and hurries off, and Sean turns to watch the two topless girls dancing on the stage in the middle of the room. He scans the room and is pleased with the vibrant crowd. He turns to Pretty Boy, and it seems Pretty Boy is impressed with the club. Pretty Boy is, but then it's his first time in a strip club.

Sean smiles and turns to Lucas, who is captivated by the girls on the stage. 'Want anything?' he asks.

Lucas can't hear Sean, so he takes a step closer to him. 'What?' he asks.

Sean dismisses Lucas with a wave, and Lucas shrugs before he turns back to the stage.

A smartly dressed young blonde woman walks up to Sean. 'Hello, Sean!' she says.

Sean turns to her and has to lean down to speak because she is short. 'Hello, Sandy,' he says. 'Where's Rebecca?'

'With a regular.'

'Put someone else on the regular,' Sean says, and gestures to Pretty Boy. 'Take the pretty boy to one of the private rooms and get Rebecca to attend to him. Anything he wants, on the house.'

'Sure,' Sandy says, and walks to Pretty Boy. She taps him on the chest, and he turns to her.

'Please, follow me.'

Pretty Boy nods, and Sandy leads him to the secluded lower ground-floor level of the club.

Sandy opens a red door and gestures into a red-themed room. 'Step in, sugar,' she says, and Pretty Boy does. 'Make yourself comfortable. One of the girls . . . our best girl, in fact . . . will be with you shortly, and I'll be back with a complimentary bottle of champagne. There's also an intercom by the sofa. Dial one for the bar and order anything you want. I'll bring it down personally.'

'Thanks.'

'My pleasure, sugar.'

She smiles and shuts the door, and Pretty Boy scans the room. He likes that the music is chilled, unlike the main room, and is impressed with the stylish decor, but he doesn't like that the east and west walls are covered with mirrors – someone might be watching behind the glass, he thinks. He takes off his jacket and lays on the sofa bed to wait for their 'best girl'.

Five minutes later, the door opens and he bounces off the bed. But Sandy walks in with a bottle of Dom Pérignon champagne in an ice bucket and two champagne flutes.

She places the ice bucket and flutes on a table beside him. 'I see you're getting comfortable,' she says, and he smiles. 'She'll be here soon. She's just getting ready. I think you'll like her.'

He nods, and she uncorks the champagne with ease. She fills both flutes and returns the bottle to the bucket. She smiles and walks to the door. But before she steps out, she turns back to him.

'Don't forget, sugar, need anything, call,' she says.

She steps out and shuts the door, and he sips champagne from a flute. He glances at his reflection in the mirror, but then he hears a soft tap on the door.

Rebecca steps in, and she's wearing black lingerie that flaunts her curves. She's beautiful too, with jet-black hair flowing down her back. She shuts the door and struts towards him, and he is mesmerised. But she stops and turns back to a control panel by the door. She dims the lights and changes the music to R&B.

'Hope you don't mind, baby,' Rebecca says with a sweet, although rehearsed, voice.

'It's all good,' he says.

'I know, baby,' she says, and smiles.

She struts towards him and this time she sways to the music, and he can't take his eyes off her.

She sits on his lap and pulls his head over her shoulder. 'I can feel you, baby,' she whispers.

Sean and Lucas sit across from each other in Sean's office, and Sean is agitated. He refills his rocks glass with whiskey from a near-empty Jack Daniel's bottle and downs it. Lucas hasn't touched his glass.

'That fat bastard got some fucking balls,' Sean mutters.

Lucas shrugs.

'Really,' Sean says. 'He fucking tried to play me.'

'Yeah, he did.'

'But I sure showed him some shit. Didn't I?'

Lucas nods.

'He's dead, right?' Sean asks.

'Should be. You fucking clobbered him. And you were going to fuck his kid up too, until, you know . . .'

'These cocksuckers gotta learn. And when word about tonight gets round . . . cocksuckers'll pay their debts real fast.'

'You sure? Cos them geezers you get at your tables think they're hard.'

'I know. You don't get many soft *geezers* putting down fifteen to twenty-five grand on a poker game . . . five on a pool game.' Sean refills his glass with whiskey. 'But your friend . . . *Pretty Boy* . . . showed some real shit tonight. Doesn't fuck around. And he's got fucking enormous brass balls. I like it.'

'Hmm.'

Sean downs the whiskey. 'I want more people like him around me.'

'Hey, Sean,' Lucas objects. 'Not him, he doesn't listen.'

'Fuck that. I know the kid's type. He reminds me of me back in the day in the South Side. You should've seen me . . . took no shit from nobody.'

'That's great, but this kid doesn't listen, does his own shit. I told you how it ended with me and him.'

'Shut the fuck up with that shit. Story changes every time you fucking tell it. I want the kid, and I need you to talk to him for me.'

'I don't think it's a good idea.'

Sean laughs. 'Does it look like I give a shit what you think?' he asks, and refills his glass. 'I don't pay you to think, Lucas. I pay you to get results, and the kid got fucking results.'

Lucas shakes his head in disgust. 'That's fucking shit, mate,' he says.

Sean bangs his fists on the desk, and that startles Lucas. 'Shit?' Sean roars, and leans towards Lucas. 'I'll shove your head up your ass, make you see shit clearly.' Sean downs his whiskey and bangs the glass on the table. 'You fucking ginger . . . bastard!'

Lucas is enraged and struggles to remain calm, and Sean laughs at him.

'What?' Sean asks. 'You going to do something, fire crotch?'

'No, Sean. No, I'm safe.'

'You better be fucking safe, cos my back's killing me. I couldn't fight your lanky ass for money right now.' Sean laughs, but Lucas doesn't even smile. 'Aww, I hurt your feelings? Cos I'm sorry, I don't want you crying and shit!'

Lucas doesn't respond.

'Where the fuck is my cheesecake, anyway?' Sean asks.

'The Rover.'

'Fuck's it doing there? Go fucking get it.'

'Just get one of the birds to go get it.'

'What? You're fucking crazy. You don't tell me what to do.

I fucking tell you what to do! Go fucking get my cheesecake now!'

Rage consumes Lucas, but he forces a smile and leaves the office. Sean laughs to himself and uses the telephone on his desk to call the bar. The call is answered, and he puts it on speaker.

'Get Sandy!' he shouts, and waits for almost a minute.

'Yes, Sean,' Sandy says.

'Get me the pretty boy.'

'Sure.'

Sean ends the call and attempts to refill his glass with whiskey, but the bottle is empty. He yells and calls the bar again.

'Another fucking regular!' he shouts.

'BEING IN DEBT TO MR POUNDS'

Rebecca is topless on top of Pretty Boy, and she grinds to the beat of the music. The intercom rings, and she pulls away.

'Fuck,' she mutters, and steps off the bed.

'What?' he asks.

'You should answer that, it's for you,' she says, and puts on her bra.

He grabs the intercom receiver but lets it ring one more time before he answers.

'I'm sorry to disturb you, sugar,' Sandy says through the phone. 'Sean wants you.'

'He couldn't wait?' he asks.

'I'm sorry, I'll be at your door in a minute to take you up to his office.'

'Okay,' he says, and drops the receiver. He turns to Rebecca, and she mutters under her breath. 'What's wrong?'

'What, you think I'm a whore?' she asks.

'Noooo.'

'You think I do that with everyone I'm in here with? I'm a dancer, for fuck's sake.'

'Sure . . . a dancer.'

'Just shut up. And you can't tell anyone this happened, okay?'

'Wait, *this* is over?'

'You don't know how *this* works, do you?' She smiles and shakes her head. 'What? You want to take me home?'

He grins.

'Fuck you,' she says.

'That's my point, I think you'd be incredible.'

She laughs. 'Cheeky one, aren't you, baby,' she says. 'I would be incredible, but you won't ever find out.'

'That's just not fair.'

She laughs again and hands him his jacket, and they smile at each other as he puts it on.

Sandy opens the door. 'Sorry, sugar, please come with me,' she says.

Pretty Boy nods and walks to Sandy.

'Bye, baby,' Rebecca says.

'Darling, you'll wait till he gets back,' Sandy says to Rebecca.

'I'm off in ten minutes, Sandy!'

'Darling, he's Sean's personal guest. I think you should wait.'

Rebecca sighs and slumps to the sofa bed.

'Gimme a second,' Sandy says to Pretty Boy and walks to Rebecca. 'You're in tomorrow, aren't you?' she asks.

Rebecca nods.

'Come in whenever you like, I'll take care of it,' Sandy says. 'Actually, just take the night off. You've earned it . . . and we should be able to survive without you for a night.'

Rebecca mouths *thank you*, and Sandy taps her on the shoulder before she walks back to Pretty Boy.

'Follow me, please,' she says, and steps out of the room.

She leads him through the lively main room, and almost everyone tries to get her attention, but she ignores them all. But then a man sweating through his business suit grabs her arm as she walks past his booth.

'Where the fuck are my drinks?' he shouts. 'I ordered them ages ago!'

Pretty Boy steps in front of Sandy and leans in to the man. 'Get your fucking hands off her now,' he says, and glares at him.

The man releases Sandy's arm and turns to his friends in the booth. 'We have Superman in here,' he says, and gestures to Pretty Boy.

They burst out laughing, and Pretty Boy watches them with a menacing grin. Sandy notices Pretty Boy's grin and tugs his arm, and he turns to her.

'Sugar, please, let it go,' she says.

He hesitates for a moment and nods.

'Thank you,' she says, and pats him on the chest.

She leads him through a sturdy door with a keypad lock in a quiet corner of the room and up the stairway to Sean's office. She knocks twice and waits for a moment before she opens the door. She gestures for Pretty Boy to walk in, and he does, but she doesn't. She shuts the door.

Sean is eating cheesecake at his desk, but he pushes it aside and stares at Pretty Boy with a smile. 'Have a seat,' Sean says, and gestures to the empty chair beside Lucas.

Pretty Boy sits and turns to Lucas, but Lucas doesn't acknowledge him.

'You want some?' Sean asks Pretty Boy and gestures to the cheesecake.

'No, I'm good,' Pretty Boy says.

'Okay. You have fun? That Rebecca's something, isn't she?'

'Rebecca?' Pretty Boy asks and smiles. 'She doesn't look like a Rebecca.'

Sean bursts out laughing, but Pretty Boy doesn't.

'Okay then,' Sean says. 'I know you don't like bullshit, so I'll get to it. What you doing with yourself? How you earn?'

'I'm good.'

'How much you earn?'

'What . . . why?'

Pretty Boy is annoyed. He glances at Lucas, but Lucas still doesn't acknowledge him.

'Relax, I'm not trying to fuck with you,' Sean says.

'What's this, then?'

'An opportunity. What you did earlier tonight was some real shit. You got results—'

'Results?' Pretty Boy interrupts.

'Yeah, results . . . and don't fucking interrupt me. I want

people like you around me.' Sean gestures to Lucas. 'But your friend here—'

'I already told you he's not my friend,' Pretty Boy interrupts.

Sean bangs the desk with his fists. 'I said stop fucking interrupting me. Shit!' he yells.

Pretty Boy is amused by the outburst, but he doesn't show it.

Sean downs a glass of whiskey and eats a forkful of cheesecake. 'Lucas says you don't listen, and you do what you want,' he says, and turns to Lucas. 'Right, Lucas?'

Lucas forces a smile but doesn't speak.

'I can't have that,' Sean says.

'Fair enough,' Pretty Boy says. 'But what makes you think I want your opportunity?'

'Cos I'll make you an offer you can't refuse,' Sean says, and laughs.

Pretty Boy is not amused, but Sean continues to laugh as he refills his glass with whiskey.

'Sorry, I'm being a bad host,' Sean says. 'Want something to drink?'

'No.'

'I like that, straight answer,' Sean says, and downs his glass of whiskey. 'The job you'll be doing for me is collection. My business involves a fair number of people being in debt to Mr Pounds.' He chuckles. *'Being in debt to Mr Pounds,'* he repeats with pride. 'I like it. You like it?'

Pretty Boy doesn't respond; he doesn't understand what Sean is on about.

'I'm Mr Pounds,' Sean says. 'Mr Sean Pounds.'

'Oh, right,' Pretty Boy says.

'Anyway, you'll get my money by any means you deem necessary.'

'Right.'

'I pay for results. Just name your price.'

'Name my price?'

'Yep,' Sean says, and nods. 'Whatever you're making now, I'll double it. And to show I'm not fucking around, that's what I'll pay for what you did tonight.'

'A thousand a job.'

Sean smirks and glances at Lucas. 'C'mon,' he says. 'That's almost double what I pay Lucas.'

'Even better.'

Sean laughs. 'Any objections?' he asks Lucas. 'Cos I don't want you crying again.'

Lucas again forces a smile but doesn't speak.

'It's a deal then,' Sean says, and picks out a roll of cash from a desk drawer. He tosses the money across the desk to Pretty Boy. 'That's a grand, but you might want to count it.'

'No, we're good,' Pretty Boy says, and puts the money into his pocket.

'Good,' Sean says, and smiles. 'Another perk of the job is that you're a contractor. You don't need to be here every day. You are welcome as much as you like, but you pay for your drinks and your time with the girls like everyone else. I call you, give you the details, you handle it, and report back here with results.'

'Okay.'

'I know the ginger bastard has your number,' Sean says, and gestures to Lucas. 'So, I'll be calling you soon. For now, you can get the fuck out of my office.'

'One question.'

'Go ahead,' Sean says and refills his glass.

'Walked through the club. Looks good . . . very busy. Off the top of my head, on a good night like tonight, I'll say you make about thirty grand.'

'More,' Sean says with pride.

'Fair enough. So why have this other business where you need to go around cracking heads to get your money? The fucking punters downstairs are competing to hand you money.'

'They not handing me shit, I'm not on that pole,' Sean says, and laughs. 'But give it time, young one, you'll learn.'

'Right,' Pretty Boy says, and stands. 'Another thing . . . Rebecca.'

Sean grins, revealing his gap tooth. 'What about Rebecca?' he asks.

'I think we have a connection. You mind if I follow up on that?'

'I'm not her dad. Long as it's not on my time, you can do whatever you want. But, just so you know, you face serious competition there. She's well-loved . . . everyone thinks there's a connection. She's talented like that.'

Pretty Boy smirks and walks out of the office.

Pretty Boy steps into his private room, and Rebecca sits on the sofa bed, drinking champagne.

'Welcome back, baby,' she says, and smiles.

'Stop calling me that,' he responds. 'You're done for the night, right?'

'Yeah,' she says, and raises an eyebrow.

'You mind if we take *this* somewhere else?'

She smiles and takes a moment to consider. 'Okay,' she says. 'I don't mind.'

'Good,' he says, and smiles.

'Where are we going then?'

'That's totally up to you.'

She stands and saunters to him. 'Okay, baby, you wait here. I'll go change. Be back soon.'

She kisses him on the cheek, and he watches her saunter out of the room.

'THAT . . . WAS INCREDIBLE'

Pretty Boy sits on the sofa bed to wait for Rebecca, and he waits for over twenty minutes before she steps in and holds the door open. She's freshened up, wearing a red overcoat, black high-heeled boots, and carrying a large Chanel handbag. He smiles and admires her.

'Shall we leave?' she says.

'Oh yes,' he says, and jumps off the sofa bed.

Rebecca and Pretty Boy walk out of the club, and the younger doorman grabs her arm. She stops. Pretty Boy walks ahead for a couple steps before he stops but he doesn't look back. He's allowing them space to handle their shit; he doesn't need the aggravation tonight.

The younger doorman glares at Pretty Boy and whispers into Rebecca's ear, and she laughs. She whispers into his ear, but he's not satisfied and attempts to whisper again, but she kisses him on the cheek and pulls away from his grasp. She walks to Pretty Boy, and she's surprised he doesn't seem upset at all.

'If you have any problems, Rebecca, just call me!' the younger doorman shouts. 'I'll be there in a minute!'

Rebecca turns to the younger doorman and smiles. She turns back to Pretty Boy, and he's annoyed.

'What the fuck is that all about?' Pretty Boy asks.

'Ignore him,' she says, and giggles. 'Let's go.' He shrugs, and they continue towards the street. 'That's just Yellow. For some reason, he thinks he's my protector.'

'Yellow?'

'That's his name.'

'Really?'

'I guess . . . that's what everyone calls him.'

'You know he just wants to fuck you, right?'

'And you don't?' she retorts. Pretty Boy is lost for words, and she laughs. 'Where's your car?' she asks.

'Not here.'

'Are you serious?'

'Yes, we'll get a taxi.'

She rolls her eyes. 'No need, my Mini is parked around the corner.'

'Mini?' he asks, surprised. 'Nice.'

'Okay, and?' she asks, and glares at him.

'Nothing, sorry,' he says, and raises his hands to apologise. 'Just didn't see you as a Mini person. Benz . . . Bimmer, yeah.'

She shakes her head. 'You're an idiot,' she says, and they laugh.

They continue to banter as they walk through vibrant Soho streets to her car, and he is captivated by her effortless, witty retorts. He tries to keep up, but he can't, and he loves it.

They get into her car. 'Where to, baby?' she asks.

'I did say it was up to you,' he responds.

'I'm hungry.'

He checks the time on his watch, and it's 23:10. 'Too late for a restaurant,' he says. 'We could go to mine, I'll cook.'

'Really?' she asks, and raises an eyebrow. 'You cook?'

'Yep. But it's your car, so I suggest we go to yours and you cook.'

'I don't cook.'

'You can't cook.'

'Same thing.'

'I guess they don't teach you to cook in dancing school.'

'Wow, that's so funny. You are so funny . . . did you go to school for that?'

'Fuck off. We'll order pizza at yours.'

'You'll order pizza,' she says, and drives.

Fifteen minutes later, Rebecca drives into the undercroft car park of a new-build block of flats in Camden and takes her time to park in her space. Pretty Boy checks her parking in his side mirror. 'Err . . . I think your back tire is in the next spot,' he teases.

'Fuck off,' she says, and they laugh.

She leads into the reception, and he scans the elegant decor as they head to the lift. 'Not bad for a dancer,' he quips.

'Says the peasant,' she retorts.

They step out of the lift on the fourth floor, and he watches her with excitement as she leads them to her flat door; she loves the attention.

She opens the door. 'My home,' she says, and gestures for him to enter.

He steps into her living room, which is only lit by the hallway lights coming through the open door. She steps in and shuts it, and the room is dark. She reaches for a light switch, but he grabs her and kisses her. She drops her bag and wraps her arms around his neck to kiss him back. They kiss and shuffle around in the darkness until they fall over a sofa to the floor. But they don't stop. They undress each other till they are naked, but then he stops and blindly searches for his jacket.

'What are you doing?' she asks.

'Getting a condom . . .'

'Leave it. I'm on the pill.'

'It's okay,' he says, and grabs his jacket. 'I've got it.'

He puts on the condom and she pulls him on top of her. They fuck, and it's passionate from the start. She grabs his arm and leads him, stumbling and giggling through the darkness, into her bedroom. He throws her onto the bed and climbs on top of her.

He slowly pulls out and lies beside her. 'That . . . was incredible,' he says between heavy breaths.

'I know.'

'Wow!'

'Baby,' she says, and caresses his abs.
'What?'
'Baby . . .'
'What!'
'What's your name?'

ABOUT TEN YEARS AGO

'Your money or his life?'

Pretty Boy and Rebecca are having sex on her bed. But a phone rings, and he stops.

She wraps her legs around him. 'Don't you dare!' she screams.

He breaks her grasp and hurries to his jeans on the floor in the middle of the room. He pulls out his ringing phone and checks at the caller ID; it's Sean.

He answers the call. 'Yeah,' he says. 'You are?'

. . .

'How did you know I was here?'

. . .

'Right.'

. . .

'I have nothing on me.'

. . .

'Okay, I'll be down in a minute.'

. . .

'She'll be cool,' he says, and ends the call.

Rebecca is furious and glares at him as he puts on his boxer briefs. 'I'll be cool?' she asks.

He ignores her and puts on his jeans and trainers.

'Fucking bastard!' she screams. 'What am I to you? You think you can just drop in and fuck whenever you like? I'm not a whore.'

He chuckles.

'What?' she screams.

He turns to her and recognises her fury. Oh, shit, he thinks; he needs to get out before she erupts. He puts on his t-shirt and grabs his leather jacket, but it's light because his wallet isn't inside. He scans the room and spots it on the bedside table beside his watch – a lavish 18ct rose gold TAG Heuer Monaco. He isn't a fan of wearing such luxury but the watch means something to him.

He avoids eye contact with Rebecca and picks it up. He puts it on, and she yanks open the top drawer to pick out a pack of Silk Cut cigarettes and a lighter. He watches her light a cigarette and take a long drag. She turns to him and blows the smoke towards his face. He shrugs and picks up his wallet. There's no cash inside. He smiles.

'What?' she demands.

'I had two fifties in here.'

'Yes, I know . . . what, you think it's free?'

He nods and walks towards the bedroom door, but he stops. 'I thought you said you're just a dancer?' he quips – he couldn't help himself.

She hurls the bedside lamp at the back of his head, and he yelps and checks for blood. He's furious but doesn't show it because he knows it'll only make her more combative.

'I was talking about the pizzas you've been eating all day, you fucking idiot,' she says. 'Bloody puppet bitch!'

He doesn't respond and walks out of the bedroom, and she screams insults at him. He approaches the front door and stops to listen to her insults.

'Cunt!' she screams. 'Fucking wasteman! I hate you, motherfucker!'

Hate, he considers and laughs to himself. That's new. He's starting to enjoy her exaggerated tirades. But she can't ever know this because she enjoys it enough already. He opens the door.

He steps out of Rebecca's building and spots the Range Rover parked underneath a streetlight, and Sean is alone in the car, which is unusual. He walks to the car and steps into the passenger seat. They greet each other with a nod. He scans Sean's clothes and fights back a smile because even though it's late spring, Sean is wrapped up in an exquisite double-breasted camel coat.

'You sure Rebecca's cool with this?' Sean asks.

'You don't give a shit.'

Sean chuckles. 'True. Ready?'

'Yeah.'

Sean nods and drives.

Half an hour later, Sean parks in front of a tower block in a rundown council estate in Harlesden. He turns the headlights off but leaves the engine running.

Pretty Boy scans the bleak street. 'I think I know this place,' he says.

'Really?'

'Yeah, and you're not going to get many people from this side of town at your poker tables.'

'You think?'

'Yeah, no one here's going to blow twenty thousand for a buy-in, unless they plan to rob you regardless.'

'You'd be surprised,' Sean says, and gestures to the glove compartment. 'Open it.'

Pretty Boy opens the glove compartment, and there is a Smith & Wesson 9mm handgun inside. 'Fuck is this?' he asks.

'Smithy.'

'What?'

'My Smith & Wesson.'

'I know what the fuck it is. W—'

'Hey! Relax. We've come a long way, Pretty Boy—'

'Stop calling me that.'

Sean takes a moment to fight back his anger at being interrupted. 'I completely trust you now,' he says. 'So, I think it's about time we take the next step.'

Pretty Boy shakes his head. 'I already told you. I'm not killing anybody for you, next step or not. Fuck that.'

Sean nods and gestures to his right hand, which is missing its pinky finger. 'I know it's hard to believe, but I used to have a pinky,' he says, and smiles. 'I had a ring on it too. Simple ring, really . . . gold with a little crest on it . . . but you see, that simple ring signified to those that needed knowing that I wasn't to be fucked with . . . that I was to be respected. I was what you'd understand to be a *made man*. I was . . . I am proud of it, cos I earned it. The hard way.'

Sean nods and reminisces. 'I was fourteen,' he continues. 'Living in the projects of South Side Chicago. Was a fucking grind, but I didn't care, I knew nothing else. The neighbourhood had been changing way before I was born, though. It used to be an Irish neighbourhood back when my dad was a kid, but black folk had always been the majority long as I remember. Then the time came when the neighbourhood was pretty much ninety per cent black, with just a few Irish knuckleheads left. But these knuckleheads, my uncle included, stayed around cos they still ran the neighbourhood. They handled the black folk with an iron fist . . . harder and harder each fucking day, probably cos they feared losing power.

'But then the inevitable began . . . black folk, they wanted power. An uprising was coming, and it was going to be bloody, it had to be. But then word came down from on high . . . prison, that is . . . that power was to be restructured. The decision-makers, who all happened to be in prison, feared for their safety if shit got wild cos the numbers in there reflected the numbers in the neighbourhood. The Irish were to relinquish control of the drug trade, prostitution, and the unions, which were the real earners. But they kept control of the gunrunning, loan-sharking, and the gambling. My uncle, stubborn fucker, never liked the neighbourhood changing in the first place and couldn't accept the power restructure. You could say he was racist or maybe just stubborn . . . probably both.'

Sean shrugs. 'Uncle was a marine. Fought in Vietnam with my father. He survived, my father didn't. He provided for Mum and me though, as well as he could. For years he ran the drug corners around us, so the restructure directly affected his livelihood. But he didn't back down. One cold night . . . can't exactly remember what I was doing up, but I was . . . I heard gunshots from the corner. BAM! BAM! BAM! BAM! Nine shots. Steady shots too, didn't seem like a firefight.

'Bout a minute later, I heard the back door of the house open, and it wasn't a break-in. This person had a key, and Mum was asleep in her room, so it wasn't her. It was all fairly loud too, I remember, but it supposedly didn't wake Mum up.' He laughs. 'I snuck out of my room and followed the sounds to the kitchen. And I saw my uncle, stood on the table hiding a black bag in the ceiling. Fuck! I snuck back to my room quick time and forced myself to sleep. Next morning it became clear what happened . . . someone shot down the boys dealing on the corner. Six black boys, youngest was thirteen and the oldest twenty-four. I knew the thirteen-year-old, Bug. We played Pop Warner football together. Know what that is?'

Pretty Boy nods.

'Yeah, those were good times. I was decent too, probably would have gotten a scholarship if I stuck with it,' Sean says, and shrugs. 'Anyway, the neighbourhood went crazy; black folk understandably wanted vengeance. Rumours were swirling around that it was this Irishman or the next one. War was coming, with only one consequence for the Irish. I knew what to do and not cos I cared about Bug. Yeah, he and

I shared a backfield, but fuck that. I saw my opportunity to be somebody, and I took it. I got the gun from the ceiling and went to the bar that was a haven for my uncle and the other knuckleheads. I walk up to my uncle, and he's happy to see me, but BAM . . . BAM! BAM! BAM! BAM! BAM! I put six bullets in his head. With that, the war ended before it began, and I earned my stripes.

'I did time. Five years in juvie and three with the big boys. But it was a fucking peach. Black folk loved me, and the Irish respected me cos they thought I did what I did for noble reasons.' He laughs. 'I got out, and I was the man. I ran the loan-sharking and gambling for both blacks and Irish.'

Sean cracks his knuckles, and the pops are louder than Pretty Boy imagined possible.

'But Mum never forgave me,' Sean says. 'Never visited me in prison. Didn't speak to me when I got out either, and I fucking tried, trust me. She never accepted anything from me. Offered to buy her a house, but nah. That fucking stubborn gene. She was born and raised in the neighbourhood, and sure as shit, she was going to die there. She got her wish. She got killed by some junkie trying to grab her bag. She fought back, and the fucker stabbed her in the neck; she bled out right there on the street. Ten hours later, the fucker was brought to me. People expected me to want vengeance, but no. Fuck vengeance. That shit never did anything for anybody. I let the fucker go. But the streets took care of him. They'll do that for you and more, you just have to earn their respect.

'Thing is, it's mostly perception, and you're more than halfway there. You've been collecting for me for bout six months now, and you've never had to really hurt any of these wretched bastards. They hear you're coming and they do whatever they need to do to get the money. Even rob the liquor store next door.'

Sean laughs, and Pretty Boy smiles.

'Damn, kid, you got that presence,' Sean says. 'Plus, you got that mysterious shit going on cos nobody knows anything about you . . . not even your name. They call you all sorts. My second favourite is *The Count*, obviously my favourite's *Pretty Boy*.'

Pretty Boy shakes his head, and Sean laughs.

'But that don't work on this side of town,' Sean says. 'Fuckers round here need action.'

'I'm not going to prison for—'

'No,' Sean interrupts. 'I get that. No one's talking about prison here. I don't want to lose you to prison. What I did, I did in daylight, and there were witnesses – civilians who testified. And one of the most important rules of this game is that you do not harm civilians, no matter what. Most times civilians won't testify cos they know who you are. But if they choose to, you let 'em be.'

Pretty Boy nods.

'This game is fucking savage,' Sean says. 'I need to know you're all in.'

Sean waits for a response, but Pretty Boy doesn't speak and just stares ahead at nothing in particular.

'C'mon, Pretty Boy, I've got to know you want this . . . I've got to.'

'I want it,' Pretty Boy says, and glances at the gun. 'But not at any cost.'

Sean chuckles. 'That is the cost, kid. All 'em chips. And I know you got this. I've never spoken to anyone out here about my life in Chicago. Just you. Cos I trust you, and more than that, you're special . . . you've got this game in you. After this, you're right beside me in everything I do. And when I go back to Chicago, you'll run everything out here cos you earned it. Remember the first day we met? I told you you'll learn, right?'

Pretty Boy nods.

'Well, you've already learnt everything I got to teach,' Sean says. 'It's your time, right now. Don't fucking hesitate, seize the fucking moment.'

Pretty Boy fights back a smile because he recognises that Sean is selling very hard.

'Trust me,' Sean says.

Pretty Boy takes a deep breath. 'Who is it?' he asks.

'That's what I'm talking about,' Sean says, and slaps Pretty Boy on the chest. Pretty Boy glares at him.

'Got excited. My bad. So, this fucker sells shit for me.'

'What?'

'Yeah, caine.'

Pretty Boy nods; he is surprised but doesn't show it.

'This fucker hasn't been paying his dues for months,' Sean says. 'Giving me stupid excuses about police raids and some other bullshit.' He points to a new BMW 3 Series parked fifty metres ahead. 'Now he drives that Beamer and is dressing flash with my money. Shit, that's just all wrong. Mr Pounds doesn't get fucked. Plus, two nights ago, one of the young kids this fucker uses to run his shit got jacked and beat to an inch of his life. You see, the folks around here haven't been happy for a long time cos he's using their kids . . . now they are fucking mad. I warned the fucker bout this, but he didn't listen. Now, it's too late.

'You take care of this fucker, you earn your stripes. Cos the streets are watching. And I'll tell you a secret – you only need to do the deed once. But do it right, and you become a legend. In a few years, you won't even recognise the story . . . it would have been embellished beyond belief. They'd make you a bona fide crusader with two Smith & Wessons and a shotgun across your fucking back.'

Sean laughs and waits for a response, but Pretty Boy just stares at the gun.

'I got you,' Sean says. 'Anything goes sideways, I'm here.'

Pretty Boy picks the gun and examines it.

'First time holding one?' Sean asks.

Pretty Boy nods.

'Know how to use it?' Sean asks.

'Point and shoot.'

Sean chuckles. 'He'll come out of that building any minute now,' he says, and points to a block of flats dwarfed by tower blocks on either side. 'It's his girl's place. She worked for me. She says he isn't packing so don't worry about that. He's a fat fuck, dark-skinned, short, shaved head.'

'How much does he owe you?'

'Why?'

'How much?'

'About twelve grand.'

'Okay. You have the bat here?'

'Sure.'

Sean pulls a metallic baseball bat from underneath his seat and hands it to Pretty Boy.

'Your money or his life?' Pretty Boy asks.

'Both, if you can,' Sean says. 'But it's more about the . . .' His phone rings, and he answers and listens for a few seconds. 'All right,' he says, and ends the call. 'He's coming down now. He's wearing a black jacket and a red baseball cap.'

Pretty Boy tucks the gun into his waistband.

'Always chamber a round, kid,' Sean says.

Pretty Boy pulls the gun out.

'You know how to do it?' Sean asks.

'I've watched all the Rambo movies,' Pretty Boy says, and chambers a round.

Sean laughs to himself, and Pretty Boy tucks the gun back into his waistband. Pretty Boy grabs the bat and steps out of the car.

Pretty Boy jogs to the block of flats and crouches in the darkness beside the entrance. A moment later, a man perfectly fitting the description strolls out of the building and heads for the BMW. Pretty Boy sneaks up behind the man and swings the bat into the man's back. The man collapses to the floor face-first and breaks his nose and a few teeth. The man shrieks in pain.

Pretty Boy drops the bat and pulls out the handgun. 'Shut the fuck up!' he commands, and aims for the man's head. 'Turn around!'

The man stops shrieking, but he groans as he turns to Pretty Boy. And soon as Pretty Boy sees the man's side profile, he recognises the man.

'Topper!' Pretty Boy shouts. 'What the fuck?'

Topper sees Pretty Boy and is shocked, but also relieved. 'Hey . . .' Topper says.

'Shut up! What the fuck's going on, Topper?'

'What, mate?' Topper asks, and crawls backwards to his car.

'Fucking hell!' Pretty Boy says, and takes a moment to think. 'I know you keep your money in your car, so you better hope you have enough in there.'

'Mate, I don't have shit. And I don't keep money in—'

Pretty Boy shoots Topper's left knee, and the loud bang reverberates through the street as Topper screams and grabs his knee.

'Shut up!' Pretty Boy shouts, and aims for Topper's crotch. 'I'll shoot your balls off if you don't shut up.'

Topper stops screaming, but he sobs and struggles with the pain.

'Where the fuck is the money, Topper?' Pretty Boy asks.

'Under the driver seat . . . but, mate, I got like twenty grand in there.'

'Twenty? In your fucking car? That's fucking stupid, Topper.'

Topper nods in agreement, and tears stream down his cheeks.

'The key and your phone. Now!' Pretty Boy instructs.

Topper pulls out his phone and car key and tosses them to the floor in front of Pretty Boy. 'Please . . . please, don't kill me,' Topper pleads. 'Please!'

'You act accordingly and maybe I won't,' Pretty Boy says, and picks up the key, phone, and bat. 'Don't do anything stupid, okay?'

'I won't. I promise.'

Pretty Boy walks past Topper to the car and unlocks it. He tucks the gun into his waistband and pulls out a black bin bag from underneath the driver's seat.

Pretty Boy drops the bag by Topper's feet. 'How much exactly is in here?' he asks.

'Everything I've got,' Topper says. 'Twenty-two thousand.'

'Fuck, Topper. You ought to be glad it's me, cos your number's up tonight.'

'Thank you, m—'

Pretty Boy swings the bat onto Topper's head, and Topper loses consciousness before his head crashes to the floor. Pretty Boy drops Topper's phone and stamps on it until it's crushed. He slots the car key into his pocket and smashes the car with the bat. He breaks the windows and lights, and as he batters the car's body, he notices the Range Rover's headlights flash. He stops and hears faint police sirens. He picks up the bin bag and runs to the Range Rover, and the passenger-seat door swings open as he approaches. He jumps into the car, and Sean speeds off even before he shuts the door.

Sean is excited and glances at Pretty Boy as he speeds away

from the estate, but Pretty Boy doesn't acknowledge Sean and fights to control his rage.

'That was fucking great!' Sean says, and pounds the steering wheel.

'You knew I know Topper.'

'Yeah,' Sean says, and smirks. 'That's the point, though. Needed to know I could fully trust you . . . needed to know the limit of your commitment. And you know Tyrone deserves to die.'

Pretty Boy glares at Sean.

'C'mon, you didn't kill him,' Sean says. 'I was sorta hoping you wouldn't too . . . he's a fucking fool, but he's an earner. You fucking set him straight though, hard too. And that's a message to all 'em fuckers round here. Don't fuck with us! Damn, that was some shit!'

Pretty Boy shoves the bin bag underneath his seat. 'There should be twenty-two thousand in there,' he says. 'Drop me off at the next station.'

'C'mon, let's go celebrate. We'll split the difference 50/50. That's five grand!'

'Just drop me off, Sean.'

'Whatever you say, kid,' Sean says, and laughs. 'I need you at the club early tomorrow. Tomorrow night is fucking big for us. We start the next step.'

'I've got somewhere to be tomorrow, so I'll get to the club when I get to the club.'

Sean laughs. 'Okay,' he says. 'There's a tube station around the corner. I'll drop you off there.'

Pretty Boy puts the gun back into the glove compartment and drops the bat in the back-seat footwell. Sean parks in front of Willesden Junction station, and Pretty Boy steps out without saying a word.

Sean grins and watches Pretty Boy walk into the station. 'You're a fucking star, kid,' Sean says to himself. 'My fucking star.'

THE NEXT DAY, TEN YEARS AGO

'You could run this city one day'

Pretty Boy steps into a chic brasserie on the edge of Covent Garden. He's five minutes early, but he spots Alan Pierce sat at a table in a corner of the room having a cheerful conversation with a waiter. Pretty Boy smiles and approaches the brasserie's hostess.

'Morning,' Pretty Boy says. 'Reservation with Alan Pierce at eleven, but I see he's already in.'

'Ah, yes, you are Alan's guest,' the hostess responds. 'He hasn't been waiting long, and either way, you're early.'

Pretty Boy nods, and the hostess leads him through the restaurant to Alan's table. Alan spots Pretty Boy approach and grins; he's glad to see him.

'My son,' Alan says to the waiter.

The waiter and hostess stare at Pretty Boy. He doesn't look at all related to Alan, and he and Alan don't seem that far apart in age for Alan to be his father. The waiter and hostess turn to Alan to confirm that he's joking, but Alan watches them with a straight face. They bury their discomfort behind polite smiles, but Alan can see beyond the smiles and enjoys watching them squirm.

Pretty Boy can sense their discomfort. 'Thank you,' he says to the hostess and smiles politely at her. He sits on the empty chair opposite Alan. 'Can I get a green tea, please?' he says to the waiter. 'No sugar.'

'Ah, that's that then,' Alan says. 'I've ordered for you, but I wasn't sure if you've graduated to coffee yet.'

Pretty Boy shrugs.

'Thank you,' Alan says to the waiter and hostess, and they leave.

'You enjoy that, don't you?' Pretty Boy says.

'Just a little,' Alan responds, and smirks. 'Anyway, happy birthday!'

Pretty Boy rolls his eyes.

'Come on! Don't be like this. You better enjoy these birthdays, till you start getting old like me.'

'You're not old.'

'Thank you. But the point remains, cheer up, enjoy your birthday. I, for one, look forward to your birthday because it's the only time I get to see you these past couple of years. Though I was worried I wouldn't reach you this year. What happened to the number you had last year?'

'Don't use it anymore.'

'No shit. But that's not what I asked.'

'I know. And there's no need to worry. I gave you my word that we'll always have this. And I always keep my word, like you told me.'

'Oh, you listened to me?'

'Yeah. To the stuff that made sense.'

They laugh.

'Don't blame you there,' Alan says. 'You were smarter than me then, and I can't imagine how smart you are now, and how smart you're going to be when you are my age.'

Pretty Boy shakes his head.

'Don't be modest with me,' Alan says. 'I know you. I've witnessed what you're capable of. You could run this city one day.'

'I don't want to.'

'I know . . . I know. But the thing is, why don't you?'

'I just don't.'

'Come on, I know you're not scared to fail. I—'

'Leave it, Alan. We can't have this conversation every time. I'm here. I'm healthy. I have no problem with your lot.'

'I know. I check every week.'

'Fair enough. And I don't need money.'

'Well . . . that brings the elephant into the room.'

Pretty Boy sighs.

'No, seriously, what do you do for money? You read a bloody fucking lot, so I set you up with the crim' barrister last year. She said you were the best apprentice she's ever had . . . for the month, before you just stopped showing up. Despite that, she's eager to have you back. I told her I'll talk to you about it today.'

Pretty Boy takes a moment to consider his response. He is grateful to Alan for the opportunity. It was challenging and exhilarating, and the barrister was great to him. But it didn't fit. And he tried hard to make it fit.

'Thank you, Alan,' he says. 'And thank Ms Fraser-Hulton . . . she's awesome. It just didn't feel right.'

Alan nods. He knows not to push Pretty Boy. The kid is a maverick, he thinks. But a maverick that easily could go down the wrong track.

'I saw you on the news a couple months ago,' Pretty Boy says. 'And in the papers. Fucking good job. Congratulations.'

'Ah, it wasn't just me. The whole Met had a part to play in that.'

'Not what I read. The kidnapper was running the show till you got involved. And it took you two days to find the girl.'

'Well . . .' Alan smirks. 'Yeah, but there's more to it than that.'

Pretty Boy knows what's more to it. The girl is the daughter of a Glaswegian property magnate in her first year in King's College University. A low-level South London drug gang kidnapped her to get her boyfriend, a second-year King's College student and part-time dealer, to pay his debts. The gang had no idea who she was, but when they found out, they got greedy and made their second mistake – they tried to ransom her to her father. All hell broke loose. He got the police, the press, and the government involved. And yet, there was no progress till Alan stepped in.

Alan reached out to a confidential and powerful contact in the underworld. Two days later, the girl was sent in a black taxi to Alan's house, and the youngest member of the gang, a sixteen-year-old teenage boy, handed himself to the police and confessed to the kidnapping. The other five members of the gang were found dead in a car in a Tesco car park the day after. As Alan says, you shouldn't trust everything you read in the papers. Their version of the story, which to be fair was corroborated by the police and the girl, had Alan outwitting the vicious teenage gang member with tracked fake cash and even a car chase.

Pretty Boy always suspected Alan had his feet in murky waters. But it didn't matter to him because Alan was nothing but a positive influence. And this taught Pretty Boy that if you look at anything carefully, you realise it's neither black nor white . . . it's some shade of grey. Pretty Boy also appreciated that Alan, on the surface, lived within his means. But he can see that Alan is not as careful anymore. He'd noticed Alan's watch the moment he sat down. The watch appears subtle, but it's worth near fifteen thousand pounds. He glances at Alan's leather shoes, and the details are exquisite. They're handmade.

Alan notices Pretty Boy glance at his shoes, and he wants to lie about them being a gift, but it has to be a good lie because Pretty Boy is . . . he spots their brunch arriving.

'Oh, good, food is here,' Alan says.

The waiter places a plate of lobster Benedict in front of Pretty Boy, and a full English breakfast in front of Alan.

'What do you think?' Alan asks, excited. 'Looks good, don't it?'

'Looks delicious! But you haven't tried it, right? Shellfish allergy and all.'

'I know. But it's what this place is known for, and I hear it's bloody good.'

'Let's see.'

They eat and banter about sports and movies. And for that time, Pretty Boy forgets he doesn't want to enjoy his birthday.

They finish eating, and their banter calms. It's time to leave. Till this time next year.

'Hannah sends her love and birthday wishes,' Alan says.

Pretty Boy laughs and shakes his head.

'What?' Alan asks.

'Hannah doesn't give a shit about me, and I'm okay with it.'

'Don't . . .'

'Stop trying to force it, Alan. I don't blame her. I understand.'

'I . . . Okay, fair enough. And for the record, I'm not saying it was her decision. She and I decided together. And she gives a shit about you . . . it was just hard, you know . . . she was . . .'

'Alan, it's okay. I'm fine.'

Hannah is Alan's wife, and there's a lot Pretty Boy wants to say about her. And about what led to *her* decision for him to leave their home. But it's best to allow Alan to come to that realisation himself. He's a detective. He ought to find out soon enough.

Pretty Boy picks out a wrapped gift box from his jacket and places it in front of Alan.

'What's this for?' Alan says, excited. 'You said no gifts, plus it's *your* birthday.'

'Open it.'

Alan unwraps the box and opens it to reveal an elegant leather wallet.

'For all the cash you'll be making as DCI.'

'What? How did you know that? I just found out two days ago, and it hasn't been announced yet.'

Pretty Boy stands. 'I keep my ear to the ground, like you told me.'

'You *did* listen.'

They smile at each other, and Pretty Boy walks away.

'I TOLD YOU HE DOESN'T LISTEN'

Yellow and Charlie, a stout professional powerlifter, flank the entrance to Diamonds.

'I told him to move, but he was talking back. So, I smacked the bloody fool,' Yellow says. 'What?'

'Bit harsh though, don't you think?'

'Yeah . . . but fuck him!' Yellow says, and they laugh.

'You hate everybody, don't you? Speaking of . . .' Charlie says, and gestures to Pretty Boy who's walking towards the club. 'Your friend's early today.'

'What?' Yellow asks, and turns to Pretty Boy. 'Oh, this motherfucker.'

'I saw you chatting to Rebecca earlier.'

'Yeah?'

'Don't do anything stupid, okay? Whatever happens between them is not your business.'

'Not yours either, is it, mate?' Yellow retorts. 'I'll handle this.'

'Sean's going to be mad if you mess with the kid.'

'I said I'll handle this.'

'Right. Just don't do anything stupid, cos I won't back you.'

'I don't need you for this, so just stay out of it.'

Pretty Boy approaches and greets both men with a nod. They nod back, but as Pretty Boy walks between them, Yellow places a hand on his chest. Pretty Boy is surprised and takes a step back.

'I need to search you,' Yellow says.

'What?' Pretty Boy asks.

'I need to search you. Pull out everything in your pockets.'

'I've been coming here for months, Yellow, never been searched.'

Yellow shrugs.

'Sean tell you to do this?' Pretty Boy asks.

'Boy, pull out everything in your pockets.'

'Yellow, answer me.'

'Boy, do what I say.'

'Yellow, don't call me boy.'

'Boy, I don't want to repeat myself anymore. Do it or fuck off, yeah?'

Pretty Boy is enraged but doesn't show it. He turns to Charlie, but Charlie doesn't acknowledge him. 'Charlie, what's this about?' he asks.

'Don't know, mate,' Charlie says, and shrugs. 'I just got to the door a minute ago.'

'Okay,' Pretty Boy says.

Pretty Boy pulls out his keys, wallet, and cell phone and places them on a small table beside the door.

'That all?' Yellow asks.

'What the fuck do you think?' Pretty Boy asks.

'Please, boy, don't give me any attitude. Take off your shoes, and—'

'Hey—' Charlie interjects.

'Charlie!' Yellow barks, and glares at him.

Charlie bites his tongue and turns away.

'Your shoes and socks . . . take 'em off,' Yellow instructs Pretty Boy.

Pretty Boy smiles and removes his trainers and socks.

'Give me the shoes,' Yellow says.

Pretty Boy offers Yellow his trainers, and Yellow snatches them. Yellow turns the trainers over and shakes them before he tosses them to the floor.

'Stretch them arms and legs out,' Yellow says.

'What?'

'C'mon, boy, I know you been arrested lots of times, you know what I mean.'

Pretty Boy nods and spreads out his arms and legs, and Yellow vigorously frisks him. Yellow becomes more vigorous around Pretty Boy's crotch, but Pretty Boy doesn't react.

'Raise your feet,' Yellow says.

Pretty Boy raises his feet, one at a time, for Yellow to see his soles.

'Okay,' Yellow says. 'Besides your little package, you clean.'

Charlie chuckles, and Pretty Boy grins.

'Pick up your stuff, boy, and get in or fuck off.'

Pretty Boy takes his time to wear his socks and trainers and return his items to his pockets. He nods at them and walks into the club. He hurries through the main room and skips up the staircase leading to Sean's office.

Sandy walks down the staircase and smiles when she spots Pretty Boy. 'Hello, sugar,' she says.

He ignores her and attempts to skip past, but she grabs his arm, and he stops. He turns to her and forces a smile, but she knows it's not genuine.

'Sugar,' she says. 'Don't go do anything stupid. Whatever it is, you take a deep breath before you step in there. Okay?'

'Okay,' he says, and nods.

She releases his arm, and he charges up the stairs and barges into Sean's office. Sean sits behind his desk and is surprised but unafraid as Pretty Boy charges towards his desk. Lucas, sitting across from Sean, spins towards Pretty Boy, looking pretty terrified. But Pretty Boy stops and glares at Sean.

Sean is perplexed. 'Okay, you're early, and that's good,' he says. 'But knock before you walk in next time. Lucas could've been deep-throating my dick.'

'Why the fuck you have them search me?' Pretty Boy asks.

'What?' Sean asks, even more perplexed.

'What?'

'Search you? Why the fuck would I do that?'

'You didn't?'

'Fuck no.'

Pretty Boy grins; he knows why Yellow did it. He grabs a beautiful pool cue that's hung on the wall and walks out of the office.

'Hey, no!' Sean shouts. 'Not my fucking cue! Fuck you going?'

'Going to kill somebody,' Lucas says, and laughs.

'Go fucking stop him then. And make sure he doesn't break my cue.'

'Sure,' Lucas says, and hurries after Pretty Boy.

Sean sighs and raises his handgun, which he'd been clutching under his desk since Pretty Boy burst in. He puts the gun back into a desk drawer and stands. 'Damn, Yellow,' he mutters, and walks out of his office.

Pretty Boy walks through the club and grabs a half-empty bottle of champagne from a booth. The man in the booth tries to chase after Pretty Boy, but Lucas grabs the man's neck.

'Forget it, mate,' Lucas says.

The man nods, and Lucas lets go of his neck. Lucas continues after Pretty Boy, but he's in no rush.

Pretty Boy steps out of the club and breaks the bottle on Yellow's head. Yellow crashes to the floor, and Pretty Boy pummels him with the pool cue. Charlie is shocked, but he gathers himself and attempts to stop Pretty Boy.

'Leave it, Charlie!' Lucas shouts.

Charlie stops in his tracks, and he's furious, but Lucas watches Pretty Boy with a smirk. The cue shatters, but Pretty Boy doesn't stop. He tosses the cue and attacks Yellow with kicks and stamps.

Sean steps out of the club and is incensed by the sight of his shattered cue. 'Shit!' he shouts. 'Lucas, I told you to fucking stop him!'

'I tried!' Lucas says. 'He didn't listen!'

'So? You want him to kill Yellow?'

Lucas shrugs.

Sean shoves Lucas aside. 'Stop it!' he shouts, but Pretty Boy ignores him. 'Fucking stop it!'

Pretty Boy ignores him again, but his kicks are nothing but taps because he's out of breath. He stops and glares at Yellow's battered, unconscious body as he catches his breath, and a crowd from inside the club gathers at the entrance. Rebecca is in front of the crowd, and she stares at Pretty Boy without an ounce of emotion. Pretty Boy walks towards her, and the crowd becomes tense, but she's not. He brushes past her, and the crowd parts for him to enter the club.

'Check for a pulse,' Sean says to Charlie.

Charlie checks Yellow's neck for a pulse and nods.

'Lucky geezer,' Lucas says, and turns to Rebecca. 'See what you done?'

'Fuck off, cunt!' Rebecca snarls.

'Both of you, shut up!' Sean says, and turns to Charlie. 'Call an ambulance, and when they ask what happened, you didn't see shit.' He turns to the crowd. 'Same thing goes for all of you, okay? Nobody saw shit. Now back inside, the show's over!' He focuses on a tall bouncer in the crowd. 'Ali, take Yellow's place at the door.'

Ali nods and steps outside as the crowd shuffles away.

'I told you he doesn't listen,' Lucas says.

'What?' Sean asks.

'He doesn't—'

'I heard what the fuck you said, you ginger cunt. Shut the fuck up and fuck off back to my office.'

Lucas nods and walks into the club.

'Make sure you take care of this, all right?' Sean says to Charlie.

'Sure, boss,' Charlie says.

'I know you guys stick together, but not on this one. The kid isn't to be touched. Yellow had this coming. And I know both of you know this.'

'Sure, boss,' Ali says.

Charlie doesn't respond.

'Charlie?' Sean calls.

'Yeah, sure,' Charlie says, but doesn't make eye contact with Sean.

'Good,' Sean says, and walks into the club.

Pretty Boy and Lucas sit beside each other at Sean's desk, and Lucas watches Pretty Boy with glee. Pretty Boy is calm, but he's struggling with the ferocity of his retaliation; he questions if it was deserved. Sean enters the office and walks to his chair but doesn't sit.

Sean ignores Lucas's grin and stares at Pretty Boy; Pretty Boy stares back. 'We've got important business to handle, so I will not waste any more time on that shit,' Sean says.

'Fine with me,' Pretty Boy says.

Lucas is surprised and considers objecting.

'But!' Sean says, and sits. 'You will pay for my cue. I loved that cue. It was my lucky cue . . . although it hasn't been bringing me any fucking luck lately. So maybe it had to go. And what better way to go than that, eh? Fucking lucky cue.'

Pretty Boy nods, and Lucas struggles to hide his anger.

'You'll still pay for it though,' Sean says.

'Only fair, I suppose,' Pretty Boy says.

'Suppose?' Sean asks.

Pretty Boy nods.

'How old are you again?' Sean asks. 'And why the fuck do you speak so fucking educated? I don't see you going to college.'

Lucas laughs.

'I read,' Pretty Boy says.

'You read,' Sean says, and smiles. 'Like books?'

'You have a problem with books?'

Sean laughs to himself. 'I suppose not,' he says.

'Both of you should try it sometime,' Pretty Boy says.

'I'm not a fag,' Lucas says.

'Really, Lucas?' Pretty Boy asks, dumbfounded.

Lucas shrugs.

'How does that even . . .' Sean says, and sighs. 'You say some real stupid shit, Lucas. You really need to read.'

'Whatever,' Lucas mutters.

'Anyway, down to business,' Sean says, and gestures at Lucas. 'Shit for brains and I have already gone through most of it, so I won't bore you with the unnecessary bits. What you need to know is we are selling a package tonight. A package of very high-grade pure cocaine that just fell in my lap. You don't need to know how it did, it just did.'

'Right,' Pretty Boy says, with more than a hint of doubt.

'Yes, right. We can't sell this package on the street. And I don't have the manpower or the patience to do what needs to be done to get it street-ready. Lucas has a connection with some Russians that can handle this sort of package. The Russians and I have negotiated a price, and all you need to know about that is after this deal, we can all retire . . . well, I can, probably not you two.'

'Lucas's connection?' Pretty Boy asks. 'I don't trust Lucas's connections.'

'Shut up,' Lucas says.

'It's all right,' Sean says to Pretty Boy. 'I did my due diligence; they seem legit.'

'Seem?' Pretty Boy asks.

'Don't question me,' Sean says. 'Deal is tonight. Go do whatever it is you do, but I want you back here at seven.'

'We need weapons?'

'What's with you today, Rambo?' Lucas asks.

Pretty Boy doesn't acknowledge Lucas, but the fact that Lucas called him Rambo makes him think Sean spoke to Lucas about last night.

'No,' Sean says. 'The Russians and I agreed there'll be no weapons, and I trust them.'

'Really? You do?' Pretty Boy asks.

'You don't listen,' Sean says, and laughs to himself. 'But don't worry, I've always got Smithy with me.'

'Okay, I'm leaving,' Pretty Boy says. 'I'll be back before seven.'

'Where are you going?' Lucas asks.

'Got drinks with Cherie,' Pretty Boy says.

'Fuck off!' Lucas says.

Pretty Boy laughs and stands.

'Wait,' Sean says, and tosses three rolls of cash across the desk to Pretty Boy. 'For yesterday. Actually, hold up.'

Sean tosses two more rolls of cash to Pretty Boy, and Lucas is confused. Pretty Boy notices Lucas's confusion, and that tells him Lucas doesn't know about last night.

'What about the stick?' Pretty Boy asks.

'It's not a stick. It's a cue,' Sean says. 'And we'll handle that later. It was custom-made, so I need to get in touch with them or find someone out here. Anyway, it's going to take a while.'

Pretty Boy nods, puts the money in his pockets, and walks out of the office. He makes a call as he walks down the stairs, and it's answered after one ring.

'Oleg,' Pretty Boy says. 'I'm good, you in the store?'

. . .

'Okay, I'm coming over now.'

. . .

'All right, safe.'

Pretty Boy steps out of the club and doesn't acknowledge Ali or Charlie, and they glare at him as he walks towards the street. But he stops and turns to them.

'Is he going to be okay?' Pretty Boy asks Charlie.

'Yeah . . . he will,' Charlie says.

'Good,' Pretty Boy says, and nods.

Pretty Boy walks towards his car and checks the time on his watch; it's 13:54.

'I HAVE IT ALL'

Pretty Boy walks into Hendon Off-Licence & Groceries. He spots Katerina sat on a high stool behind the cash register, and she looks vibrant with her long blonde hair tied up in a bun. Their eyes meet, and she's happy to see him.

'Hello,' she says, and her Russian accent is as strong as ever.

'Hello, Kat,' he says. 'How's our princess?'

She laughs. 'Anastasiya is good,' she says. 'Home with her nana.'

'Good. Your husband in the back?'

She nods. 'I'll open the door,' she says.

'Thanks,' he says, and walks through the aisles to a door at the back of the shop. He pushes the door open, and the entire shop is flooded with the noise from a loud television inside the back room. He hops in and shuts the door behind him. The room is filled to capacity, but immaculate. It's split in two, with the shop's merchandise on one side and Oleg's personal space on the other. Oleg's space is busy, with an array of sturdy metal lockers, a home cinema system, a long sofa, and a desk with a computer.

Oleg turns to Pretty Boy and smiles. He mutes the television and walks towards him with outstretched arms. Pretty Boy smiles; not only because he's happy to see Oleg, but also because he's amused by Oleg's daily attire. A sharp office shirt, slim black trousers, and black oxford shoes, regardless of the occasion.

'Welcome, my friend,' Oleg says, and they embrace.

'Thanks,' Pretty Boy says, and gestures to the home cinema system. 'I see you've upgraded.'

'Yes, my friend, I have Russian television now.'

'I noticed. Good for you.'

'I told you. If you want it, I'll get it.'

'What about my golden gun then?' Pretty Boy asks, and they laugh.

'If it exists, give me time, I'll get it for you. But it will cost you.'

'Everything does.'

'This is true. So, this is friendly visit, or you need something?'

'Planned to be a bit of both, but it took me like an hour to get here.'

'Yeah, the traffic around this time crazy, my man. Let's relax and talk.'

Oleg leads Pretty Boy to the sofa, and they sit.

'I need a weapon,' Pretty Boy says.

'Gun?' Oleg asks with enthusiasm. 'About time . . .'

'No. Something else. Something small. Something I can easily hide.'

'Still no guns, eh?' Oleg says, and shakes his head, disappointed. 'I have the new X26 Taser, what about that?'

'That'll work.'

Oleg bounces off the sofa and walks to the largest of the metal lockers. He pulls out a bunch of keys from his pocket and picks out the right key in an instant. He opens the locker, and there is a large safe inside. He enters the code and pulls open the thick door. The safe is split in two, and the smaller top compartment is filled with cash of different currencies, jewellery, and several sealed A4 envelopes. The bottom compartment houses an assortment of weapons. He picks the X26 Taser from an array of handguns and gestures for Pretty Boy to come over; he does.

'You like this?' Oleg asks, and hands him the Taser.

Pretty Boy examines it, and it looks and feels like a handgun.

'You know how to use it?' Oleg asks.

Pretty Boy smirks; it's the second time in as many days he's been asked that question. 'I guess,' he says. 'Like a gun, point and shoot.'

'I've never used one, but I think that's correct.'

'What's the range?'

'I hear around twenty feet, but I have not checked. You will need cartridge.'

Oleg picks up a Taser cartridge and hands it to Pretty Boy, who inserts it into the Taser.

'How much?' Pretty Boy asks.

'For you, my friend, five hundred.'

'Okay.'

Pretty Boy pulls out a roll of cash and hands it to Oleg. 'Here's a thousand,' he says. 'For the Taser and some credit.'

Oleg nods and puts the money into his pocket. 'I see we are doing well,' he says.

'I'm not doing bad, that's for sure.'

'So why you need Taser?'

'Leave it, Oleg.'

'C'mon,' Oleg says, and grins. 'You can tell Oleg.'

Pretty Boy smiles. 'I have a related question anyway,' he says. 'You know any Russians looking to get into the cocaine business in London?'

'Are you serious, my man?' Oleg asks, and laughs. 'We are talking Russians here.'

Pretty Boy nods and chuckles.

'But I've been hearing about some scary guys just arrived from Moscow. Red mob, we call them . . . cocaine is serious business for these people. Could be them.'

'Well, we're meeting some Russians tonight . . . Lucas's connection.'

Oleg shakes his head. 'No! No! Not that bastard,' he says. 'I don't trust him, and I know you don't trust him.'

'Sean does.'

'To hell with Sean! I have warned you about Lucas. You should have killed him that night. Now—'

'I know,' Pretty Boy interrupts. 'He's harmless now, though.'

'Harmless?' Oleg scoffs. 'There is no such thing as harmless, my friend. You never underestimate your enemy.'

Pretty Boy nods in agreement, and Oleg's eyes light up.

'You know some Russian guy came to me the other day for serious firepower,' Oleg says. 'Never heard of this man before, but Katerina's brother sent him to me, and he had a lot of money to spend. Bought five assault rifles, three handguns. Didn't even *hagger* price.'

'Haggle.'

'Yes, haggle. Negotiate, yes?'

Pretty Boy nods. 'You think he's with Lucas's Russians?' he asks.

'I don't know, my friend, but I think so. And I tell you I don't trust Lucas.'

Pretty Boy sighs.

'You know what, my friend?' Oleg says. 'I have a little pistol. It'll be perfect.'

'Already told you, Oleg, I don't want a gun.'

'Shut up! If you meet these Russians, you will need it. And don't worry, it won't cost you.'

'Don't want it, Oleg.'

Oleg picks up a pistol smaller than his palm from the safe and offers it to Pretty Boy, who is astonished by the size. Pretty Boy hands Oleg the Taser and takes the pistol. He examines it, and Oleg watches him with a smile.

'Wow,' Pretty Boy says. 'Never seen anything like this before.'

'I have it all,' Oleg says with pride. 'It's called Seecamp.'

Pretty Boy looks at Oleg with a raised eyebrow.

'Yes. Seecamp,' Oleg says. 'Just for close range and only six rounds. But as you can see, it is easily hidden.'

'Thank you.'

'You're welcome.'

Pretty Boy slots the Seecamp into his jacket.

'Still want this?' Oleg asks, and gestures to the Taser.

'Yeah.'

Oleg hands Pretty Boy the Taser, and Pretty Boy tucks it into his waistband.

Pretty Boy checks the time on his watch; it's 15:13. 'I've still got time, but I'm hungry,' he says. 'Got anything to eat?'

'Sure, I'll order something.'

'No, it's okay.'

'Stop it!'

'Thank you,' Pretty Boy says, and smiles.

'Good. And how's that beautiful girl I saw you with the other night?'

'Rebecca. She's fine.'

'Rebecca . . . yes,' he says, and smirks. 'She is more than fine, my friend. She's a fucking beauty.'

'Whatever you say.'

'Whatever I say?' Oleg asks, and chuckles. 'Where did you meet her?'

'The club,' Pretty Boy says.

'Oh,' Oleg says, and his smile disappears.

Oleg turns to close the safe, but he bursts out laughing and Pretty Boy laughs as well.

'Fuck you,' Pretty Boy says.

'Enjoy yourself, my young friend. You want to watch some American TV?'

'Sure.'

Oleg closes the safe and locker, and he and Pretty Boy walk back to the sofa.

'You have ESPN?' Pretty Boy asks.

'American sports channel? I think so.'

Oleg picks up a sizeable remote control from the sofa armrest and changes the channel to ESPN.

'Yep! ESPN,' Pretty Boy says, excited.

'Of course, don't test me,' Oleg says, and they laugh. 'Enjoy, I'll go get us some food.'

'Thanks.'

'No worries, my friend.'

Pretty Boy watches two hour-long episodes of SportsCenter back to back, and that dampens his excitement. Now he's midway through the repeat of an NBA game played the night before. And he's not enjoying it because the result and highlights have already been revealed on SportsCenter – twice. He's enjoying a bag of Haribo Starmix though, and that always keeps him content. He eats the last sweet in the packet and turns it over to be sure there is nothing left. He checks the time; it's 17:36. He turns to Oleg, who's sitting beside him and watching the game with even less interest.

'Got to go,' Pretty Boy says, and stands. 'Thanks for

everything, and please let me know soon as you speak to your TV guy. Need this at mine ASAP.'

'Sure, my friend,' Oleg says, and stands. 'And you better take care for tonight. Be sharp.'

'I will.'

They embrace, and Oleg smiles as he watches Pretty Boy walk out of the room. His smile disappears once the door shuts behind Pretty Boy, and he is worried. So much that he fabricated the story about the Russian guy buying serious firepower from him. He hates to lie to his young friend, but he'll do anything to keep the young man safe.

It's an unusually warm spring evening a couple days after Pretty Boy's seventeenth birthday, which he spent executing a meticulous jewellery heist. The heist was at the playboy son of a Qatari billionaire's penthouse in Kensington.

The playboy tried to hire Pretty Boy to steal a handmade watch from his younger half-brother's King's College London residence. The watch is worth just over a hundred thousand pounds, but that's not why the playboy wanted it. He wanted it because it belonged to their father who gifted it to his brother for achieving a first-class degree in his undergraduate course. But his brother didn't appreciate the watch; he never wore it, and just left it in its box somewhere in his room.

Pretty Boy refused the job on principle, and also because the playboy was an asshole. Pretty Boy decided to rob the playboy instead. The heist was Pretty Boy's sixth and his most audacious, but also the most fruitful by a large margin. And even more important, Pretty Boy learnt that he's fuelled more by principle than money.

Pretty Boy walks into an off-licence looking to buy a packet of Haribo Starmix. He'd been waiting in a coffee shop around the corner for one of his unreliable fences, who didn't show up or answer the phone. Pretty Boy nods at the pregnant young woman sitting on a high stool behind the cash register, and she acknowledges him with a smile.

He scans the shelves in front of the register and is surprised not to find Haribo with the other sweets and chocolates. But he walks through the aisles and is elated when he finds a shelf near the back of the store dedicated to the largest selection of Haribo products he's ever seen in an off-licence. He picks up a packet of Starmix and checks if the sweets are soft; they are. He picks up three more packets and heads for the cash register.

Suddenly, two short middle-aged men burst into the store and charge at the cash register. The men wield weapons – the stocky bald man has a butcher knife, and the slender man with a full head of black hair has a ball-peen hammer. They surround the cash register with their weapons raised and bark at the pregnant woman in Russian. But she isn't flustered and watches them with only mild interest.

'Where is Oleg?!' the stocky man demands in Russian.

She doesn't respond, but the slender man swings the hammer into the cash register, and she flinches. She examines the broken register and then glares at the slender man, but she doesn't speak.

'Tell us where Oleg is, or I will break your head!' the slender man shouts in Russian.

She shakes her head with disdain, and the stocky man swings the knife towards her neck and stops the blade just underneath her chin.

Now she is frightened but doesn't show it. Instead, she glares into the stocky man's eyes. 'You buy something, or you get out,' she says in English.

'What?' the stocky man shouts in English and continues in Russian. 'Are you crazy, woman? Where is Oleg?'

Pretty Boy hides behind the shelves, watching. He considered staying back till they finished robbing the cash register, but it's clear the men aren't here for the broken register. Pretty Boy doesn't have a weapon on him, just a backpack full of stolen luxury jewellery from the playboy's penthouse. He glances at the playboy's Breitling watch on his wrist; it's worth five thousand pounds at least.

Pretty Boy places his backpack on the floor and walks towards the register. 'Hey!' he calls.

The men turn to Pretty Boy. The slender man looks to the stocky man to handle Pretty Boy because the stocky man is the alpha of the pair and the one with the best understanding of the English language. But the stocky man understands just the bare minimum needed to work in a North London abattoir, and he struggles to articulate in English what's at the tip of his tongue in Russian.

He grunts and points his knife at Pretty Boy.

'Hey, Boris,' Pretty Boy says. 'Calm down.'

The slender man laughs. 'Why always Boris?' he asks the stocky man in Russian.

The stocky man ignores the slender man. 'Get on the floor!' he growls at Pretty Boy in Russian, and spit flies out of his mouth.

'Calm down,' Pretty Boy says again, and removes the Breitling watch. He offers it to the stocky man. 'Breitling . . . very expensive . . . five, six thousand pounds.'

The stocky man doesn't acknowledge the watch and glares at Pretty Boy.

'Seriously, Boris?' Pretty Boy asks, and gestures at the watch.

The slender man laughs again, but the stocky man glares at him, and he stops. The stocky man turns back to Pretty Boy and shakes his head.

'Okay, not good enough,' Pretty Boy says, and puts the watch back on. 'All right, I'll go get my bag, there's a lot more inside, good shit too!'

The stocky man doesn't respond.

'You don't understand me, do you?' Pretty Boy asks.

The stocky man doesn't respond.

'Okay. Idiot . . . bald tosser . . . fucking bastard . . .'

The stocky man grunts.

'Ah, you understand that. Fair enough, you stupid cunt. So, sweetheart, I'm going to get both these idiots to focus on me and then you run out, get to safety, and call the police. Okay?'

She shakes her head to refuse, but Pretty Boy doesn't notice because he's not looking at her; he's focused on the stocky man. It wouldn't matter even if he saw her anyway, because he's made up his mind and he's a stubborn fucker.

'Where is Oleg?' the stocky man barks at the pregnant woman in Russian and gestures to Pretty Boy. 'And who is this monkey?'

'Please don't do anything. I'll be fine,' she says in English.

'It's all right,' Pretty Boy says, and turns to the slender man. 'Oleg. You, Oleg?'

The slender man nods, even though he doesn't understand what Pretty Boy said.

'Cool,' Pretty Boy says. 'Boris and Oleg . . .'

'You! Where Oleg?' the stocky man asks Pretty Boy in English.

'What the . . .' Pretty Boy says, and gestures to the slender man. 'I thought he was Oleg.'

The stocky man grunts.

'Shit, calm down, fucking dumb and dumber over here,' Pretty Boy says, and gestures at himself. 'Me.' He gestures towards the end of the room. 'I go get bag.' He gestures to the watch. 'More inside.'

Pretty Boy turns and walks through the alcohol aisle.

'Stop! Stop!' the stocky man shouts in English.

Pretty Boy ignores him, and the stocky man charges.

Pretty Boy grabs a bottle of vodka and flings it at the stocky man's head. The bottle hits the stocky man flush in the face and breaks his nose and bursts his lips, and he stumbles backwards towards the register.

The slender man leaps onto the wine shelf to avoid a wild swing of the stocky man's knife, and the pregnant woman dives out from behind the register just before the stocky man crashes into it.

Pretty Boy charges at the slender man, but he trips on one of the wine bottles that has tumbled off the shelf and falls head-first onto another bottle. The slender man swings his hammer towards Pretty Boy's head, but Pretty Boy dodges the swing, and the hammer smacks onto the floor. The impact sprains the slender man's wrist, and he releases the hammer and screams in pain.

Pretty Boy tries to push off the floor, but his hand slips off another bottle. He falls onto his elbow, and the slender man kicks him in the chin. The slender man kicks him in the ribs and he groans. He tries to kick Pretty Boy's head, but he blocks with his arms. Pretty Boy clamps his arms around his head and curls up for protection, and the slender man continues to kick him in a frenzied attack. The slender man tries to step into a final ferocious kick, but he trips over a bottle and falls onto his sprained wrist. He clutches the wrist and writhes in pain.

The stocky man fights to his feet and staggers towards Pretty Boy. He's dizzy, bleeding from his nose, and struggling to breathe through his mouth. He stands over Pretty Boy and gathers himself before he raises his knife, but the steel barrel of a revolver nudges the back of his bald head.

The pregnant lady holds the gun to the stocky man's head, and a man in a sharp office shirt, slim black trousers, and oxford shoes holds a pump-action shotgun to the slender man's head.

'Boris, the Petersburg butcher,' the man with the shotgun says to the stocky man in Russian. 'I know things have changed for you here in London, but some things never change . . . you do not bring a knife to a gunfight, and you do not fuck with Oleg Jogovich.'

A few hours later, Pretty Boy lies on a sofa in the store's back room with a bag of ice on his swollen forehead. Oleg sits on a stool beside the sofa, watching television and holding another bag of ice on Pretty Boy's ribs. Pretty Boy wakes up with a groan and reaches for his ribs, but Oleg grabs his hand.

'Don't move,' Oleg says, and places Pretty Boy's hand onto the bag of ice on his forehead. 'Hold that, okay?'

Pretty Boy stares at Oleg for what seems an eternity before he nods. He tries to sit up, but he's in too much pain. He tries to scan the room, but he can't move his neck. He sighs and tries to speak, but his throat is too dry.

'Ah, I knew I forgot something,' Oleg says, and places Pretty Boy's other hand onto the bag of ice on Pretty Boy's ribs. 'Hold it. I'll be back with some water.'

Oleg hurries out of the room, and Pretty Boy fights through the pain to sit up. He scans the room as Oleg walks back in with a bottle of water.

'Hey! No, don't move,' Oleg says.

Pretty Boy ignores him and attempts to stand, but he can't.

'Take it easy or you hurt yourself more,' Oleg chides.

Oleg makes a point to show that it's a fresh bottle of water before he opens it. He hands the open bottle to Pretty Boy, who gobbles down half the bottle.

'Thanks,' Pretty Boy says, and stares at Oleg.

'Is everything okay?' Oleg asks.

'Where's my bag?'

'Ah,' Oleg says, and gestures to a desk behind Pretty Boy.

Pretty Boy turns around to see his backpack on the desk beside his watch. He turns back to Oleg and attempts to nod, but grimaces in pain.

'You are brave,' Oleg says. 'And that is half the battle.'

Pretty Boy shrugs.

'But you need to learn to fight,' Oleg says.

Pretty Boy smiles, and Oleg smiles back.

'Where am I?' Pretty Boy asks.

'In my office . . . also the stockroom, as you can see.'

Pretty Boy nods.

'I'm Mr Jogovich,' Oleg says. 'But my friends call me Oleg. You call me Oleg for the rest of your life.'

'Okay, Oleg.'

'But my wife, she prefers that you call her Katerina . . . not sweetheart.'

Pretty Boy chuckles.

'I apologise for that,' Pretty Boy says.

'Oh, I don't mind. But Katerina, you don't want to mess with her.'

'I'm sure.'

They both smile and Pretty Boy finishes his bottle of water.

'You want another bottle?' Oleg asks.

'Nah, I'm good.'

Oleg nods. 'So, my friend,' he says, and gestures to Pretty Boy's bag. 'I can help you with that. It's what I do.'

Pretty Boy fights back a smile. 'Okay, Oleg,' he says. 'I'm listening.'

18:44

'Trust goes out the window'

Pretty Boy checks his watch as he walks towards the club; it's 18:44. He greets Ali and Charlie with a nod, and they both nod back before he walks inside. He goes through the main room, which is busier than he expected for the time of the day, and stops at the bar. A bartender hurries to him.

'Hey, George,' Pretty Boy says. 'Could you please send a glass of orange juice with ice up to Sean's office?'

'Sure,' George says.

Pretty Boy reaches for his wallet, but George stops him.

'It's for me,' Pretty Boy says.

'I know,' George says.

Pretty Boy nods and heads up to Sean's office. He knocks on the door and waits for a couple seconds before he opens it and walks in. Sean turns away from the television to Pretty Boy, and Lucas looks up from a magazine.

'Early again, kid,' Sean says, and mutes the television. 'Love the enthusiasm.'

'Where did you go?' Lucas asks.

'He's reading,' Pretty Boy says to Sean and gestures at Lucas. 'That's quick.'

Lucas raises the magazine to display its pornographic cover.

'Right,' Pretty Boy says, and sits beside Lucas.

'Where did you go?' Lucas asks again.

'Fuck off, Lucas.'

'Where did you go?' Sean asks.

'You too?' Pretty Boy asks Sean.

Sean shrugs. 'Lucas thinks you went to get a weapon,' he says.

'Really?' Pretty Boy asks.

'Yeah, I do,' Lucas says.

'Our relationship with the Russians is based on trust,' Sean says. 'We agreed no weapons. When we meet they might search you, and if they find a weapon . . . not good. Trust goes out the window . . . the relationship is fucked. I'm sure you understand.'

'Fair enough. And yes, I did go get a weapon,' Pretty Boy says, and places the Taser on the desk.

'I fucking told you,' Lucas snarls.

Sean laughs. 'To be honest,' he says to Pretty Boy, 'I would have been disappointed if you didn't. I would have.'

'Fuck that,' Lucas says. 'He could've fucked things up for us. We are talking serious money here.'

'I know, I know,' Sean says.

'What the fuck is that going to do, anyway?' Lucas asks, and gestures to the Taser.

Pretty Boy shrugs and picks up the Taser. 'We can try it on you,' he says, and points the Taser at Lucas's head.

'What the fuck!' Lucas screams, and raises his arms to protect his head.

'Stop!' Sean shouts.

Pretty Boy laughs, but he notices that Lucas is horrified. 'C'mon, Lucas, I wasn't going to do it,' he says.

Lucas lowers his arms, but he is seething.

'Shit, Lucas, I was just fucking about,' Pretty Boy says.

Lucas nods, but it's obvious he's still mad about it.

'Okay, then,' Pretty Boy says, and turns to Sean. 'What are we waiting for?'

'A call,' Sean says. 'They'll call Lucas at seven and let him know where we meet.'

Pretty Boy is surprised. 'They decide where we meet?' he asks. 'You really trust these guys.'

'Yeah, I do,' Sean says.

There is a tap on the door.

'It's for me,' Pretty Boy says, and stands.

Pretty Boy hurries to open the door, and a half-naked waitress stands outside with his glass of orange juice. He takes the glass and gives her a tenner as a tip, and she smiles before she saunters off. He shuts the door and walks back to the desk.

'What's that?' Sean asks, and gestures to the glass.

'Orange juice,' Pretty Boy says.

'Plain?'

'Yeah.'

Sean shakes his head. 'Get some alcohol into your system,' he says. 'It helps.'

'Yeah, and then I'll end up like Lucas,' Pretty Boy says, and they all laugh.

Sean unmutes the television and watches CNN. Pretty Boy watches as well as he enjoys his glass of juice, but Lucas ignores it and flicks through his *Penthouse* magazine.

Several minutes later, Lucas's phone rings, and Sean and Pretty Boy turn to him with anticipation. Lucas checks the caller ID and nods, and Sean mutes the television. Lucas answers the call, and Sean leans forward as if trying to listen in.

'Yeah, we're ready,' Lucas says into the phone. 'Yeah, I know the place.'

. . .

'All right,' Lucas says, and ends the call.

'Where?' Sean asks.

'Wapping,' Lucas says.

'Where's that?' Sean asks.

'By the docks in East London,' Pretty Boy says.

'East London?' Sean asks.

'Yeah,' Lucas says. 'When we get close, I'll call them, and they'll direct us.'

'Let's get it on!' Sean shouts, and switches the TV off.

They stand, and Lucas leads them out of the office, but Sean stops.

'Head down to the car, I'll be there in a minute,' Sean says, and steps back into the office.

'We'll wait,' Lucas says, and attempts to follow Sean back into the office.

'For what?' Pretty Boy says. 'Let's go, mate.'

'You heard the man,' Sean says, and shuts the door in Lucas's face.

Pretty Boy and Lucas head down to the Range Rover, which is parked in front of the club. Pretty Boy waits by the back door, but Lucas doesn't unlock the car. Lucas is distracted watching the entrance for Sean.

'You're going to open the door, right?' Pretty Boy asks.

'Yeah . . . yeah,' Lucas says, and unlocks the car.

Pretty Boy steps into the car, but Lucas stays outside. Pretty Boy watches Lucas, and it seems Lucas is anxious, which worries Pretty Boy. But Sean walks out of the club, and Lucas relaxes before he steps into the driver's seat.

Sean enters the passenger seat, and as he puts on his seat belt, he notices Lucas watching him. 'Why the fuck you staring so hard?' he asks. 'C'mon, fucking drive, let's go.'

Lucas nods and drives, and Sean pulls a CD from his pea coat. Sean inserts the CD into the stereo, skips to the sixth track, and turns the volume up. He closes his eyes as the ominous and experimental sounds of Phil Collins' 'In the Air Tonight' begins, nods along as it builds, and grins with excitement when Phil Collins starts to sing.

Sean's grin transforms into an intense glare as the song fires him up, and Pretty Boy watches the transformation with mild amusement. He shrugs and turns to watch the street.

'NEVER HAVE, NEVER WILL'

Lucas parks underneath a flickering streetlight on a quiet Wapping street, and Sean turns down the stereo which has been blaring 'In the Air Tonight' on repeat for the entire journey.

Lucas calls the Russians. 'We're here,' he says.

. . .

'All right, we'll be there in two minutes.'

. . .

'No need,' Lucas says, and turns to Sean. 'We're close.'

'Fucking move then,' Sean says.

Lucas drives. 'So bloody excited, I need to piss,' he says.

'You're going to have to hold it, mate,' Pretty Boy says.

'You're going to have to fuck off, mate,' Lucas retorts.

Two minutes later, Lucas turns into a long gravel driveway that leads to an abandoned warehouse and parks beside a black Lexus GS. 'We're here,' he says.

They step out of the car, and Sean can't contain his excitement. Pretty Boy scans the derelict building; he's anxious but doesn't show it. Lucas is a bag of nerves.

'Get the bag,' Sean says to Lucas, and strides to the warehouse entrance.

Sean steps into the warehouse and stops due to the darkness. He waits for his eyes to adapt to the darkness and spots three men underneath the only ceiling light switched on in the vast open space. Pretty Boy steps in and Sean leads them towards the men.

The three men are on one side of a stack of heavy-duty slabs, and the man in the middle sits on a folding chair, oozing elegance. He's tall, with long, flowing blond hair, and looks like he was born in his charcoal grey three-piece suit. He's in his mid-twenties but has the refinement of a cultured middle-aged gentleman. Both of the men standing beside him are robust and wrapped up in long black overcoats. The older man is in his mid-forties and doesn't have a hair on his head beside his icy-white eyebrows. The younger man is in his twenties and doing his best to emulate the elegant man's hairstyle. They are the Russians. The elegant Russian stands as Sean approaches.

'Hello, Viktor,' Sean says, and they hug.

'Hello, Sean,' Viktor says. His accent has only a hint of Russian. 'You find the place easy?'

'Yeah,' Sean says, and nods.

'Good. We don't have too long, the police patrol the area often.'

'No problem.'

Viktor gestures to a folding chair on the other side of the slabs, and Sean nods. Sean leads Pretty Boy to their side, and Viktor walks back to his chair. Sean and Viktor sit across from each other, and Pretty Boy stands to Sean's right, across from the younger man.

'My associates,' Viktor says, and gestures to the older man. 'Dmitry.'

Dmitry greets Sean and Pretty Boy with a nod, and they nod back.

'Egor,' Viktor says, and gestures to the younger man.

Viktor waits for Egor to greet Sean and Pretty Boy, but Egor just glares at Pretty Boy. Viktor turns to Sean and waits for Sean to introduce Pretty Boy, but Sean couldn't care less about that.

'Where is Lucas?' Viktor says.

Before Sean answers, Lucas steps into the warehouse with a red duffel bag and hurries towards the table. Viktor watches Lucas with a smile and stands. Lucas smiles back and walks to Viktor; they hug.

'Hello, Lucas,' Viktor says.

'What's good, Viktor?' Lucas asks.

'Everything, always,' Viktor says, and turns to Sean. 'I love this guy . . . funny guy.' He runs his hand through Lucas's hair. 'And we don't have many redheads in Moscow.'

Egor speaks in Russian but everybody hears him say the word 'nigger'. Viktor, Lucas, and Sean turn to him. He doesn't acknowledge them and stares at Pretty Boy, but Pretty Boy doesn't look his way. After a few tense seconds, Pretty Boy turns to Egor, and Egor grins at him.

Viktor forces a laugh to break the tension. 'Egor says he's thankful that we don't have that many . . .' he says, and considers his next words, '. . . *black people* in Moscow.'

Lucas and Egor laugh, but Viktor is embarrassed, and Sean is infuriated. Pretty Boy is not fazed; it'll take a lot more than that to rile him up. Dmitry is unconcerned by it all, but he's impressed with Pretty Boy's stoicism.

'Any toilets in here?' Lucas asks Viktor.

'I told you,' Viktor says to Sean, and gestures at Lucas. 'Funny guy.'

'Like, really,' Lucas says, and grabs his crotch.

'C'mon, Lucas, look around you, this place is abandoned, there's nothing in here,' Viktor says. 'Go outside. No one here cares to see your little cock.'

Egor laughs, and Lucas forces a smile. Viktor sits, and Lucas walks around the slabs to stand beside Sean and across from Dmitry.

'Shall we get to it?' Sean asks.

'I love your accent,' Viktor says. 'Where's it from exactly?'

'Chicago.'

'Real nice.'

Sean doesn't respond; he's bored with the preamble.

'Ah, yes,' Viktor says with excitement. 'Did you vote for George Bush?'

Sean is confused. What the fuck is this Russian fuck on about? he thinks.

'The last couple of years I've met a lot of Americans,' Viktor says. 'Not one of them like George Bush, and they all say they didn't vote for him. But then that's not possible because he is your President. Personally, I like him. He's a strong leader. Responded well after 9/11. But you Americans now complain that the response was excessive.' He shakes his head. 'Usual American bullshit, because that's what all of you wanted after the attack . . . vengeance . . . furious vengeance. Now you don't like how it makes you feel.'

Sean takes a deep breath; he's uncertain how to respond.

'Did you vote for him?' Viktor asks.

'Didn't vote,' Sean says.

'Why?'

'Don't know. Never have, never will.'

Viktor is annoyed by the response, and Sean struggles to remain calm. Lucas forces a smile and attempts to break the tension, but Viktor shushes him with a finger-wag.

'Fair enough,' Viktor says. 'I hope Bush wins re-election. We need strong leaders right now to eradicate this wave of terrorism. Like with us back in Russia with the Chechens, we—'

'Viktor,' Sean interrupts. 'I didn't come here for a lecture on communism.'

'Communism?' Viktor asks. He forces a smile, but it's clear that he's annoyed. He opens his mouth to speak but doesn't and takes a moment to calm down. 'What do you know about communism?'

'Not much,' Sean says, and gestures to Pretty Boy. 'But I'm sure the kid could tell you all about it. He's one of them clever ones.'

Viktor nods and turns to Pretty Boy. 'So, what do you know about communism?' he asks.

'Communism is a form of government largely derived from Marxist theory,' Pretty Boy says. 'Ideally, everything is equally shared among all citizens to create a classless, moneyless society. But nothing's ever ideal, as evidenced by the fall of the Soviet Union.'

Viktor grins.

'Told you he's a clever one,' Sean says.

Viktor nods. 'I like you,' he says to Pretty Boy. 'But you remind me of my brother. I'll bet you always think you're the smartest person in the room.'

Pretty Boy doesn't respond, and Viktor studies him.

'Really nice watch,' Viktor says, and raises his watch. It's the same as Pretty Boy's – a TAG Heuer Monaco V4. 'Do you mind if I ask where you got yours? Cos it's very rare and very expensive. And I'm not suggesting you can't afford it. Just, you might know someone that knows someone that could get me a good deal. I'm sort of a collector.'

'I don't,' Pretty Boy says. 'And I didn't buy it either. I got it from a . . . let's call him a friend.'

'This *friend* just gave you a watch worth eighty thousand pounds?'

'Something like that,' Pretty Boy says, and shrugs.

Egor speaks in Russian, and again everybody hears the word 'nigger'.

Sean and Viktor glare at Egor, and Lucas fights back laughter.

Pretty Boy chuckles and shakes his head with disdain, and this seems to infuriate Egor.

Egor opens his mouth to speak, but Viktor raises a hand to stop him.

'Egor,' Viktor says, 'thinks you stole it.'

'He understands English then?' Sean asks.

'More or less,' Viktor says. 'But he can't speak it.'

'I usually wouldn't bother with your question, but I think the answer's pertinent,' Pretty Boy says to Viktor and points to Egor. 'Especially for the Hitler Youth.'

Viktor smiles.

'This watch belonged to the last person who called me nigger twice,' Pretty Boy says.

Viktor's smile disappears. 'You killed him because he called you nigger twice?' he asks.

'I've seen a good number of cocksuckers killed for saying it just the once,' Sean says.

'I think he gave me the watch because he thought it'd stop me killing him,' Pretty Boy says.

'Did it?' Viktor asks.

'Not exactly,' Pretty Boy says. 'Cos I wasn't going to kill him, anyway. We ran into each other at a bar in Chelsea. I was meeting somebody about a thing. When the meeting was done, I stayed for a bit to enjoy myself. So, I'm at the bar waiting to order a drink, and this belligerent posh git is waiting impatiently beside me with a couple of his friends. The Erykah Badu-looking bartender . . .' Pretty Boy stops and turns to Egor. 'I'm sure you know who Erykah Badu is,' he says, and turns back to Viktor. 'Anyway, Miss Badu serves them their drinks, but she got the order wrong, and the posh git screams at her. She apologises and goes off to correct the order, but he turns to his friends and calls her a *"fucking dumb nigger"*. I heard it, but she didn't, so I wasn't bothered. His friends though, they stiffen up and gesture over his shoulder to me as they urge him to calm down. But no calming him, he turns to me and says, *"So, nigger, what the fuck are you going to do about it?"* I just smile, but still, he says, *"I thought so, nigger."* He gets his drinks and swaggers off to his table. I get my virgin mojito . . .'

Pretty Boy smiles because Viktor is evidently perplexed by his choice of drink.

'I know,' Pretty Boy says. 'I don't drink alcohol. Nothing much to it, I just don't.'

Viktor nods.

'Anyway,' Pretty Boy continues. 'I enjoy the mojito and go wait for the posh git in my car. About an hour later, he stumbles out of the bar with a girl. They get in a taxi, and I follow them back to a house in Chelsea. I wait outside till ten the next morning when the girl leaves. Now I'm sure it's the git's house, so I make a note of his home security system. The next Monday, I break into his house about noon. I make sure he lives alone, then I disable the security system. I sit in the dark in his bedroom until he returns from work. It was quite late too; he's a hard-working investment banker at Goldman's. He steps into his room, and he is exhausted, maybe even a little tipsy. He switches on the lights, and there I am, and he's fucking terrified because he recognises me.

'He cries and begs for his life, but I never touch him. I just tell him to gather every item of value in the house and put them into a bag, and I walk around the house with him as he does it. You see, he had no idea that I'd disabled his security system, so I let him trigger every silent alarm in that house. It made him very compliant because he was expecting the police to turn up at any moment.

'After we'd gathered all his valuables, we settle in his beautiful kitchen. He's getting antsy now because he's thinking I'll escape with all of his precious shit before the police turn up. But no, I ask him to light a fire in the sink, and that's when it dawns on him that I wasn't going to be taking anything away. He becomes distraught, and I can see that he's thinking about grabbing a knife from the block on the counter. But I know he won't do it; he doesn't have it in him. Plus, he's still hoping that the police will arrive at any moment. He begs and begs. And then he offers me this watch.'

Pretty Boy taps his watch. 'He says it was his dad's. Some shit about his dad leaving it to him when he died. He swears it's the most valuable thing in his life. I tell him to place the watch on the counter and fucking light the fire already. He does as he's told. He lights the fire, and I drop the bag in the fire.

'We watch it burn for about five minutes, and I have to tell you that smell was fucked up. But even more fucked up was the look in his eyes when he realised there was no one coming to help . . . the look when he lost all hope. That's what all of it was for. Because that feeling will live with him forever. He'll never *ever* feel safe again.'

Pretty Boy takes a deep breath and looks at everyone; they are all captivated, besides Dmitry, who couldn't give a shit.

'When the fire went out, everything was destroyed. Some shit burnt, some melted together. Sad sight, really,' Pretty Boy says. 'I thanked him for not resisting and promised to check in on him the week after. I picked up the watch, thanked him for that too, and walked out of his front door.'

'Did you go back?' Sean asks.

'Yes. I went back the next Wednesday, but the house was empty. He was gone.'

'You should have just killed him,' Viktor snarls.

'Why?' Pretty Boy asks, and turns to Egor. 'He only called me nigger twice.'

Viktor yields with a nod, but Egor's fury threatens to boil over, and Sean watches Pretty Boy with a proud smile.

'Shall we get to it then?' Sean says to Viktor. 'You said we don't have much time.'

'Sure,' Viktor says, and nods at Dmitry.

Dmitry places a black duffel bag on the slabs, and Sean reaches for it.

'No,' Viktor says, and wags a finger. 'Put your bag on the table first.'

Sean nods, and Lucas drops the red bag on the table. Sean opens it and grins as he looks through the neat bundles of fifty-pound notes. But Viktor opens the red bag and is expressionless as he scans the bricks of cocaine.

'As you see,' Viktor says, and closes the bag. 'Doing business with me is easy.'

'I do,' Sean says.

'I will not waste your time checking the product. We both know what happens if it is not what you say it is.'

'Okay. But you'll have to bear with me cos I've got to count this. I don't mess with my money.'

'Okay,' Viktor says, and smiles.

Sean turns the bag over, and the bundles fall onto the slab. He licks the thumb and index finger of his right hand and counts the heap of cash.

'This is going to take forever,' Lucas says. 'I'm going outside to piss.'

'Just wait till he's done,' Pretty Boy says.

Lucas ignores Pretty Boy and walks off, and Sean is too engrossed counting the money to care. Pretty Boy watches Lucas walk out of the warehouse and then focuses on Egor. Pretty Boy is anxious but fights to appear calm, and Viktor smirks because he senses Pretty Boy's anxiety. Pretty Boy notices the smirk, and it exacerbates his anxiety. He slots his hands in his jacket pockets, grabs the Seecamp, and holds his finger over the trigger, ready to shoot at a moment's notice.

'Kid, fifty multiplied by seventy-five?' Sean asks.

'What?' Pretty Boy asks, and turns to Sean.

Egor reaches into his coat to pull out a long-barrelled gun, but Pretty Boy spots him and pulls the Seecamp quicker. Pretty Boy shoots twice before Egor raises his gun, and one bullet pierces through Egor's forehead. Pretty Boy hears a shotgun blast and feels Sean's head explode onto him, but he doesn't cower and turns to Viktor. Viktor is unarmed and recoils in fear. Pretty Boy shoots him in the mouth. Pretty Boy hears a shotgun pump, but he shoots Viktor in the neck before ducking behind the slabs, and a shotgun blast barely misses his head.

Dmitry pumps his shotgun and shoots through the slabs at Pretty Boy, but the shot doesn't penetrate. Pretty Boy raises his head over the slabs and shoots as Dmitry pumps the shotgun, but he misses him. Pretty Boy shoots again, and the bullet grazes Dmitry's arm.

Dmitry shoots back at Pretty Boy, but Pretty Boy ducks in time to evade the blast. Pretty Boy jumps to his feet and aims at Dmitry's head as he pumps his shotgun. Pretty Boy pulls the trigger, but there is no gunfire because he is out of bullets. Dmitry aims for Pretty Boy's torso, and Pretty Boy turns away as Dmitry pulls the trigger, but there is no blast because Dmitry is also out of rounds.

Pretty Boy is stunned, but he snaps out of it and reaches for the Taser in his waistband. The Taser's not there, and he remembers he left it on Sean's desk.

He watches Dmitry reload the shotgun, and his heart pounds out of his chest. Suddenly, it feels like time slows for him, and his vision widens to become almost panoramic. He scans for a weapon and spots a Desert Eagle beside Egor's dead body. He hears Dmitry pump the shotgun and flings the Seecamp at Dmitry's head before he dives across the slab. Dmitry shoots, and the blast misses Pretty Boy's legs by inches. Pretty Boy crashes onto Egor and grabs the Desert Eagle. He spins to Dmitry as Dmitry pumps the shotgun and shuts his eyes as he shoots back.

Pretty Boy shoots until the Desert Eagle is out of bullets, but he can still hear Dmitry moving. He opens his eyes to see Dmitry staggering after being hit by all nine shots. One in the neck, one above the cheek, seven in the chest, and two of those pierced through Dmitry's bulletproof vest. Dmitry falls to his knees and nods at Pretty Boy before he collapses.

Pretty Boy jumps to his feet. He's covered in other people's blood from head to toe but couldn't care less until he sees what's left of Sean's head. His euphoria is replaced with rage, and he heads to the entrance with the Desert Eagle raised, forgetting it's out of bullets. He peeks out the warehouse and scans the driveway, but he can't find Lucas. He steps out, but he hears a car approach on the gravel driveway and darts back into the warehouse.

A black Ford Focus with tinted windows parks behind the Lexus, and a tall, broad-chested man with piercing eyes steps out of the passenger seat. He's casually dressed in dark colours but wearing unusually expensive trainers, especially for a man in his forties.

The man examines the Lexus and the Rover. 'Lucas,' he softly calls.

There is no response, and the man walks towards the warehouse, but the Lexus's boot pops open. He grabs a handgun tucked in his waistband and approaches the boot, and it opens just enough for Lucas to peek out.

'C'mon, Lucas, it's me, Jack,' the man says, and tucks his gun back into his waistband. 'Get out of the boot.'

Lucas pushes the boot open and scans the driveway before he climbs out. Lucas is frantic, and this worries Jack.

'What's going on, Lucas? What happened?' Jack whispers.

'It wasn't my—' Lucas responds.

'Lower your voice. Is Viktor alive?'

'I . . . I don't know . . . I don't . . . it was a shoot-out in there!'

Jack pulls away from Lucas, and Lucas attempts to speak, but Jack raises a hand to stop him.

Jack ponders for a few seconds. 'If he's dead,' he whispers, 'we're all fucked. You. Me. Everyone. Fuck.'

'I know.'

'Fucking hell, Lucas. Both your guys had guns, then?'

'I don't know, Jack. I—'

'When was the last gunshot?'

'Err . . .'

'Don't tell me you don't know. Think.'

'Five minutes . . . less, maybe . . . maybe not . . .'

'Stop. Five minutes it is. You have a gun?'

Lucas shakes his head, and Jack nods. Jack walks to the Ford Focus, and the passenger-side window lowers as he approaches. He leans into the car, and Trevor, a strapping black man in his late twenties, sits on the driver's seat. Mustafa, a lanky full-bearded Arab man in his late twenties, and Glenn, a tall hairy man in his early thirties, sit in the back. All three are casually dressed in dark colours as well.

'Boys,' Jack says with a natural air of authority. 'Job's changed. It's no clean-up anymore. We don't know what's happened, so we'll need to go in ready.'

'What the lad say, gaffer?' Trevor asks, and gestures at Lucas.

'There was a gunfight—'

'Wait,' Glenn interrupts. 'Gunfight? I thought—'

'Yes, Glenn,' Jack says. 'That's why the job's changed. The lad's guys had guns too.'

'I didn't—' Glenn says.

'Not now,' Mustafa interrupts.

'No, it's okay,' Jack says. 'Let him finish.'

'I didn't sign up to step into no bloody gunfight,' Glenn says. 'You said this was easy money, Jack. The wife's eight months along.'

'I understand, Glenn. I really do,' Jack says. 'But before you do or say anymore, you need to know that if we don't do this proper, we're all dead. And not just us either . . . our families, everyone we care for. Think about it. People who pay twenty grand each for a clean-up job do not fuck about. We're nothing to them. But someone very special to them is in that warehouse. We need him to be alive . . . we need him to need our help . . . or else we're dead men walking.'

Jack glances at Trevor and Mustafa, and both seem eager. But Glenn is still anxious.

'And if you leave now, Glenn, and we get it done,' Jack says, 'they'll want their money back from you, and they'll come for it the only way they know. Plus, they'll make an example out of you. That's just how this works. You make a deal with the devil, you best deliver.'

'How's it back there, Musti?' Trevor asks.

'Just fine, Trev,' Mustafa says.

'Watch your feet, though,' Trevor says. 'You don't want to step in Glenn's piss.'

Mustafa and Trevor laugh, but Jack doesn't react because he's observing Glenn. Glenn doesn't respond either because he's focused on the warehouse and consumed with fear.

Glenn turns away from the warehouse and sees Jack watching him. 'Fuck yourself back to Africa, Akabusi,' he says to Trevor.

Trevor and Mustafa burst out laughing, and Glenn forces laughter.

Jack knows Glenn's laughter isn't genuine, but he smiles at him anyway. 'We're all in, boys?' he asks.

'Yeah, boss,' Trevor says, and Glenn and Mustafa nod.

'Guns and extra ammo,' Jack instructs Mustafa.

Mustafa pulls a gym bag from underneath the driver's seat. He picks out a handgun and tucks it into his waistband. He gives Glenn and Trevor a gun and two extra magazines each and gives Jack two magazines. He puts two magazines into his pocket and shoves the bag back underneath the driver's seat. Jack opens the glove compartment and picks out a flashlight and his Metropolitan Police ID card, which is attached to a lanyard.

'We wear our badges,' Jack says, and wears his ID around his neck. 'Go in clean-like, but with guns ready in case things go south in a hurry.'

They wear their police IDs and chamber a round in their handguns.

'Follow my lead, boys,' Jack says. 'And I'll get you through this safe and sound, like always.'

They nod and step out of the car, and Jack leads them to Lucas.

'We're going in,' Jack says to Lucas. 'You first.'

Lucas is horrified and attempts to object, but Jack shakes his head and gestures for Lucas to lead. Lucas curses underneath his breath and leads them to the warehouse entrance. He steps in, and it's pitch-black because all the ceiling lights are switched off. Lucas attempts to turn around, but Jack places a firm hand on his back to stop him. Lucas continues for a few more steps before Jack grabs his shoulder, and he stops.

'It's the police,' Jack shouts, and his voice echoes around the vast room. 'Is anyone here?'

There is no response.

'We received reports of loud disturbances coming from this location, consistent with gunfire,' Jack says. 'If you are hurt, we are here to help. But if you are armed, put your gun down and surrender. Now!'

There is no response. Jack switches on his flashlight and searches the room, but there is no movement. Jack directs the bright beam of light to the dead bodies around the slabs. 'Move,' he instructs Lucas.

Lucas leads the way to the bodies, and Jack focuses the light on Viktor's lifeless body slumped on the chair with blood trickling from his mouth and a hole in his neck.

'Dead, innit,' Mustafa says.

'Nah, lad's just taking a nap,' Trevor quips.

'Fuck,' Jack says, and chuckles. 'We'll probably join the slick motherfucker real soon too.'

Jack examines the other bodies with the light.

'And I just paid the deposit on a house,' Mustafa says.

'Really?' Trevor asks.

'Yeah.'

'You're single, what you need a house for?'

'I'm Moroccan, bro, my mum could marry me off tomorrow.'

'This is not funny,' Glenn says. 'This is fucked!'

'All right, calm down, Chewbacca,' Trevor says.

'Fuck you, you heartless fag!' Glenn barks.

'Damn, take it easy, mate,' Trevor says and chuckles. 'And who I fuck is not your business either . . . plus, Musti loves my heartless bangs. Right, Musti?'

'Oh yes,' Mustafa says. 'But if anybody asks, Musti only like pussy.'

'Stop,' Jack commands, and directs the light to the four bodies. 'There are only four bodies.'

'He's alive!' Lucas screams.

'What? Who?' Jack asks.

All the ceiling lights in the warehouse switch on and off in an instant, and the intense flash of light temporarily blinds them. Glenn blindly opens fire, and Trevor and Mustafa shoot indiscriminately as well. Bullets ricochet around the room, and ceiling lights and windows shatter.

'Stop!' Jack commands.

The shooting stops, and Jack scans the room with the flashlight.

'You see him?' Jack whispers.

'No,' Trevor whispers.

'I didn't,' Mustafa whispers.

'Where was he, Glenn?' Jack whispers.

'I don't know,' Glenn whispers.

'But you started shooting,' Jack whispers.

'I thought . . . I thought I heard him,' Glenn responds.

Jack fights to hold his tongue because he knows Glenn heard nothing. 'What's this boy's name again?' he asks Lucas.

'Err . . . Pretty Boy,' Lucas says.

'What the fuck, Lucas? I want his fucking name, not what you lot call him in bed.'

'I don't know it.'

'Really? Fucking hell,' Jack says, and scans the room with the light. 'Boy! We're not here to hurt you. We're just here doing our jobs. My coppers were just spooked by the lights, that's all that was. I see all the bodies here . . . all the bullet wounds . . . and I know you couldn't have done all this yourself. Whatever your part was in this tragedy, I'll bet it's justifiable . . . self-defence and all. But you'll have to surrender peacefully and talk to me. I'll take care of you, I promise. Just walk into the light.'

There is no response.

'Boy, I don't think you know what you're into,' Jack says. 'It's best for you to come with us. We can protect you. Cos the dead Russian here in a million-pound suit is pretty much royalty. His people will hunt you down and kill you . . . your family . . . everyone you care for.'

Again, there is no response.

Jack switches off the flashlight. 'Lucas,' he whispers.

'Yeah?' Lucas responds.

'The light switch is probably by the door. You go over there—'

'I can't . . .' Lucas interrupts.

'Shut up,' Jack says and grabs the back of Lucas's neck. 'You'll do it. It's easier than you think. Just walk towards the light coming through the door. The light switch ought to be on one side of the door. You feel for it and switch the fucker on. Okay?'

'I don't—'

Jack squeezes Lucas's neck. 'Now.'

Lucas nods, and Jack releases his neck. Lucas creeps towards the entrance, but there is a gunshot. Trevor howls and falls, and Jack switches on the flashlight in the gunshot's direction and shoots back. Glenn cowers and shoots wildly.

Mustafa hurries to Trevor. 'I need the light!' he shouts.

Jack stops shooting and turns the light to Mustafa and Trevor, but Glenn continues to shoot until he is out of bullets. Trevor clutches his chest in despair, but Mustafa pushes Trevor's hands apart and unzips Trevor's hoodie. Mustafa spots the bullet lodged in Trevor's bulletproof vest and he slaps Trevor across the face.

'Shut up,' Mustafa says. 'Your vest stopped it.'

Trevor checks his vest and sees the bullet. 'Facking hell!' he screams, relieved, and Mustafa helps him to his feet. 'I'm going to fucking murder this cunt.'

'We will,' Jack says with conviction.

Jack moves the light to Glenn, and Glenn is frantic. Glenn

didn't bother to check on Trevor; he just reloaded and stayed alert. Jack seethes and searches the vast room with the light, but there is no sign of Pretty Boy.

Jack switches off the flashlight. 'Huddle up,' he whispers.

Mustafa and Trevor hurry to Jack, but Glenn shuffles backwards to him.

'Glenn, you go to the north wall,' Jack whispers. 'Musti, you're east. Trev, west. I'll go south. Make sure there is nothing between you and the wall, then walk clockwise along the wall for two corners. Be as silent as you can and take care with every step. Only shoot when you're sure because the gunshot will give away your position. We do this right, and we'll have the cunt, easy. He is desperate, but he's just a boy.'

'What if we don't find him after two corners?' Glenn asks.

'We will,' Jack says.

'This is a big place, Jack.'

'Okay, then. If we don't, we meet right here and do it again, and again, and again . . . as many times as it takes to get this fucker. Then we smash the heads of the corpses, break their teeth, and burn this fucking place to the ground. That's what we're going to do. Any more bloody questions?'

There are no more bloody questions.

'Good,' Jack says. 'We're on.'

They separate and sneak towards their assigned wall.

Mustafa approaches the east wall, but he steps on broken glass, and it shatters underneath his feet. He freezes and waits for ten seconds before he continues, but he hears glass crunch a few steps away. He spins to the crunch and opens fire, but he's shot in the head from behind and collapses, dead.

Jack, Trevor, and Glenn wait for Mustafa to let them know he is okay, but there is just silence.

'Musti?' Trevor calls, but there is no response. 'Fuck!'

Trevor opens fire and charges towards the east wall. Glenn shoots and runs also, but Jack doesn't shoot and walks towards the wall, cautious with every step. Trevor approaches the wall, and a gunshot takes off half his ear. He ignores the pain and shoots back, and there is a loud groan and a fall. But the fall is followed by a gunshot that whizzes past Trevor's legs. Trevor lowers his aim to the floor and shoots three more times before a retaliating gunshot pierces through his right eye and lodges in the top of his skull. Trevor is dead on his feet and crashes to the floor.

Glenn stopped in his tracks when the gunfight began and doesn't move after the shooting stops.

'Trevor?' Glenn calls.

'Be quiet,' Jack whispers.

'Trevor!' Glenn screams. 'You—'

Jack covers Glenn's mouth with one hand and pushes his gun into Glenn's ear. 'Glenn,' he whispers. 'Shut up, or you'll get us both killed. Okay?'

Glenn nods, and Jack releases him.

'I think they're dead,' Glenn whispers, his voice trembling with fear. 'We should leave. Just torch this place now.'

Jack doesn't respond.

'Jack, I can't die here,' Glenn says. 'I can't leave—'

'Glenn,' Jack interrupts. 'I'm going to switch on the flashlight in a second and you shoot anything that moves, okay?'

Glenn is about to object, but the flashlight lights up the east wall for a moment before Jack switches it off. But there is no reaction to the light, and several tense moments pass before a flashlight switches on closer to the east wall. Glenn jerks his gun towards the light, but just before he pulls the trigger, his brain registers that it's Jack.

Jack holds the light over Trevor's dead body, and he struggles to control his emotions. He moves the light to Mustafa's dead body a few steps ahead and closes his eyes to hold back tears. He hears Glenn approach and shifts the light to Sean's bloodstained Smith & Wesson a few feet ahead. There is a pool of blood by the gun, and a blood trail leading away.

'The boy's hurt bad,' Jack says. 'And he doesn't have a gun anymore.'

'How do—' Glenn asks.

'That's his gun, and Trev and Musti still have theirs.'

'They are dead, right?'

'You'll follow the blood trail. I'll lead you with the light—'

'I'm not—'

'Glenn—'

'I'm not doing that!'

'You are. Cos if this boy still has any fight left, he'll come for the flashlight. I'm holding it. I'll be the bait. You just be ready to end the boy. Unless *you* want the flashlight?'

'Okay. Okay,' Glenn says, and takes a moment to gather his nerves. 'I'm ready.'

'Good.'

Jack tracks the blood trail with the light and Glenn follows a couple steps behind. Jack tucks his gun into his waistband and picks up the Smith & Wesson. He aims for the back of Glenn's head and pulls the trigger, and there is a sharp click as the firing pin ignites, but no gunfire because the gun is out of bullets. Glenn spins to Jack, and Jack switches off the flashlight, but Glenn shoots and hits Jack in the left shoulder. Jack yelps and falls to his knee, and the flashlight rolls away.

Glenn continues to shoot at Jack, but he misses because he can't see. Jack tosses the Smith & Wesson, pulls out his gun, and takes his time to aim as bullets whizz past him. He shoots three times in a quick burst. The first bullet misses Glenn, but the next two bullets pierce through Glenn's cheek and forehead. Glenn collapses to the floor, dead.

Jack is in excruciating pain and can't move his left arm. But the physical pain is insignificant compared to his anguish. He tucks his gun into his waistband and pats the floor around him for the flashlight, but he can't find it. He grimaces and fights to his feet.

'Boy!' Jack screams, and pulls out his gun. 'Look what you made me do! I'm going to fucking rip—'

Pretty Boy charges at Jack, but he's not quick enough because he has a bullet wound in his left leg, and Jack hears him coming. Jack braces and absorbs the collision, but his gun flies away from his grasp. Jack wraps his right arm around Pretty Boy and lifts him into the air. He drives Pretty Boy's head onto the floor, but Pretty Boy moves his head in the nick of time and lands on his shoulder.

Jack drops all of his weight onto Pretty Boy and shoves his right forearm into Pretty Boy's neck. Pretty Boy tries to fight off Jack's arm, but he's too strong.

Pretty Boy desperately feels the floor around him for Jack's gun, and a piece of glass gashes his palm. He grabs the glass and drives it into Jack's neck. Jack is stunned by the sharp pain, and Pretty Boy pushes the glass further into Jack's neck. Jack collapses.

Pretty Boy tries to push Jack's body off him, but can't move the body because it's heavy, and he's exhausted. He stops to catch his breath and tries again, but he's drained of all energy. Lucas stands over Pretty Boy and listens for more breathing. Lucas can't see, but he uses Pretty Boy's frenetic breaths to track the only sign of life in the warehouse. Lucas can no longer hear any breathing, but he shoots twice, and each time there is a thump from the bullet hitting a body.

Lucas hurries to the slabs and uses his phone's screen for light. He tucks the gun into his waistband and pushes Sean's annihilated head off the empty black bag. He drags the cash into the blood-soaked bag and puts the bag over his shoulder. He slings the red bag over his other shoulder and hurries towards the exit.

'Five!' Pretty Boy screams.

Lucas is overwhelmed with fear. He drops the bags, pulls out the gun, and shoots. But it's an aimless shot because he has no idea where Pretty Boy is.

'Four!' Pretty Boy screams.

Lucas spins and shoots, and again it's aimless. But he is sure Pretty Boy is creeping towards him because Pretty Boy sounds closer than before.

'Three!' Pretty Boy screams.

Lucas shoots twice in random directions; he's terrified because Pretty Boy's voice seems so close.

'Two!' Pretty Boy screams.

Lucas runs just before Pretty Boy swings the piece of glass towards him, and he unknowingly avoids the glass. Pretty Boy falls with the momentum of his wild swing and watches Lucas run out of the warehouse.

'One!' Pretty Boy screams.

Pretty Boy struggles to his feet and limps towards the entrance. 'Zero!' he screams. 'Lucas, your time's up, I'm coming! You can run . . . you ought to run! You can hide . . . you should hide! But it won't fucking matter, cos I will find you, and I will fucking kill you!'

Pretty Boy approaches the entrance and stops because he hears a swarm of oncoming police sirens. He seethes with rage and considers continuing after Lucas, but he knows he has to leave now to escape the police. Lucas's time will come, he'll make sure of it. He limps as quick as he can towards a large broken window on the other side of the warehouse, but he stops. He hurries to the bags and puts them across his back.

Pretty Boy climbs out through the broken window and

hurries through a wild field behind the warehouse. He pulls out his phone and calls Oleg. 'Oleg,' he says. 'I need—'

He trips over a rotted piece of scrap metal and falls into the tall grass.

01:08

'No mercy'

I pull my head off the steering wheel and scan the car park; it's serene. I check the digital clock on the dashboard, and it's 01:07. I check my cracked watch, and it's 01:08. I shake my head with disappointment because that's the second time I've unintentionally fallen asleep today. But then it's been one hell of a fucking day. I stretch my sore legs and drive out the car park.

Thirty minutes later, I turn into a quiet semi-rural neighbourhood and park in the short driveway of a detached cottage house. I grab my bag, step out of the car, and plod to the front door, feeling every step. I enter the house, disarm the alarm system, and walk to the stairway without switching on any lights. I take a deep breath and drag myself onto the steps, and I hear a cat meow. I smile and skip a step because that's where Sandy is; it's her spot.

'One of these days, I'm going to step on you,' I say.

Sandy stands and brushes against my legs as she follows me up the stairs.

'I see you're happy I made it back.'

Sandy climbs up the stairs and waits at my bedroom door.

'You really couldn't give a shit, eh? And how you get in without setting off the alarm? Mrs Lewis will be really worried that you're lost too. I'll call her in the morning . . . well, whenever I wake up.'

I open my bedroom door, and Sandy hurries onto my bed. She settles in the middle, and I chuckle. I drop my bag, pull my trainers off, and head straight into the shower. I let the hot water run through my clothes before I undress, and I sit on the floor to savour the hot shower.

I crawl out of the shower and climb onto the bed beside Sandy. I close my eyes.

Three black BMW X5s with tinted windows drive through a semi-rural street with headlights off. The cars park in darkness away from streetlights, and the passenger window of the first car lowers to reveal Alan. He has a black eye and bruises on his face, and his right arm is bandaged in a sling, but his hair is impeccable.

Alan scans the modest cottage houses on both sides of the street and doubts this is the right location, but it is where the trace has led them. He turns to Franka, and she shrugs – she shares his doubt.

Alan steps out of the car and walks to the back window of the last car. The window lowers to reveal Michael.

'That's the house,' Alan whispers, and gestures to a detached cottage house further down the street.

Michael leans forward for a better look. 'You sure?' he asks.

'Yes. According to the trace.'

'Really? You're sure?'

Alan takes a moment to bury his annoyance. 'Yes, according to the trace,' he repeats.

'I don't get it. What's a geezer from round 'ere doing fucking around all the way in London?'

'I don't know. But we'll find out soon enough.'

Michael turns to the woman sitting beside him, and she's dressed in black with a wide-brim hat covering her face. 'Baby,' he calls. 'This is the place.'

She nods and raises her prosthetic left hand. She moves the fingers, and the mechanism is mesmerising, but it's slow and lacks the rhythm of real fingers. She raises her right hand and twirls the fingers. 'Kill him,' Meiling says.

'You heard her,' Michael says. 'You make sure they cut him up real good. I want all his limbs ripped apart. And you bring me his head, Alan. I want his facking head.'

Alan nods and walks to the passenger side of the second car. The window is down, and a fearsome elderly Japanese man scans the street. Alan nods at the man and walks to the first car. He taps the backseat window, and three sturdy men hop out. They wear balaclavas and are dressed in black. Another three sturdy men in identical attire hop out of the back seat of the second car, but the old man takes his time to step out. The old man is dressed identically to the men, and he is just as sturdy.

The men gather around the old man, and he puts on his balaclava. All seven become indistinguishable. They look like ninjas, and, for all intents and purposes, they are modern-day East London ninjas. They approach Alan and bow; he bows too.

'Anybody you see in there,' Alan whispers, and points to the house, 'kill. No mercy. And bring me his head.'

The men pull out katanas and charge towards the house; they don't make a sound.

The men circle the house – each at a potential point of entry. The man at the front door disables the house alarm with a handheld device and signals the others. He and the man at the back door pick the locks, and the men by the windows use suction pads to detach the glass. They signal each other and charge into the house. But the moment they enter, muffled pops erupt around the house and continue for about ten seconds before it stops.

Silence.

Five minutes pass before Alan approaches the house wielding a handgun. He sneaks to the open front door and peeks in. He can't see anything because it is pitch-black inside, and he can't hear anything either. He slides through the open door, and someone sticks a gun to the back of his head and shuts the door.

'Drop the gun,' Rebecca says.

Alan does as he's told.

'Not laughing now, are you?' Rebecca says. 'And where is your stunning driver?'

'Didn't bring her. Thought the ninjas—'

'Alan?' Pretty Boy says, and switches on the hallway lights.

Alan recognises Pretty Boy's voice and turns to him.

They stare at each other and smile.

'Happy birthday.'

ACKNOWLEDGEMENTS

I'm eternally grateful to everyone who has supported me to make *A Good Day to Die* a reality. I'm a boy from Lagos, so as you might imagine, there are a lot of people to thank. Probably a chapter's worth. I hope you all know who you are.

Finally, this book is a testament to perseverance and the virtue of others. Follow your dreams, and don't be afraid to share them. Nothing is impossible with commitment and the right support.